The Balance Wars

Book III

Equilibrium

Robert C Littlewood

To my son Alex and to Teara
who registered with Stellar Star Registry
Binary Star #3051671 – Triangulum Australis
as 'Avlar' and 'Colunda'.

Thank you guys!

'The Balance is All'.

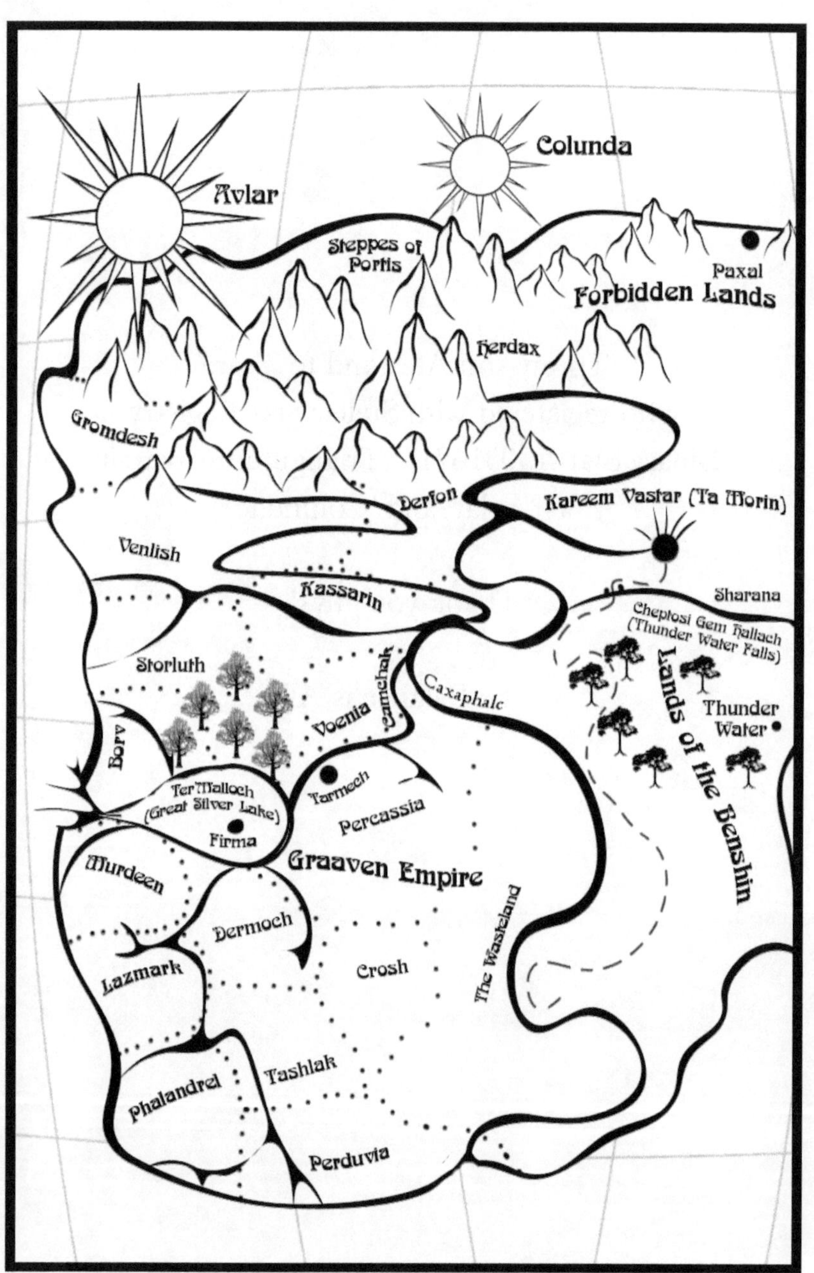

Avlar
Colunda
Steppes of Portis
Forbidden Lands
Paxal
Herdax
Gromdesh
Derion
Kareem Vastar (Ta Morin)
Venlish
Sharana
Kassarin
Cheptosi Gem Hallach (Thunder Water Falls)
Storluth
Caxaphale
Thunder Water
Voenia
Tarnehak
Borv
Lands of the Benshin
Ter'Malloch (Great Silver Lake)
Tarmech
Firma
Percassia
Murdeen
Graaven Empire
Dermoch
The Wasteland
Crosh
Lazmark
Tashlak
Phalandrel
Perduvia

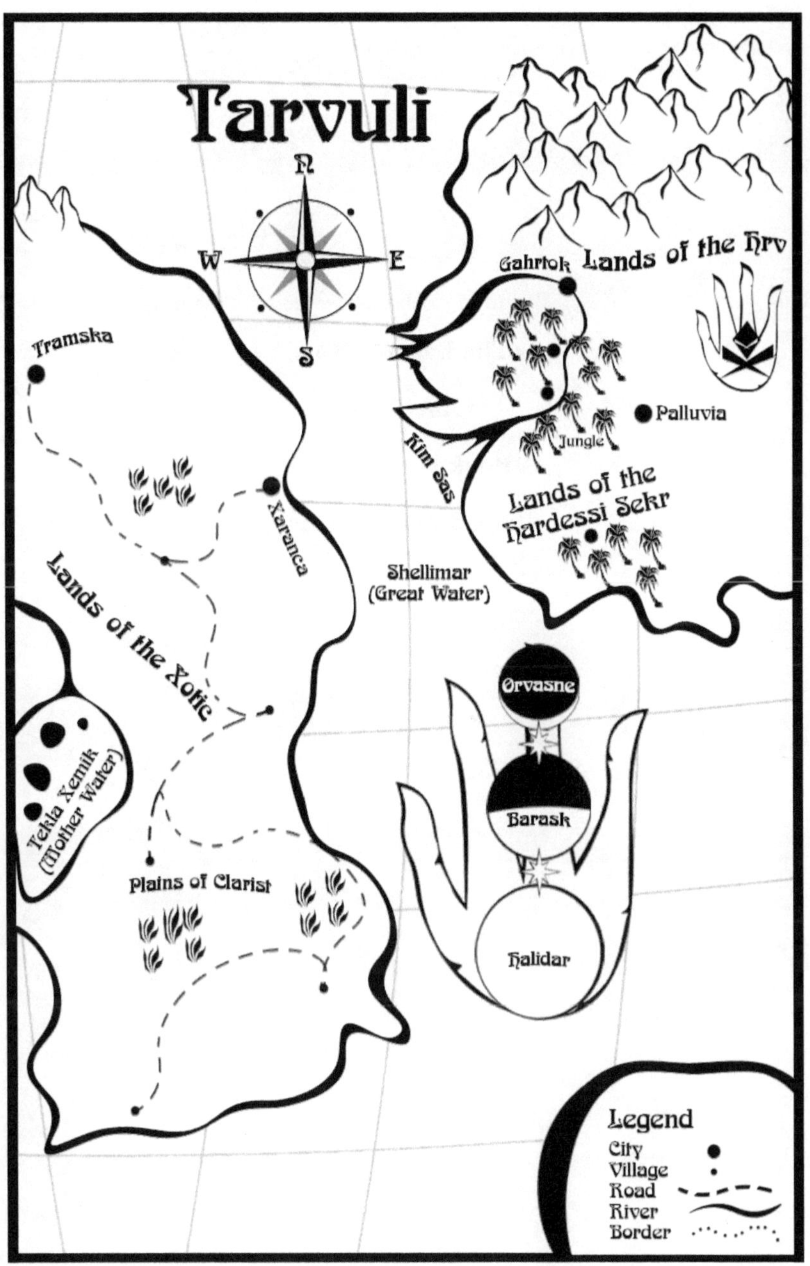

Tarvuli
N
W
E
S
Tramska
Xaranca
Kim Sas
Gahrtok
Lands of the Hrv
Jungle
Palluvia
Lands of the
Hardessi Sekr
Shellimar
(Great Water)
Lands of the Xotie
Tekla Kemik
(Mother Water)
Plains of Clarist
Orvasne
Barask
Halidar
Legend
City
Village
Road
River
Border

GLOSSARY

PLANETS, MOONS and SUNS

Name	Meaning	Pronunciation
Tarvuli	The Mother, home planet of the Graaven peoples	**TahFOOLee**
Avlar	'Brightest' – one of the two suns of Tarvuli	**AFlar**
Colunda	'Fading Star' – second of the two suns of Tarvuli	**KoLOONdar**
Halidar	'Queen of Night' – moon of Tarvuli, the first to rise and set	**HARleedar**
Barask	'She Who Shines Coldly' – moon of Tarvuli, the second to rise	**BAHrask**
Orvasne	'He Who Waits' – moon of Tarvuli, the last to rise and set	**OrVASHhneh**

SEASONS

Name	Meaning	Pronunciation
Hordeth Gar	Season of Storms	**HorDETH Gar**
Veremis Gar	Season of Weeping	**FerEEMish Gar**
Talloch Gar	Season of Renewal	**TAlock Gar**
Carminac Gar	Season of Abundance	**KarMEEnac Gar**
Nahver Gar	Season of Waning	**NahVEER Gar**
Techmun Gar	Season of Desolation	**TeshMUN Gar**

THE SEVEN PROVINCES of the GRAAVEN EMPIRE

Name		Pronunciation
Percassia		**PearCASHeeah**
Dermoch		**DAREmock**
Voenia		**FoEENeah**
Kassarin		**KashARin**
Storluth		**SsDORlute**
Tashlak		**TARSHlak**
Crosh		**CROWsh**

THE TWELVE VASSAL STATES of the GRAAVEN EMPIRE

Name		Pronunciation
Perduvia		**PearDOOfeeah**
Phalandrel		**FARlandrel**
Lazmark		**LATHmark**
Murdeen		**MOORdeen**
Borv		**Borf**
Venlish		**FenLEESH**
Herdax		**AIRdarz**
Gromdesh		**GROOMdesh**
Derfon		**DAIRfoon**

PLACES and LOCATIONS

Name	Meaning	Pronunciation
Kareem Vastar	A City–State	**KAReem VASHtar**
Palluvia	A City–State	**PaLOOveeah**
Paxal	A City–State	**ParkSHARL**
Tekla Xemik	The Great Water Lake	**TEKlah SHEMik**
Ter'Malloch	Silver Water Lake	**TEar MAHlok**
Firma	Large island set in the waters of Ter'Malloch	**FEERma**
Cheptosi Gem Hallach	The Thunder Water Falls	**ChepTOsee Ghem HALack**
Sharana	The Black Water River	**ShaRARnah**
Xerfun	The Underworld	**SHERfoon**
Tarmech	Capital city of the Graaven Empire	**TAHmesh**
Camchak	River of Life	**KamCHACK**
Steppes of Portis	Unconquered lands to the north	**PORtish**
Plains of Clarist	Desert region to the far east of the Empire	**CLARisht**

PRINCIPAL GRAAVEN GODS BEFORE the FALL

Name	Meaning	Pronunciation
Slax Ar Terrun	Goddess of Death	**SLArx ar TERoon**
Bekkor	The Seven-faced God	**BEKor**
Bringarell	God of the Underworld	**BrinGAHREL**

GRAAVEN MEASURES of TIME and DISTANCE

Spahn	Roughly equivalent to 12 inches	**SHParn**
Talit	Roughly equivalent to one inch	**TARlit**
Persangh	A Graaven mile	**PearZang**
Chaal	A Graaven hour	**CHarl**
Dak'chaal	A Graaven day	**DAHK CHarl**
Meh'chaal	A Graaven week	**MURK CHarl**
Bach'chaal	A Graaven month	**BAHR CHarl**
Sem'chaal	A Graaven year	**ZEM CHarl**

GRAAVEN MILITARY STRUCTURE

Name	Meaning	Pronunciation
Shu Tek	Greatest of 25	**SHOO Tek**
Shu Mut	Greatest of 50	**SHOO Moot**
Shu Lan	Greatest of 100	**SHOO Larn**

GRAAVEN MILITARY STRUCTURE (cont.)

Name	Meaning	Pronunciation
Kalvak	First of 500	**KULvark**
Met Stragosh	'Little' General	**Met STRARgoash**
Stragosh	General	**STRARgoash**
Impisch	Unit of 10 000	**IMpeesh**
Impisch tarn	Unit of 1000	**IMpeesh TAhn**
Praka	Unit of 25	**PRAka**
Praka xem	Unit of 50	**PRAka SHEM**
Praka vek	Unit of 100	**PRAka Fek**
Praka haram	Unit of 500	**PRAka ARam**
Hoplex	Graaven foot soldier	**HOplecks**
Sagit	Graaven archer	**ZAYgit**
Baran Mec	Imperial guard	**BAHrarn Mek**
Zaltec	Supreme military leader	**SAHLtek**

PROLOGUE

It fled in confusion and pain, repulsed by a power that was unexpected and unfathomable.

It fled without thought as to its destination, fuelled by an all-consuming rage. Finally, it came to rest, substance without form, a vast pool of blackness so dense that, had there been eyes to see it, it would have stood out even against the blackness of the space that surrounded it. There it floated in silence, reassessing and probing the stored memories inherited from its parent.

Despite its efforts, nothing solid could be gleaned as to the identity of the force it had so recently and painfully encountered. Tantalising pieces of information offered promise but, like pursuing the trail of some mythical creature, they all disappeared into a maze of rumour and legend.

Still, its own power was growing and as its might grew, so too arose a new definition of itself. And with growing awareness came the realisation that it was not so much the offspring of its parent, but rather an altered state of it, bonded yet independent. Not tied to the planet of its birth like its alter ego, but able to travel through space as it willed. Shapeless, structureless, it was nonetheless real, totally malevolent and completely consumed by its hatred of all life and its overwhelming desire to dominate.

Its sense of identity grew stronger, seeking an expression of itself to give it form and focus. From its vast reservoir of knowledge, a single concept arose and it contemplated this idea:

Chaos.

Yes, this was its perfect manifestation and it began to think of itself as a single, implacable entity given form in a language whose origins were but an echo of an echo:

Apocris.

Empowered by this revelation of itself, and as it mused over seemingly imponderable matters, Apocris became aware of something else. Leaving its memories, it instead reached a probing filament of energy into the empty space around it. Yes, there was something there! Invisible, indefinable, a part of reality and yet separate from it, so close and yet resistant to all initial attempts to touch it. No sooner had Apocris grasped it than it slipped away. Not to be deterred, however, continuous delicate probing slowly eroded resistance until it became apparent that this was another thread of energy unlike anything encountered before. And not just one strand – one among thousands.

Apocris refocused and intensified its energies. Now multiple strands of thought swept out like a net until, at last, it managed to grasp hold of a single thread. The impact was staggering. A web of power seemingly without end or beginning, connecting all things. Myriads of threads, a vast system of energy, its structure very like the roots of a gigantic tree. Apocris sent tenuous threads of its own energy along the line it had captured and a new and satisfying idea began to form. Fixing a firmer grasp on the strand it held in its power, Apocris poured hatred and malice into it. The strand, which pulsed with a bluish intensity, now dimmed and blackened. Apocris's negative energy flowed into it, to be instantly swept along its vast length. As the darkness grew, so other lines were corrupted by it. Like some horrific leech, Apocris concentrated its will, forcing darkness and corruption into the strands, causing an imbalance which grew apace.

Apocris had found its purpose. It drew energy from its alter ego just as the parent did in turn from all its offspring, feeding on the life energy of millions; newly empowered, it poured into its network of corrupted strands the darkness of despair and misery in the depths of space.

It gloated as its evil spread.

CHAPTER ONE

As Tishan and Menkh sped along the Threadway, it became immediately apparent to Menkh that something about it had changed. Where before its energy strands had been a kaleidoscope of colours, some were now dense black, a phenomenon that Menkh had not discerned before. Although a less experienced traveller on the Threadway, Tishan had also noticed the dark strands, and they gave her a sense of extreme disquiet. Their presence disturbed the harmony of colours and drawing near to one created an unpleasant physical effect, a feeling entirely absent from any other thread. However, there was no interference in their journey to the Balancepoint and they both materialised in the huge anteroom within the Complex that was, in so many ways, remarkably similar to its imitation located in the heart of Ta'Morin.

Tishan looked around in amazement. In this, her first journey to the Balancepoint, she realised there was nothing in Menkh's descriptions that did it justice, particularly the floor she now stood upon. Knowledge of the Eye of Malavak was no preparation for actually seeing or standing upon it, and she stared amazed as planets and other celestial bodies moved slowly beneath her feet.

Before her, several individuals were gathered in welcome.

'Greetings Menkh and to you, Tishan Dar,' said Frzath the Abbot. 'We had foreknowledge of your journey to us. Allow me to introduce the Adepts who stand before you, Tishan.'

Introductions and greetings took some small amount of time before T'klath spoke; her voice a deep contralto: 'The Way has been prepared for you Tishan Dar; if you would like to accompany Morgath, he will take you to the portal.'

Morgath bowed slightly and gave Tishan a small smile.

'I'm sorry: The Way?' asked Tishan.

'It is the chief reason you are here, Tishan Dar. In the battle to come, you must be fully prepared and as protected as possible. Knowingly or otherwise, you are now an Adept, but you are yet to be truly bonded.'

'And this is necessary?'

'It would be a reassurance to me, Tishan,' said Menkh. 'I think what has gone before was only a taste of what is yet to come.'

The Adepts all nodded in agreement.

Tishan looked deep into Menkh's eyes and then at the others waiting expectantly around her. She could think of no logical reason to refuse and could not argue with the comments made by Menkh.

'If you would come this way, Tishan Dar.'

Without waiting for a response, Morgath turned and headed towards a series of doorways which, in place of physical doors, were instead filled with many-coloured swirling bands within the confines of their frames. To Tishan's eyes, the swirling patterns were bewildering, but as they drew nearer, she could see that each doorway had an unvarying mix of colours slightly different from every other so that each doorway was unique unto itself, the pattern repeated over and over again.

Morgath's voice entered her mind: <It is interesting, isn't it? As you realise that each doorway has a particular pattern and palette

of colours, so you begin to recognise that each has a different meaning. This tells you what lies beyond each portal.>

<Yes, I can see that. Although knowing there is a pattern and understanding what it means are two different things entirely. Did it take you long to work it out?>

<A novice spends much time in the company of Adepts who know their way around. There are currently 110 doorways I am aware of, each connecting to parts of the Balancepoint. Some of them lead to areas which are present in our reality, while others are inter-dimensional. The Balancepoint occupies many places. While taking the wrong doorway is never lethal you can end up in some very interesting locations.>

Tishan's mind veered away from the concept of inter-dimensional doorways and instead focused her eyes on the portal they were now approaching.

<I would imagine then from your remark that you have experienced this?>

Morgath's laughter echoed in her thoughts. <Oh yes, all of us have experienced it at one time or another. It pays to be concentrating on where you wish to go before you enter the doorway. Being distracted by other thoughts or problems is not advisable. However, I can assure you that your journey today will be through the right portal.>

No sooner had Morgath finished this remark, than they were standing in front of a doorway, which, now that it was before her, seemed to be much bigger than it first appeared. Swirling bands of magenta and green shimmered in a complex series of spirals which twisted and turned before breaking apart, only to re-form in a hypnotic dance which drew the eye deep inside it.

Tishan looked back over her shoulder at Menkh and the other Adepts. Remarkably they seemed to be a very long way from where she now stood, as if the short journey in Morgath's wake had in fact covered a much greater distance than the number of steps would indicate.

<Fascinating and disturbing at the same time.> Tishan's thoughts manifested a sense of deep reflection.

<Yes. Living within a Balancepoint is to live on the edge of mystery. But come Tishan, a deep breath and step forward. I wish you well.>

<No clues then as to what awaits?>

<Not through this doorway. It is always different for whoever enters. Suffice to say that upon returning you will be 'different' from what you were before you entered.>

Tishan turned to question Morgath, but the words died on her lips as he no longer stood alongside her. Looking back over her shoulder there was only darkness; it was as if she was no longer in the same place at all. Before her the portal appeared even larger. Tishan fought down trepidation and fear; she felt totally alone and sure that, somehow, this was part of a test. Though to what end, she did not understand.

After several long moments wishing she was somewhere other than here, she followed Morgath's advice, drew in a deep breath and, not without some qualms, stepped into the portal.

Having spoken with Menkh at length about his experience in the Balancepoint, and her familiarity with those on Tarvuli, Tishan thought she knew what to expect as she passed through. As with all gateways, she felt a moment of intense coldness combined with a slight dizziness, causing her to briefly close her eyes. Upon opening them, she expected to see some kind of vast cavern filled with crystalline protrusions as Menkh had related, but she was instead confronted with nothing. Absolute emptiness stretched out in all directions. It was a completely disorienting experience; if it were not for the sensation of standing on solid ground, she could have been floating in a void. A faint greyish illumination allowed her to see her body when she looked down, but even the ground beneath her feet was no different in aspect to the rest of her surroundings. The overall effect made her unsteady.

Not sure what she was supposed to do, she turned around thinking that she might step back through the doorway but, to her consternation, that too had disappeared. Turning back, she fought down a sense of panic and took deep breaths to steady herself. The complete absence of sound – or indeed of anything – was deeply unsettling; even her breathing did not seem to make a sound in this eerie place.

Suddenly, just at the point where she felt she wanted to scream out loud; she discerned movement. The floor around her seemed to ripple and, in the far distance, it reared up like storm waves on the surface of the Great Water and swept toward her in a surge that grew and grew until it towered over her to an impossible height.

Tishan stood rooted to the spot, only her years of military training and a hundred desperate engagements where she had emerged alive, stopped her from running in terror. Though where she could have run to in that empty place was a thought she acknowledged with wry humour, and quickly banished.

Just as she felt sure she would be overwhelmed, the wave abruptly halted, perhaps some twenty paces from where she stood. Dramatically subsiding, it formed a vaguely humanoid shape and flowed towards Tishan till it was within touching distance.

A voice spoke to her, though there was no mouth to issue the sound. Neither male nor female in tonality it seemed as if many voices made one utterance and that a myriad of voices combined into single flowing speech.

'Greetings Tishan Dar, Adept of the White. Are you ready to journey with us?'

Tishan's thoughts scrambled. Adept of the White? What did that mean? After the last few moments, she wasn't sure she was prepared for anything and yet she herself say aloud, 'I am ready,' and if her voice was not exactly rock steady it sounded calm enough to her ears.

Hundreds of voices echoed her response, this time they did indeed sound as if they came like an echo from some vast cavern. 'She is ready, she is ready.'

The liquid shape flowed up above her. 'Very well. Do not be afraid, Tishan Dar.'

Before Tishan could even think of a response the wave crashed over her. Her senses reeled as she disappeared inside it.

This was like nothing Tishan had ever experienced. From a brief moment of panic as the wave engulfed her, she found herself floating, suspended inside a warm and intimate space. A comforting sound, not words or music, but more a sibilant sighing, echoed around her. The closest she could liken the sound to was the quiet lapping of waves on the shore, or slow and steady beathing. In a way that she could not define, it was deeply comforting. Perfect peace and contentment flowed over her. Like a waking dream, she felt a strange languor, as though she could walk away whenever she wanted to – but had no desire to do so, being perfectly content to remain where she was.

While her mind drifted, a part of it sought a way to rationalise her surroundings. She happened upon a thought that at first she rejected, but which became more insistent. Reflecting on it allowed it to grow and, as it coalesced, she realised it was what she imagined – or perhaps even vaguely remembered – an embryo in the egg might experience. Growing, changing, safe from all disturbances. As the thought crystallised, the comforting sound around her changed. Now it sounded to her more like a lullaby and once again she was swept away, deeper, into a state of complete serenity.

She awoke to a sense of loss; no longer was she floating in that warm void. Instead, she now lay in warm sunshine on a thick carpet. Around her she saw a great wall of stone blocks patterned with flecks and bands of colour, predominantly blue and silver, which rose over her head into great arches supporting a vast roof of interlocking ribs that resembled the limbs of enormous trees. Although the architecture was of a grand scale, the resulting space did not feel cavernous or impersonal; curiously it had rather the opposite effect on her senses.

Despite her prone position on the floor, she could see out through large open windows over a vast expanse of shimmering liquid. Given its size, she assumed it must be a sea or lake, but as no land was visible it was impossible to tell if it was somewhere she recognised or was indeed an alien landscape beyond her experience. As if in response to her unspoken thoughts she saw in the distance huge mountains towering upwards to an extreme height, their pinnacles reflecting the light of a red sun that hung low in the sky beyond them. Despite the window appearing to be open to the elements, the air around her was warm and heavy with the scent of what she supposed was a flowering plant.

Drowsily she yawned and stretched and realised that she was very hungry. She had no idea where she was or how much time had passed, but she had never felt such contentment. Perhaps, she thought, she had died and had come to the Land Beyond as the Graavens called the place that all ultimately journeyed to. Her musings did not elicit any sense of sadness or despair; she was content merely to be in the moment, knowing that explanation would come in its own good time.

After some moments of quiet reflection, her thoughts were interrupted by tinkling laughter and Tishan sat upright to locate its source.

As her eyes focused, she saw before her an enormous dais made of the same stone as the walls and upon it there sat an equally large blob of…jelly. It was the only way she could describe it to herself. It seemed to have no discernible features at all, other than pulsing lights of many colours which she could see flashing deep inside of whatever it was. The tinkling laughter seemed to emanate from it and she observed that the pulsing lights themselves seemed to brighten and diminish so that they mirrored or echoed the cadence of the laughter.

She watched as the jelly-like matter melted and re-moulded, slowly assuming a humanoid form. Tishan watched in fascination, it was like seeing a skilled potter create a delicate vase from a shapeless lump of clay. The features sharpened until a figure akin to a very large Graaven sat cross-legged on the dais before her. Lights still pulsed beneath its skin but, rippling down from its shoulders, its outer body was rapidly covered by a diaphanous material that shimmered in the light from the open widows. A musical voice, feminine in tone and pleasing to the ear, spoke:

'There you are Tishan Dar, is that better to your eyes?'

'I don't know what to say,' Tishan responded. 'I am curious about your other form; is that your natural body?'

The tinkling laughter sounded again. 'I am an Acclydian, Tishan Dar. Our natural ability is to assume any shape or form we choose and, for the current purpose, to make you feel more comfortable in these undoubtedly unfamiliar surroundings. So, it has fallen to me to educate you.'

'I am sorry, this is so confusing – who are the Acclydians? Why am I here? In fact, where is *here*?'

'There is no need to be sorry child, it is only natural that you should feel disorientated. After all, you have just experienced re-birth, which is a unique experience all by itself.'

'Rebirth?'

'You could not be here Tishan Dar, had you not. Have you looked at your hands or considered the way your body is feeling?'

In response Tishan lifted her hands in front of her face, and was shocked to realise that the markings of her skin, which were her Graaven heritage, had disappeared. Her skin was now smooth to the touch like glass and gave off a pearly white luminescence. Careful consideration of her legs and those parts of her body she could see, confirmed that she had changed dramatically. Internally she felt the same and yet, as she pondered this, also different. More alive, stronger somehow.

'Yes,' said the creature. 'You are now truly a bonded Adept of the White.'

Tishan looked up in surprise, but on further consideration, found the comment made sense and explained a lot about what had happened to her.

'I remember Menkh telling me that he had to die before he could transform.'

'Die? Who said anything about dying? Menkh is of the Red. Reds tend to be much more, shall we say dramatic, than the White. They do love their little 'surprises' as they call them. We of the White are more nurturing. Rebirth is more gentle, profound of course, but still much calmer.'

Here the creature paused in reflection and Tishan could find nothing to say in response. Her mind whirled, trying to sort out confused thoughts and reconcile the experience she had been through into a logical sequence.

The creature interrupted her silent reverie. 'By the way, are you hungry? Yes, I am sure you are, here – try this.'

Without waiting for any response, it waved its left hand and a low table spread with several dishes, whose contents sent tendrils of steam into the air, appeared before Tishan. The aroma was tantalising and piqued her appetite; she realised she was indeed ravenous.

'You eat, I will talk. Now, who are the Acclydians you ask? Hmmm….it may be better to ask *what* are the Acclydians, yes.'

The creature mused for several moments. 'Let us say that we are instruments of the Intelligence. We go where we are required. Here in this Construct, I am required to assist you.'

'Construct?'

'Yes indeed. This place is not real. I know it feels real, but, well there you are. So *where* we are is nowhere at all really. Oh dear, I'm not explaining this at all satisfactorily, am I?'

'Well, I am sure it must be a difficult concept to explain. So, is *where* we are something like being in the In Between? Like being just outside of reality?'

The creature clapped its hands in delight. 'Oh yes, well that is very good, yes quite like that. Not exactly but close enough. Here we are outside of time. We could spend several of your peoples' lifetimes here and you would find that virtually no time at all had passed once you came back into phase.'

'I see,' said Tishan. 'And do you as an Acclydian have a name at all? You know mine and seem to know something about me.'

'Not a name as such, they are rather superfluous for my kind. Let me think.' Here the creature paused once again for some moments. 'How would you feel about calling me Thatras?'

'The Graaven word for teacher? Well, that would seem to be appropriate. Thatras it shall be. So, you spoke of educating and assisting me. Exactly what are you going to assist me with?'

'Before we begin have you eaten enough? Is there anything else you require?'

'No thank you, I am quite replete. The meal was delicious.'

'Excellent. Then I am to assist you with this.'

The Royal Diadem of the House of Dur floated in mid-air before Tishan's eyes, its jewelled and faceted surface reflecting the light from the windows. In its depths could be seen a dark shadow. Tishan reached up and took it in her grasp. It seemed larger to her eyes than the last time she had seen it and it gave off a faint warmth that she had not noticed before. As ever, it seemed to draw her gaze deep into its depths and she felt that, if she allowed herself, she could fall into it. With difficulty she drew her eyes away.

'Do you know what this is?' Thatras asked.

'I believe so. Once I knew it as the Royal Diadem and heirloom of the House of Dur. Since then, I have learned from Menkh that it is in fact the Orb of Kalash. An artefact of great power.'

'Yes,' Thatras said. 'Certainly, that is what the Adepts of the Balance Point call it, though how Kalash came across it is a mystery lost in the depths of time; it was certainly Menath or one of her siblings who took it when they fled the Balancepoint in the long ago. But that is not what I asked you. I asked, do you know *what* it is?'

'Other than that Menkh used it to entrap the Dorath Mar and remove the threat it posed – no.'

'I would be surprised if you did.' Thatras paused before proceeding. 'You see this object is quite alien in its origin.'

Tishan laughed and then apologised. 'I am sorry Thatras, but I would have thought that was obvious. It is certainly an alien artefact.'

Thatras nodded. 'Yes, but you have limited your definition of that term. When I say alien, I mean not of this reality. It should not be here at all. How it got here is a wonder in itself and certainly conflicts with one of the five Immutable Laws, the rules that govern our universe.' Once again, Thatras drifted off into contemplation leaving Tishan grasping at concepts that were as difficult to comprehend as they were momentous.

'Not of this reality? I don't quite grasp what you're saying.'

'Yes. It is a difficult concept to fathom, but one that you should have knowledge of as an Adept, even if the understanding of it has yet to manifest. Let us say that its origins lie outside of this Universe. However this object came into being, whether by natural means or crafted by beings unknown, we cannot say, but nevertheless here it is. That it is has remained stable for so long is another mystery.'

Tishan battled confusion and a thousand questions.

'But surely Varnahrin knew this when Menkh used it to entrap the Dorath Mar?'

'Things are moving toward a climax tens of thousands of cycles in the making, Tishan Dar. All we can determine is that this object is here for a purpose. Perhaps Varnahrin has determined what that purpose is, or perhaps merely saw it as the solution to an immediate problem. It also presents an opportunity for you.'

'How so?'

'Somehow its power was activated by Menkh the moment he used it to trap the Dorath Mar offspring on your World. We can utilise that power as it provides us with the means to overcome the threat of the Dorath Mar, once and for all.'

'But I don't see how,' said Tishan. 'How can the Orb defeat a creature the size of a small planet, let alone the manifestation of dark energy that has sprung from it?'

'One thing at a time child. Besides, you are allowing your physical senses to dictate and shape what you believe this artefact is capable of. The fact that you can hold it in your hand does not limit its capacity to absorb and contain matter of unlimited size and capacity. The space inside it, while not infinite, could contain whole worlds. More than anything it is a storage device, holding the objects it contains in a kind of stasis. But it is becoming unstable; we know this because as you yourself have observed it is increasing in size. This will continue until it reaches a certain point where it will expand at a huge rate. This final stage will disrupt its integrity.'

Tishan shook her head in confusion. 'You mean it will explode.'

'Yes child, that is what I just said. Although the word explode does not really convey, in any sense, the cataclysmic effect of its disruption. Entire worlds will be destroyed in the initial burst of released energy, and then it will suck the disrupted matter back into itself before it ceases to exist in our reality.'

'You mean it will disappear?'

'Indeed child, did I not make that clear? You really must try and keep up. Theoretically, the result of the disruption should end in its complete dissolution. In one sense the after effects of initial disruption will be greater than the initial explosion. The power being such that, for a fraction of time, the barrier between our reality and the next will be open and, we surmise, the Orb will return whence it came.'

'I see, I think. Then, assuming that all this supposition is correct, you are telling me this so we can turn the outcome to our advantage?'

'Absolutely. If we – and by *we* I mean *you* of course – deliver the Orb at the right moment to the place where the creature is located, it will destroy it utterly. As the worlds around it are devoid of life, nothing living will be affected by the disruption. We also believe the energy pulse will be so strong that all the threads of power connecting it to its offspring will be charged with a lethal bolt of energy that will annihilate them. In one stroke, part of the Balance will be restored leaving only its alter ego to deal with.' Thatras's voice carried a note of supreme contentment.

'And what happens if I get the timing wrong? Is it part of the plan that I too cease to exist?'

Thatras was immediately contrite. 'No, no child, not at all! You and I will plan in detail what needs to be done to maximise your chances and I will know exactly when the task needs to be undertaken. I will not deny there is a risk, as there is in all dangerous undertakings, but you have the strength to carry out this task. Your successful completion of the challenges presented to you when the shield was activated on Tarvuli are testament to this.'

'And how did you know that I would go along with this plan? Was there any intent to ask me if I was willing?' Tishan's tone was sharp with annoyance at the presumption that she would go along with any plan that could lead to her own demise.

Thatras paused before responding. 'You are quite right to re-buke me, Tishan Dar. If I have given you the impression that your views are not to be considered, I am sorry. Sometimes we Acclydians overlook the feelings of other sentient beings we encounter. I hope you may forgive me?'

It was clear to Tishan that Thatras's apology was sincere and she admitted to herself that her reaction was due partly to her pique that it was a given that she would meekly go along with the plan laid out before her.

'There is no question that I will not wholeheartedly assist in restoring Balance, even if it does end in my death. It's just that all this has been so overwhelming; things seem to be moving at a pace that doesn't allow me to reconcile what is happening to me.'

'Of course Tishan. That is why we are here in this Construct. Here we can take as much time as required, for we are outside of reality and the Orb is held here in stasis. Once you leave though, the Orb will react accordingly; it is likely that its time here will escalate the speed at which it approaches disruption once it is back in phase.'

'Well then, let us plan our approach and perhaps we can walk together as we talk? I feel the need to stretch my legs and at the same time, explore this Construct as you call it, a little more.'

'Yes, let us do that. We can also talk about how we might coordinate our efforts with that of Menkh and Crixac to further secure our success.'

Tishan stood up and, together with Thatras in deep discussion, strolled up what now proved to be a long stone gallery interrupted by many large unglazed windows.

'You may have wondered why this entity has the capacity to disrupt the Balance to such an extent?'

'If I am being perfectly honest Thatras, the speed with which events have moved have left me more in the mode of reacting to matters than dwelling on other issues. Now you have raised it, yes, I would be very interested in gaining some insights,' said Tishan.

'Then let us discuss the nature of consciousness and you may begin to understand. You see there are seven levels of awareness. The first is the most primitive level and one which manifests in all living things: the need for food, the need to reproduce. Even plants and growing things have a level of awareness and react to changes in their environment in order to survive and flourish. Above this level is an awareness of self and of others that goes beyond mere adaptation to one's environment. Animals of all kinds have this level of consciousness, interacting as they do within herds and other groupings. Many mate for life, for example, or will defend their young and that of others within their group against predators and interlopers. Some animals have complex family groupings and exhibit primitive levels of communication.

'Above this is the next level, where a true sense of oneself as an individual becomes apparent. Here we can see the emergence of entire cultures that seek to explain and rationalise their surroundings: the development of languages, the art of storytelling and the transmission of learning from adult to child are evident at this level, and can affect whole populations of sentient beings in a very rapid time frame.'

'I see. So, you understand this as being common to all life?'

'Oh yes very much so,' said Thatras. 'Of course, my explanation is simplistic because all these things are shaped also by the environment in which life has evolved and these, as I am sure you are aware, are many and varied. Now, however, we start arriving at levels of consciousness which become much more centred on individual beings. We see the development of rational thought, an emotional intelligence that includes justice and empathy at a much higher level. The development of science, art and culture, and a consideration of the concept of good and evil. Sentient beings develop higher-level consciousness at different rates; a single individual can have a profound effect on their society or on others within their circle of influence, for good or ill.'

'I see,' said Tishan. 'I'm not getting how this has any bearing on the Balance and the particular entity we are discussing.'

'I have said there are seven levels of consciousness. To arrive then at the sixth level requires all of the entity's awareness to be fully developed. The sixth level is enlightenment. A profound understanding of the nature of the Universe and the place of Balance in regulating it.'

'And the seventh level?' Tishan asked.

'Yes, the seventh level.' Thatras paused for several moments. 'A level of consciousness that requires no physical manifestation. The ability to conceptualise infinity and to traverse the multiverse. The power to manipulate time itself. To fundamentally alter reality.'

'To be a god!' Tishan's voice was hushed at the enormity of Thatras's explanation.

'If you will, child, although even your concept of what a god is, is limited by your current understanding, such as it is at this moment. So now think: here you have an entity that has absorbed the life-force of millions. In consuming that energy, it has also absorbed the knowledge and understanding of millions and in so doing, by a freak act that I doubt even it fully grasps, it has created a living alter ego, free to roam at will. Your Dorath Mar has gone from a primitive level of awareness to a supreme level of consciousness in what amounts to the blink of an eye. Its conscious development is *untempered* by an accompanying development of compassion, love, justice, or any of those qualities that might balance its actions. It cares only for itself and seeks unlimited power over all life.'

Tishan nodded her head in agreement; this was momentous news and explained much.

'Now I see why the Balance is so threatened.'

'Indeed. If we cannot overcome this power, we will not be able to ensure equilibrium; everything will be affected and the Universe will descend into chaos.'

'Then,' said Tishan, 'we must prepare our plans well to give us the best chance of success.'

'Yes,' agreed Thatras. 'There are two phases to this. The first is the destruction of the source of energy; in so doing, all its offspring will be eliminated. There is no doubt that this will also impact its alter ego but in what ways we cannot predict. Perhaps it too will cease to exist.' Thatras's tone conveyed uncertainty.

'But you don't think so.'

'No, it would be too much to hope. I think I can safely predict, however, that its fury will be unbounded and the first and most obvious target of its wrath will be Tarvuli. If it overcomes Varnah-rin, I don't even want to think about the consequences.'

'No more do I,' said Tishan and she shuddered inwardly at the terrible potential should that come to pass.

'So let us continue our walk, and look at our options to achieving success in the first phase.'

As they walked and formulated their plans, Tishan occasionally looked out of the window openings they passed. The corridor seemed to go on endlessly, only relieved by the windows to her left. Abruptly, she observed that from one window to the next the panorama changed: one vista showing a jagged range of mountains, the next a yellow sea occupied the entirety of the frame, its waters raging under a sky filled with ominous clouds, seemingly capable of driving through the window. Mighty waves rose up under what seemed to be gale force winds, and occasional flashes of lightning lit up the seascape. No sound could be heard, however, and the corridor where they stood remained still and quiet. Tishan's thoughts stopped in confusion and she backed up several steps while Thatras watched her with an amused expression.

Yes! Here in this window the mountains could be seen once again and yet ten steps later the raging sea appeared in the next opening.

'Thatras what is this?' Tishan asked in amazement. 'I thought these were windows looking out from wherever we are to the world outside.'

'And so they are Tishan. Although the word windows does not adequately capture what they are and if you substitute *world* for *worlds* then yes, your thoughts are correct.'

Tishan crinkled her eyes in concentration. 'So, this place where we are, looks out across many worlds and every few steps these worlds change?'

'Indeed, you have grasped it exactly,' said Thatras.

Tishan shook her head resignedly. 'Well, I may have grasped it, but I don't understand it at all!'

'Look at it this way. *Where* we are has adapted itself to your experience and the nature of *who* you are. Hence, a long corridor and windows are constructs you can understand and which lie within your concept of reality as you know it. For another creature, the construct would be completely different. This place is a physical manifestation of the Threadway and these windows are, in effect, a gateway to each of the worlds that you can see through them.'

'So anyone can use them?'

'No. To access this place you must have a sufficient degree of, what shall we call it?' Here Thatras mused for a few moments. 'Yes, let us call it enlightenment, and of course a key to enter it.'

Tishan closed her eyes, grappling with another profoundly confusing concept. 'Key?'

'Key,' agreed Thatras.

'But I don't have a key!' Tishan retorted in frustration.

'Of course you do, Tishan Dar. *I* am your key.'

Thatras nodded to itself and turning away from Tishan continued walking on alone down the corridor.

Tishan paused for several of her own moments and then, sighing in exasperation, moved off after the slowly diminishing form
of the Acclydian, passing ever more windows that looked out on
ever more worlds, her mind a whirl of thoughts.

CHAPTER TWO

Draachnull sat cross-legged and watched Avlar lift its head above the horizon. He was perched on a rocky ledge that overlooked the fern forest spread as far as the eye could see beneath his feet. At this early hour of the day, at the very edge of his hearing the muted roar of Cheptosi Gem Hallach – the Thunder Water Falls – could be heard as a whisper on the air.

Despite his particular fondness for this place, Draachnull did not come here often. On reflection, his previous trips had taken place when something troubled his thoughts. Indeed, his first meeting with Menkh ab Dur had been as the result of a careless fall that happened on his journey back to his village. A momentous event indeed and one which he felt fate, or some other power, had had a hand in.

His thoughts turned to the Graaven people, now the Benshin's closest friends and allies. The Benshin had learned much, some of the knowledge uncomfortable to the forest dwellers, but they had profited greatly from the association and new vistas had opened for his people. In turn, the Graavens had come to the know the ways of the Benshin and their bond with the land. Mutually bene-ficial exchanges between their peoples had grown. The establishment of the gateways which allowed one to travel great distances in just a few steps was one such example, so wondrous at first and which now seemed commonplace.

However, it was not concern for the Graaven people that had disturbed his thoughts and drew him to this place of solitary contemplation. No, it was something else, something hard to define, tenuous, hardly discernible, but there nevertheless. Draachnull stilled his mind and let his consciousness flow outwards. Now he sensed it in greater detail and his brow wrinkled in thought. Yes, there it was, a kind of taint, something unwholesome on the air. Draachnull's skin shivered in response; he could not guess at what effect this taint would have on Tarvuli, but knew it was nothing good.

Draachnull felt another presence in his mind and a quiet unearthly voice spoke to him.

<You are perceptive, Draachnull of the Benshin. Not many beings on Tarvuli can sense what you do.>

<Greetings Spirit of Ta'Morin,> he responded formally. <I am honoured that you would speak to me. What do you know of this taint?>

<You may call me Varnahrin and it is I who am honoured. Your affinity with the land and with your people gives you a rare insight. This taint is a new and disturbing occurrence. I am filtering the worst of it so its impact here is milder than it would otherwise be, but it is potent for all that. Even now Menkh and Tishan journey to combat this thing and will strive to overcome it.>

<And will they succeed?>

<Ultimately, that is a question of Balance. Not even the Intelligence can accurately predict the outcome. I will aid as I can, though that is limited. My primary task is to defend Tarvuli and the City of Ta'Morin. Menkh and Tishan are both powerful Agents of Balance and they have many allies, but that which they face is

also very powerful. Perhaps a new and chaotic order may be established. If so, it is not one that you or I will be a part of.>

<No? Why not?>

<Because, Draachnull of the Benshin, I will obliterate this planet if the enemy is victorious. A more merciful end than the terror and evil to which you and all the peoples of Tarvuli would be subjected to. No, this new order would be the end of all things as we know them.>

Draachnull rocked back in horror, struggling to collect his thoughts.

<What of you, Varnahrin? Would you be obliterated also?>

<Me? It is strange to think in terms of myself as a single entity. That which I once was is changing, I have Tishan Dar to thank for that.> There was a silence which Draachnull did not interrupt. Eventually Varnahrin spoke again.

<In the destruction of Tarvuli, in this reality, I will return to the base matter which originally formed me and perhaps will once more become a part of the Intelligence. That too will be fundamentally different from what it is now. So, you see we must hope that Menkh and Tishan triumph and equilibrium is restored. An equilibrium that has a future in it for me, the Benshin and all the people of this planet.>

<From what you are saying, it will not just be those of us here that will have a future. I think this taint will have an effect beyond my ability to grasp it.>

Varnahrin gave a low laugh of genuine amusement. <Yes, perceptive beyond many indeed. Come, let me show you something that will expand your 'limited understanding'.>

Before he could form a coherent thought Draachnull felt as if his very life essence was drawn out of his body and he seemed to shoot upwards. In amazement he watched his seated self rapidly diminish, and while there was no sensation of movement, soon he hung in space far above Tarvuli, which now rotated slowly far beneath him.

Strangely, he felt no fear. He thought that if his time had come this was a transcendent way to end his existence. Soothing words entered his mind.

<You are safe with me Draachnull. No harm will come to you, I have you in my grasp. Look.>

Draachnull, while knowing full well that his physical body still sat on the ledge far below, could still 'see' his surroundings. It was a wondrous site. Here floating in space far above his home world, whole new vistas opened before him. The moons of Tarvuli seemed so close he could touch them and, as his focus went beyond those familiar celestial bodies, other planets, moons and stars drew into sharper focus as if they too moved closer to him so that Tarvuli seemed but a tiny pinprick against the multitude of stars surrounding him.

Once more Varnahrin's voice entered his mind. <This is the physical plane, Draachnull. You can see these things with your own eyes and had you the means, journey outwards and visit them. Watch now.>

No sooner had Varnahrin spoken than Draachnull's perceptions seemed to shift and while he could still faintly discern the planets and stars he had observed before, the whole was replaced by a complex web of light. Threads of energy seemed to surround everything, stretching off into the infinity of space.

<Behold that which we call the Threadway. Living energy created by all life. The Threadway connects all things everywhere. Adepts like Menkh may journey at will on the Threadway to travel across vast distances in the blink of an eye.'

Draachnull was too overwhelmed to form any rational thought. It was altogether a wondrous thing, both exquisitely beautiful and altogether mysterious. As his consciousness observed the threads, he was able to see that they pulsed with different colours of the spectrum; alive with energy, they danced and swirled like a ballet whose intricate steps he could not follow. As he looked further, he could see also that some threads out of the multitude before him were bereft of colour. Black as night, they gave off a different aura and as they danced among the multicoloured threads, those they came into contact with also darkened. Even absorbed in wonder as he was, Draachnull felt the inherent wrongness in the darker threads.

<Behold the taint, Draachnull. That which your senses informed you of.>

<But what is it, Varnahrin? I can now sense even more its malevolence, as if it was a living thing.>

<It is a living thing,> Varnahrin answered. <It is chaos. Unchecked, its taint will grow in time, corrupting the Threadway. Balance will be overthrown and all will be changed forever. Its effects will flow everywhere, infecting the physical plane and those which exist above.>

<Above?>

In answer, Draachnull's perception shifted yet again. This time all that he could see was replaced by something else entirely. A colourless void in which vague shapes moved. He knew that he was somewhere but it was out of focus and try as he might, he could not concentrate his mind enough to bring the clarity needed to see exactly where this was.>

<Wait, Draachnull. On this plane you will need my assistance.>

No sooner had Varnahrin uttered these words than it was as if an opaque liquid flowed away from his living eyes. The space around him filled with light and colour. If the Threadway was wondrous, this place was magical. Great bands of colours collided, producing a rainbow of new light. On the very edge of hearing there was music; not the music of any known instrument but a complex harmony, somewhat to Draachnull's mind like voices singing. If he had been physically present in this place he would have wept, not with sorrow but with unalloyed joy.

<What is this place Varnahrin?> Even Draachnull's thoughts were hushed and his question was as a whisper.

<This is the place where thought is manifested. It is created by all sentient life. Here, thoughts, ideas and dreams coalesce. Here is where inspiration is created and all sentient life interacts with it to a greater or lesser extent. The physical plane interacts with the Threadway, and the Threadway in turn feeds both into and off this plane. All things are connected and all is held together by Balance.>

Draachnull's thoughts spun around these new revelations. <So then the taint, will also impact this place.> It was a statement not a question.

<The taint will eventually corrupt even this place and in turn that corruption will flow upwards.>

<Upwards? You mean there is a further plane above this one?>

<Indeed. In that place all three planes below blend and interact and there you will find the Intelligence. Or at least one form of it.>

<Can I see it?>

<You are not yet ready to travel to that plane. Though in time all life travels there.>

<But are you not of the Intelligence? Can you not take me there?>

<Of the Intelligence, yes, but separate now in a fundamental way as indeed you are too, Draachnull. My crystalline form is a physical manifestation of the Intelligence and is the means by which it sustains a presence in your reality. This assists in maintaining Balance.>

Draachnull's mind spun. <Why have you shown me this place?>

<Because you are perceptive. Because you, the Benshin and all sentient beings on Tarvuli, have a role to play in what is to come and in resisting the taint. Because, in a way that cannot be explained to you, it felt the right thing to do and finally, to show you how the spread of this taint will affect everything. Not just the physical plane on which you exist.>

Draachnull considered this. His knowledge had increased a thousandfold but he was not sure that he could ever fully understand what he had been shown.

<Thank you, Varnahrin. I little thought when I travelled to that ledge in the heart of my Country what I would learn today. I am ready to return. If the Benshin can assist in any way in this great battle then we will do it.>

<There was never any doubt in my mind that your people would do so, Draachnull. In unfathomable ways your connection to place anchors and grounds the Benshin in a manner that does not exist for many. We will speak again.>

As if waking from a dream, Draachnull opened his eyes. His senses returned; he observed Avlar still peeping just above the horizon and realised that only a very short time had passed while he journeyed with Varnahrin. He took a deep, calming breath and looked out once more across the fern forest with new eyes, his perception of reality changed forever by the Spirit of Ta'Morin.

Draachnull shook his head to clear his thoughts. The struggle ahead, as it had been revealed to him, would be both difficult and dangerous. He sighed. Perhaps the end of all things was in sight; such thoughts were overwhelming. Standing upright, his hands clenched into fists. He would die fighting this evil if that was required, and he would give everything he had, including his life, so that his people and all their friends should not perish.

With grim determination he struck out for his home village. He had a strong need to hold his granddaughter in his arms.

ooooOoooo

Garfun Bendax brought the ImXin to a gentle stop and activated the shield which hid it from prying eyes. He was still somewhat baffled that no one had yet discovered the machine or if they had, the knowledge was being held for some reason he could not understand. As far as he was aware, the ImXin was the last of its kind in Kareem Vastar and he had only discovered its whereabouts by an extraordinary set of circumstances some time ago. The city defences were certainly sophisticated enough to alert the Council to its movements, and so Garfun suspected that he was being aided, why and by whom he could not say. He had some suspicions as to where that source of aid emanated from but had rejected them as fanciful; as to the reasons for it, these were completely beyond him.

Garfun had been undertaking these clandestine trips for so long without problems that, while he was by no means blasé about discovery, his confidence had grown – not enough to completely dispel the fear of exposure, but enough to encourage him to continue, at least for the present. Besides, even if his suspicions were correct, the crystal that formed the real power source of the city had for years beyond count completely shut itself off from contact and was, to all intents and purposes, unreachable.

As Garfun crossed the fields back to the outskirts of the upper city he ruminated on his recent trips. Many years before he had discovered a vast swampland far to the north and it was here that he had come across a type of creature that intrigued him from the outset. A species of amphibious humanoid without record within the Complex archives. This alone was a fact of interest as historically, certainly before the slow decline of the city had begun and enmity with Paxal and Palluvia had gradually increased, exploration of the lands around the three cities had been commonplace. To have missed these creatures seemed a remarkable thing to him.

Naturally over time, he had surreptitiously brought back several of these creatures and, had smuggled them, heavily sedated, into his laboratory. As Kareem Vastar's chief geneticist, Garfun had been unable to resist tampering with their genetic code, even to the extent that certain of his experiments, if discovered, would have led to very serious problems with the Council of Kareem Vastar, leading to potentially fatal consequences for himself. However, in his 130 years of life, Garfun had become a master of secrets and subterfuge and with a patient and well devised plan, knowledge regarding his experiments had become quietly disseminated among the Kareems. A harmless but ultimately pointless experimentation, only of interest to those of an academic bent. Of course, none of the Kareems had any idea what he was really up to and due to his cunning, their reaction to the presence of these creatures had been a patronising tolerance.

While the other Kareems referred to these creatures as his pets they would have been alarmed had they realised exactly what he had done to them. Bigger, stronger, smarter and more able to think and to communicate complex ideas, Garfun himself could not exactly explain why he had done what he had done. He brushed these musings aside. What was done was done and he found that he had grown very fond of his pets as his colleagues referred to them. His own thoughts and feelings were much more profound.

As he entered the city, his thoughts turned to the slow decline of Kareem Vastar. The upper city these days was so under populated as to be almost deserted in a sense. Certainly, the Council members and his fellow scientists preferred the lower city, if they left the Complex at all. While the upper city was more utilitarian in function, catering as it did for the more 'common' people, it was the lower city that boasted spectacular private dwellings, theatres and art installations. Garfun shook his head; there was no obvious explanation for the decline in numbers, the simple fact was that while Kareems might indulge in sexual activity, there seemed no result other than gratification of desire; certainly no offspring resulted, or at least very few. It was just another imponderable. The decline in population was accompanied by a gradual loss of interest in scientific research and discovery. He presumed the Paxals and Palluvians were similarly affected.

Now, research was almost exclusively limited to military applications and defence. Gone was the curiosity to explore and expand knowledge. He recalled wistfully reading in the archives how the Kareems were poised to engage in the exploration of space. An endeavour which never, as far as he could determine, proceeded, except for some installations established on the moons of Tarvuli in the very earliest days of the three founders. And no one now living was exactly sure as to what these 'installations' had been built for. Despite his persistence, any archives pertaining to their construction appeared to have been lost, so research even into this was impossible.

Sighing in frustration, he nodded to a few Kareems as they hurried past him to take a meal in one of the several refectories that could only be found in the upper city. The Kareems of the lower city were far too important to take a meal rubbing shoulders with the common, preferring to eat in one of the dining establishments that had become a feature in their select area of the city.

Still musing, Garfun trudged up the span of the first causeway bridge where the turbulent waters of the seven streams converged, plunging under the Complex to drive the huge turbines deep beneath the structure, before exiting into the lower city, the force of the waters greatly diminished. Flowing through the upper city in a series of cascades, the streams had been integrated into parks and plazas expressly constructed to capitalise on water displays, before they plunged underground, emerging in the lower city as a single course that eventually disappeared into the land way beyond the city's limits.

The intricate arrangement of the city's canals was a marvel of engineering, built during the very beginnings of Kareem Vastar. A huge underground basin had been discovered in the nearby range of hills. Tapped, its waters were channelled into seven pipes feeding into the city, the power and energy of the subterranean flow gaining in strength as it streamed downhill, before lifting to ground level in the seven great channels which flowed through the upper city.

The name Kareem Vastar meant the 'Place Where Waters Meet' and so the inhabitants became known as Kareems. Over many cycles, they became inured to the wonder of the seven streams and the engineering marvel that created them and hardly noticed the ceaseless flow of the waters which journeyed through their city.

Garfun sighed again. Having no desire to see anyone, he skirted the Complex, and the paved plaza with its wonderful depiction of the heavens, and trudged onto the second causeway bridge. Here he entered the lower city and made his way to the modest building he thought of as home besides the apartment he occupied in the Complex when working long hours in his laboratory.

He hadn't even had time to settle down to rest when the front door alarm indicated the presence of a visitor. Peering through the door monitor, he saw his visitor was none other than Kamion, a prominent Council member – and a complete boor.

He had no sooner opened the door than his greeting was cut short by a surly command.

'The Council wishes to see you, Garfun. About these experiments and so-called pets of yours. Present yourself in Chambers when the gong strikes nine tomorrow.'

Garfun's mouth had dropped open. This could mean a number of things, and none of them were good.

'Well?' Kamion's voice was tinged with impatience.

'I will be there, of course.'

Kamion's eyes swept over him from head to toe. His expression told Garfun he didn't like what he saw.

'Make sure you are.'

Without a further word, Kamion swept round and strode off, expressing arrogance in every step.

Garfun thought of several words that could adequately describe his visitor. He was not looking forward to this meeting. Regrettably, Kamion's demeanour was merely a reflection of the rest of the Council members' attitude towards himself.

CHAPTER THREE

Menkh threw a casual glance towards Tishan as she walked away, within moments however, that casual look was replaced by intense scrutiny. Although Menkh could clearly see the steps that Tishan and Morgath were taking, they seemed to rapidly diminish – as if those same steps covered a much greater distance than their length indicated, until, in a very short space of time Tishan seemed to be fading beyond sight. The walls and doorways that had seemed so close just moments ago, seemed also to be very much further away than before. It was an optical illusion and Menkh's attention was fully engrossed while his mind grappled with the impossibility of what his eyes were witnessing. So focused was he that it was only after some moments he noticed the other Adepts had stopped speaking and were looking at him with wry amusement.

'So Menkh, you see at first-hand the wonder of the Eye of Malavak. While our own eyes measure the distance from here to the surrounding walls as but a few steps, the reality is that the distance across the Eye is much greater. Albeit the phenomenon is barely noticeable when you walk it yourself.'

'Yes, it is fascinating. But then so much about the Balancepoint borders on the inexplicable.'

'That is very true, friend Menkh,' said Denith. 'However, let us draw our minds back to the realities of the situation we are facing.'

'Yes, your last attempt to destroy the Enemy – together with Crixac – teetered on the edge of disaster.' Frzath's words were somewhat scathing.

'That may be so,' replied Menkh. 'But that is not to say that the plan was not a good one. Merely that we had totally underestimated the power of that which opposes us. None of us could have foreseen the emergence of its alter ego or its malevolence and capacity for harm.'

T'klath nodded her head. 'You are, of course, correct. We also know that this other power is currently pouring its malice into the very essence of the Threadway. To this end we may assume that it is totally absorbed in this task and therefore the opportunity to destroy its noisome parent may be manifest.'

'I hear your words T'klath, but making assumptions about this entity, whatever it is, may be dangerous in the extreme,' said Menkh. His past experience lent an edge to his remarks.

As T'klath was about to respond, a voice entered their minds.

<My friends. While Menkh's point is true, without detailed information which we have no power to acquire, and without expending time that we simply do not have, we must act on assumptions. Both Tishan Dar and Menkh have been tasked with the destruction of the parent Dorath Mar. If this can be successfully achieved, then the problem of its alter ego may be tackled after that point. We must act proactively in the case of the former, and reactively in the case of the latter. We cannot accurately predict the consequences of the Dorath Mar's destruction as it relates to this being, but we can assume that its rage will be all-consuming. In that event, there is an obvious target for its wrath. While there may be other outcomes, it would seem that the world of Tarvuli

will be the ultimate battleground. Overcoming this evil is therefore the final test. Failure to achieve either task is not an option.>

There was a long period of silence while Varnahrin's words were digested and the consequences of failure fully realised for perhaps the first time.

Frzath's thoughts came in response.

<Clearly, we Adepts here must play a more direct role in supporting success.>

<You speak truly, Frzath. Even now, Tishan bonds to the White. She will travel to the Dorath Mar home world and obliterate it.>

Menkh absorbed this information calmly. While it was not wholly unexpected, he nonetheless felt a frisson of fear at the danger to which Tishan, alone and unaided, would be exposed. He gathered his thoughts and spoke.

'But how is that even possible? She is but one individual; what power can she wield even in her changed form that would enable this?' Menkh's fear for Tishan was palpable.

<Your fears are understandable, Menkh. But believe me when I tell you that Tishan will have an object with her that has capability way beyond your understanding. Even so, she is but one individual, as you say. How then might you here aid her in her task?>

Varnahrin's questions led to a deep discussion among the Adepts in considering the options at their disposal.

After lengthy deliberation Frzath spoke aloud:

'Clearly, and as all have agreed, we need a distraction. If we here can coordinate the obliteration of the Dorath Mar on the Chosen home world, with Tishan's assault on the Dorath Mar parent, it may be of assistance to her in achieving success.'

'An interesting proposition Frzath, but what plan do you have in mind to accomplish this distraction?' asked Menkh.

'We know the Allroians are still engaged in their war against the Chosen and even now prepare an assault. The destruction of their deity may provide a fitting distraction to the Enemy in aiding its annihilation.'

Menkh pondered these remarks while the Adepts spoke in hushed tones among themselves.

'This is a huge task, the dangers of which are clear to us all. While I fear for Tishan, there is no other being I would trust with this mission. But how do we successfully coordinate our separate attacks to ensure the success and achievement of both aims?'

'As to that,' said Denith, 'we can employ the Eye of Malavak. We know that the Allroians have been concentrating their forces for a direct attack on the Chosen System. As we have considered, if you insert yourself into this attack, we think there will be ample opportunity to exploit the situation and eliminate the Dorath Mar.'

'And,' added Morgath, 'the sudden obliteration of their deity will likely have a profound effect on the Chosen as well, though exactly how that would manifest is anyone's guess.'

'There are several issues here that we will need to address if we are not to rely on blind chance,' said Menkh. 'The attack of the Allroians must occur at the same time as Tishan begins her mission. Then I will have to affect the demise of the Dorath Mar at exactly the right moment. Are you still confident that you can manage communication to enable this?'

'We have the means, Menkh,' said T'klath. 'On this matter, if you consent to trust us, we will work to facilitate your actions and that of Tishan Dar.'

Menkh bowed his head to the group of Adepts. 'It goes without saying that you have my complete trust, but let us say that Tishan and I achieve this thing. Do we then assume that its alter ego will also be destroyed?'

'It is a possibility, certainly,' replied Morgath, 'but not one that we are overly confident about. By whatever means this power came into being, we believe we must work on the assumption that it will remain. The destruction of its parent must therefore lead to an immediate and violent retaliation.'

'That being the case,' said Denith, 'as Varnahrin has indicated, while there may be other alternatives we can expect that its wrath will be turned against Tarvuli – and Varnahrin in particular. This is where the final battle must occur.'

Menkh nodded. 'Then we must ensure that we are fully pre-pared. While the power of Varnahrin is beyond our understanding, I believe that the presence of Tishan and myself must be there to assist.'

<You speak truly Menkh, for you and Tishan both have a role to play in the battle to come. Your plan is not without risk, yet it is sound for all that. News of Tishan Dar will come to me and information as to her actions will be passed on. You must be pre-pared for the unexpected and adapt accordingly. May the Intelligence guide you in your endeavours.> The voice of Varnah-rin resonated in their minds, and was gone.

'Very well,' said Frzath. 'While we await further knowledge of Tishan Dar let us see where our friends the Allroians are up to in the preparations for their campaign against the Chosen.'

'I for one, would like to see a little more of their home planet and judge what manner of beings they are,' said Menkh. 'Having some insight into them as a Race and the weapons they will be deploying, will be of great value. While I have knowledge of them through Crixac's memories, they are not recent. Some first-hand experience would be of immense value in what is to come.'

The voice of Crixac entered Menkh's and the Adepts' minds: <Well, as you have seen from my memories, they are certainly not humanoid, Menkh. The Allroians' home world is almost com-pletely covered by water and as you glimpsed before, they resemble huge jellyfish. They communicate in a series of clicks and pulses of sound, as well as through intricate movements of their several

tentacular appendages. As strange as they are to our eyes, they are highly intelligent and generally peace-loving creatures.>

'All that Crixac has conveyed to you is true,' said Frzath. 'Their war with the Chosen was initiated by that Race who abhor any form of life different from their own. In attacking the Allroians, they created an implacable enemy.'

'If they have established interstellar relations with nearby systems, surely they must have found a sophisticated means of communication?' suggested Menkh.

'Indeed,' replied Denith. 'Remember that their Hegemony was established over many hundreds of years' development as well as scientific and technological advancement. The Allroians are masters of artificial intelligence and they mostly use highly sophisticated androids to achieve their ends. Having said that, they also have translation devices so they can easily communicate with other life-forms. But come, let us take a look at their home world. The Allroians eschew names for individuals, places and all things. Theirs is a shared intelligence; a thing either is or is not. They have a profound sense of what a thing is and so feel no need to name it.'

Menkh's face crinkled in bemusement.

'But surely not naming something must lead to difficulties. If I was telling you about a tree and yet neither it nor its constituent parts had names, then surely communication would be extremely difficult, if not impossible?'

'Yes, that would be true if you were communicating in words, Menkh,' Frzath said. 'But the Allroians do not use words at all, the bulk of their communication is telepathic. They communicate in concepts, pictures if you like, with some sounds and gestures to add further clarification. There is no need for words because each Allroian perfectly understands what is being conveyed. Take your tree example, although I am simplifying it for ease of our own understanding. You would not need the word for tree because in the

Allroian awareness a perfect picture of a tree and all its parts would arise in the minds of those in the discussion.'

'That is why we so often use mind-speech, Menkh. That way, we utilise the same ability without the limitation of words. If I wish to express profound joy to you, how much more powerful is mind-speech in communicating that as opposed to trite statements in words such as, "I am so happy", or however we might express it vocally?'

Menkh nodded his head in understanding.

'You have given me much to think about and piqued my curiosity even more to see this home world of theirs. If they have no name for it, do we use one at all?'

T'klath laughed and turned to mind-speech.

<We do indeed Menkh, we call it Pell Hamsh which in the language of my people means Great Ocean, rather apt given that nine-tenths of their world is covered by a vast sea. But come, let us show you their world, and you will see for yourself.'

Once again Menkh experienced a sense of movement, even though he was stationary. Planets and planetary systems flowed at great speed beneath his feet and he felt a plunging sensation as one particular planet seemed to surge up from the depths and, like a plummeting comet, Menkh was swept down through dense layers of cloud until he spied a vast grey sea. Huge waves whipped up by winds that blew unimpeded across a limitless ocean-scape leapt up to meet him, until he plunged beneath the waves. Or at least that is how it seemed. Deeper and deeper he descended but rather than the light diminishing in the depths, it increased. Not the bright light of day certainly, but a clear illumination that allowed him to see into the distance.

<Remarkable, isn't it?> T'klath's thoughts entered Menkh's mind.

<The light is provided by the plants which grow here in the depths. There are four main types: one is a gigantic seaweed that

reaches up into the shallower waters far above us. As the light of the sun above waxes and wanes, there is a photochemical reaction in the plant and it gives off a phosphorescent light. In the depths of the ocean there are three species of plant-like creatures which absorb that light. These grow at different levels and while they resemble plants in a number of ways, they are actually aquatic animals that feed off tiny fish and other minute forms of life. They produce light as a side effect of their digestive processes. The end result of all this, is that the great deeps of this world are not buried in darkness but are illuminated throughout the day, causing other plants and animal life to thrive in turn.>

<Amazing. I have never really thought about what grows beneath the surface of oceans, but of course whole ecosystems flourish in the deep waters. Remarkable is an understatement. Do *we* have a name for these plants?> said Menkh.

<We have christened the seaweed *kelix* and the three types of aquatic life we identify as *questil* in the shallower waters, then *mital* and finally *doxtal* which live in the great deeps. The light they produce is slightly different and it is one way of assessing how deep you are. Of course, the Allroians have no need for anything as primitive as words to describe them.>

The Eye moved them across a vista of underwater mountain ranges, followed by great plains covered by a species of sea grass. Everywhere were fish of dazzling variety, some preferring the ocean floor while others swam in great schools high above. Once an enormous shape passed over their heads, seeming to take forever to pass by, such was its size. Before Menkh could comment, they floated stationary above a vast city, the like of which Menkh had never imagined possible.

The buildings of the city were bathed in the light which emanated from thousands of the questil and mital plants that covered their outside surfaces. The structures themselves were multiple and varied: some many storeys high, rising to peaks like mountain summits, while others were domelike, boasting but two or three storeys. All had what appeared to be windows, but these seemed to be naturally occurring apertures in the buildings' surfaces; albeit they were many, some much larger than others acting as entry and exit points. What streets there were seemed to be more as a result of gaps between one structure and the next rather than intentionally planned as in terrestrial cities. But, Menkh supposed, what need was there for roads when everything he could see simply floated between the buildings.

Great schools of multi-coloured fish swam freely, adding further colour and movement to the ever-unfolding scene and among all this, Allroians – singles and small groups – could be seen passing into and out of buildings or merely floating, engaged perhaps in a discussion or other activity which did not require movement.

Above their heads silvery vessels, which he had at first thought were some other type of aquatic creature, proved to be a form of transportation. They employed a method of propulsion which expelled water at great speed from rear apertures, thus taking travellers to far-flung corners of the vast city or to other locations in the depths.

<This city looks more like it has grown rather than been built. I've never seen its like!> Menkh's thoughts echoed his surprise.

The Adepts stood by, quietly enjoying Menkh's reaction until Denith spoke:

<The cities of the Allroians are entrancing, are they not? Well may you think they look as if they had simply grown because in reality that is exactly what has happened. They are all created by the work of another creature, actually countless millions of tiny creatures naturally occurring on the planet. The Allroians learned long ago how to shape the growth of these creatures into habitable structures and they grow at a ferocious rate, two to three of your Graaven spahn each day. If you spent more time here you would find what you might mistake as long ranges of hills which are in

fact merely the growth of these creatures. Of course, the material they form attracts the growth of plants and fish, so that the cities of the Allroian are bathed in life and light and movement.>

Menkh nodded in response, his eye now drawn to the Allroians themselves. While their overall size varied, the majority of those he could see would have been no larger in mass than a Benshin adult. Their long-tapered bodies glistened in the water and were all of a uniform opaque whiteness. Two very large black eyes were located just behind several long tentacles that finished in delicate, finger like protrusions. As with the vehicles he had seen earlier, their movement through the water seemed to involve some sort of natural propulsion where seawater was expelled thrusting them forward, which Menkh observed could be at great speed where required.

It was difficult to take it all in and Menkh spent long moments trying to order the spectacle of movement and colour into a comprehensible form. As his eyes began to focus and filter, his attention was drawn to several vehicles apparently transporting materials, harnessed to large fish. These were being shepherded by an Allroian holding prods in two of its tentacles to guide the much larger creature on its journey. The teardrop-shaped vehicles were silvery and almost transparent, so that the cargo inside could be clearly seen, though what it was Menkh had no idea. The towing creature was similar in shape to the vehicles it pulled, but was a pale blue in colour and it moved both itself and its cargo by means of strong vertical beats of its finned tail.

<I echo your amazement Menkh, I feel as if we could spend many dak'chaal simply observing this world and these creatures,> said Crixac. Menkh could only nod in fascinated agreement.

The voice of T'klath echoed in Menkh's mind.

<Now let us travel above the surface of this world and there you will begin to grasp the technological advances of the Allroians.>

In moments, they floated far above the Allroian home world. There, suspended in space, was an enormous wheel-like construction slowly rotating before their eyes. A blue aura surrounded it, whether as a protective shield or the means by which atmosphere was maintained was open to surmise, but it was clear that this was a city markedly different to that which they had so recently observed. Here could be seen mighty towers and tall cellblock buildings clustered around a central open space. From above, to Menkh's mind, it resembled a city bordering a lake. Adding to this image were sophisticated protrusions similar to long wharves or docks that stretched out around the edges of the open area.

<Your thoughts are accurate, Menkh> said Crixac. <This is where incoming craft from the planet below berth, and where travellers make their return journey. The wharf-like protrusions are actually airlocks where travellers can safely embark or disembark without compromising the integrity of the city itself.>

Crixac had no sooner completed his thought than an approaching craft loomed large as it entered the central hub of the city. Coming to a complete stop, a connection was made and presumably passengers and cargo were even now being offloaded.

The Eye of Malavak descended further; the Adepts pierced the blue aura and entered the confines of the city proper where Menkh was in for another surprise.

<This whole place is filled with water!>

<Yes> responded Morgath. <But then the Allroians are aquatic.>

The city itself was alive with movement. The same silvery vessels they had so recently observed on the home world could be seen entering and exiting the myriad towers and buildings of the suspended city. As they neared one of the tower blocks, they became aware of a number of creatures apparently standing guard; somewhat different in appearance to the Allroians, having fewer tentacles, they floated upright in the waters.

<These creatures are different in aspect to the Allroians. Are they standing guard?> Menkh's thoughts were hesitant, as he was unsure of their purpose.

<Quite right Menkh. However, as we said before, these creatures as you see them are actually a kind of artificial intelligence developed by the Allroians. In a sense, they are like your tetrans back on Tarvuli. The Allroians manufacture many different kinds, developed for a wide range of applications. These act, as you correctly thought, as security guards. Others are much more sophisticated: under controlled circumstances, they are capable of manufacturing duplicates of themselves. It is these creations which provide the bulk of the crews required to operate Allroian battle fleets and trading ships. You recall we observed how our friends sacrificed their ships in the battle to entrap the Chosen and fire their new weapon?> said Crixac.

<I do indeed. Initially I thought them cold and calculating, but it was a clever ploy. I am reassured that they did not intentionally sacrifice their own.>

<The Allroian mind is capable of controlling several droids at any one time and those selected for this task are trained rigorously from their earliest years. To this end there is a hierarchy of control built into the command structure of their creations. Not unlike a military hierarchy. Each AI operates according to its internal programming and subject to the orders issued to it, just like your tetran forces.>

<What happens if the Allroian controllers are killed?> inquired Menkh.

<A good question,> said Frzath. <This is actually a rare occurrence. In any battle fleet, the Allroians themselves sit at the heart of their formations, protected by a ring of powerful escort craft. If the battle goes against them, they withdraw and their AI forces also automatically withdraw in a rear-guard action. Multiple strategies have been anticipated and the AI are programmed to adapt

to the situation they find themselves in. If the Allroians themselves are killed then a similar response ensues, but if the AI are unable to withdraw, they mount a full counterattack until they themselves are destroyed.>

<It would seem that with a force of combatants with neither emotional attachment nor fear of death, they would be invincible if they turned their minds to conquest,> Menkh mused.

<That is so,> said Denith. <But the Allroians have never as a race desired conquest. Trade, yes. They have an insatiable appetite for the import and export of goods and materials and as a result they are great explorers. This obsession is combined with high intelligence and respect for life. That is why their war with the Chosen is unusual to say the least. However, it would be evident that they have recognised in their enemy a hatred so deep that the loss of the war must end in their own extermination. This threat has magnified since the Chosen became the disciples of the Dorath Mar.>

<This city in space bears little resemblance to the dwellings of the Allroians on their home world. I assume that this is an adaption required to allow for travel in space?>

<To a degree, Menkh,> Denith said. <But this city, as you call it, is fixed in a stationary orbit. From here you can travel to several of the planets that neighbour Pell Hamsh, colonised by the Allroians long ago. It is there that they have facilities to construct interstellar craft.>

<Of course,> Frzath added. <The construct you have previously observed prior to your very unfortunate encounter with the Enemy, apart from acting as a Waystation, also has the capacity to both repair and manufacture spacecraft of different kinds.>

Menkh considered these words and then Crixac interjected.

<It is clear then that the Allroians are both sophisticated and intelligent. So, where are they up to in their conflict with the Chosen?>

In response to this thought everything around Menkh swirled and became unfocused for a brief moment until they stood above the Eye of Malavak once more in the Balancepoint.

<We have been observing the Allroian build-up for some time; this is why the idea of a coordinated attack with Tishan is feasible,> said Denith.

T'klath nodded in agreement.

<Three battle fleets have been amassed by the Allroian with the purpose of assaulting the Chosen home world.>

Before Menkh could form the question, Denith spoke. <We do not believe that their intention is the destruction of the planet. Rather they seek to destroy the Dorath Mar that bides there and to cripple the Chosen's ability to make war. This will be an offensive with multiple objectives in mind.>

<What of the Chosen? Surely they cannot be ignorant of the power set against them?>

<The Chosen are blinded by their own arrogance, enhanced by their 'deity'. We believe that they have no idea that the Allroians have the ability to penetrate their outer defences.>

<Still, they must be making preparations themselves. What have you observed of them?>

Here the several Adepts exchanged looks.

<Regrettably,> said Frzath <we have been unable to observe them. By some unknown means it would appear that their Dorath Mar master has screened them so that even the Eye of Malavak cannot penetrate the shield that surrounds them.>

<Then clearly Crixac and I must travel to the location of the Allroians. Powerful as the Allroians are, the Chosen may yet have developed a counter to them.>

<You speak truly and it is a concern that we here can do little about,> said Frzath. <It is our belief that the Allroian target is Katlun, the Chosen home world and where the Dorath Mar bides. The Allroians are readying their battle fleets in the space around a

planet within their system which we have named Men'Harast. It is home to several mining colonies, but is otherwise uninhabited. Well inside Allroian space, they are safe from detection there. Their attack is imminent; close observation of this location should give us what we require.>

<Very well, then perhaps we can take a look?> suggested Menkh.

Frzath nodded in agreement and Menkh steadied himself as the Eye of Malavak re-oriented and they appeared to float once more in a new quadrant. As the planet Frzath had referred to, came into focus, they could see that dozens of huge ships were massed together with what appeared to be a similar number of smaller craft either returning to the surface of Men'Harast or coming from it. Still others were locked on to vessels slowly orbiting far above the planet's surface.

<Supply vessels,> said Crixac. <There are enough Allroian battle cruisers here to constitute three separate attack groups.>

< How can you tell that? All I can see is a great mass of ships, > Menkh asked.

<Look carefully Menkh. Do you observe any differences in the appearance of the larger ships?>

Menkh turned his attention to the mass of craft in front of him. In the rays of light from the distant sun they appeared uniformly white. Great tubular vessels, each having a hollow centre down its full length which emitted a muted glow of purple light. The surface of the vessels was smooth, but in orderly rows across them were a series of ridges that bulged slightly outwards as they wound around the circumference of the vessel. A series of regularly spaced peaks, like hilltops, emerged at the summit of these, giving off a silvery luminescence. What the purpose of the ridges were, Menkh had no idea.

<That is easily answered Menkh,> said Crixac. <These ridges and the summits they contain are where the shielding and cloaking

devices for each vessel are located. Each ship can be disguised to blend into the background of space, thereby rendered invisible from attackers. In battle the ridges are the focal point for energy shields to protect each craft. But are they all the same?>

Menkh continued his observation, his curiosity heightened by Crixac's question. It was confusing, amid the array of so many identical vessels masked to some degree by the constant movement of smaller supply craft. However, after several moments he perceived that what he had first thought was a random collection of vessels, began to take on a discernible pattern. Menkh pulled his focus back from individual craft and looked at them as a whole. Now it was clear that there were three formations; an array of craft arranged spherically around a central vessel. As his perspective changed he saw that at the heart of each formation reposed a ship of very different proportions and appearance.

<Now you see them Menkh; these are the control ships. The craft that carry the living Allroians who oversee and coordinate the vessels that form each school of craft.>

<So you mean that each battle group is like a school of fish?>

Crixac laughed. <Well they are aquatic creatures, Menkh, so – yes, exactly like a school of fish moving in close coordination. The outer craft also protect the Allroians from attack.>

Menkh was fascinated. The three vessels Crixac had referred to were constructed of a material that seemed to absorb the light around it. In addition, each craft was more spherical in shape and, unlike all the other vessels, did not have a hollow centre.

<Yes, the hollow centre you can see on the other craft is the heart of their weaponry. From out of that core, where the purple light pulses, the Allroians have developed a lethal energy. The weaponry of individual craft can also be combined with the power of other ships in the fleet,> said T'klath.

Now Morgath's thoughts entered Menkh's mind. <So in effect each vessel can attack individually, or can combine with other craft to increase the power of their attack.>

<I see,> said Menkh. <Then presumably when an entire fleet of ships combine, the concentrated power must be overwhelming.>

<As you have seen, Menkh. The new weapon that we observed them deploying against an earlier Chosen force was the culmination of many attempts to combine the might of all their ships at one time. These spherical formations allow both for maximum protection of the Allroians and also to provide the most effective way to combine the destructive force of their weaponry. One gigantic energy beam that has the capacity to obliterate an opposing force.>

<Assuming of course that the enemy counters with their own battle fleet,> mused Menkh.

<Yes, that is my thought. There may still be a vulnerability in their formation if the Chosen develop a different strategy,> said Crixac.

<Well,> said Denith, <the Allroians must be confident that the might of their three battle fleets will be enough to overpower whatever the Chosen try. Up to now they have always reacted in the same way to an attack.>

During the time of the Adepts' observation through the Eye of Malavak, the constant movement of the smaller supply craft had gradually diminished until the three battle groups floated alone. Against the backdrop of space and in the reflected light of the distant star, the sight was awe-inspiring, both beautiful and terrible at the same time. The ships evoked a sense of menace and the technology used to create them reflected the pinnacle of Allroian power and ingenuity. There was a time, not so long ago in his life, when the sight of such things would have seemed to be the magical works of the gods. Now Menkh knew differently and that these vast machines were the creation of creatures who, while very different from himself, were still of flesh and blood.

Then, within moments, the fleets began to move. The individual ships of each formation reacted just as a school of fish, turning as one in a single movement without in any way losing their tight formation. Faster and faster they moved until, reaching what must have been a defined point, they abruptly accelerated and vanished from sight.

Around Menkh, the Eye of Malavak swirled, triggering the usual feeling of momentary dizziness until they all stood once more on solid ground above it.

<Now I believe it is time for Crixac and I to depart,> said Menkh. <I had hoped that Tishan might have returned to us, but it may be that she already moves. I believe we cannot linger and I have the strongest feeling that the need for our aid may be imminent.>

<Then you must follow your instincts in this,> said T'klath. <We will observe events through the Eye. Wait for our communication before you directly attack the Dorath Mar on Katlun. Tishan will play her own part, but it will take a little time for her to adjust to the changes she has undergone, just as you did Menkh when you became a bonded Adept. Our thoughts and prayers travel with you,> said Frzath.

<Thank you, all of you,> said Menkh. <As the Allroian target is the Chosen home world, it seems obvious that Crixac and I will travel to the edge of Chosen space. From there we should be able to locate the Allroian battle fleets as they emerge.>

<Fare you well Menkh ab Dur and Crixac. May the Intelligence guide you. The Balance is All,> declared T'klath. As one, the Adepts bowed to Menkh, their hands clasped in a prayer-like attitude.

Drawing the Threadway to him, Menkh echoed their words. Focussing his thoughts on the Chosen planetary system, he summoned his staff and ascended, disappearing from the relocated Balancepoint, and passed like a thought into the ether.

As the form of Menkh departed from view, Frzath clapped his hands. 'Come my friends. We have a vital role to play in this task. We must meld our minds and use all our powers to assist. Morgath, you have knowledge of Tishan's current location?'

'Given the door that was used here, there is only one possibility. After her transformation she will have revived in the Anshar Construct.'

The Adepts nodded their heads as one. 'Of course,' said Denith. 'The gateway to all worlds. From there she can emerge without detection.'

'Yes, which makes our task somewhat more difficult,' said Frzath. 'Come, the sooner we meld, the sooner we can link to the Intelligence. We must find a way to ensure that Tishan exits the Anshar at the right moment.'

As Frzath spoke, the Adepts walked together towards one of the many doorways that surrounded the Eye of Malavak and, passing through, vanished one by one.

CHAPTER FOUR

arfun left his dwelling in the lower city very early to attend the required meeting and made his way to the Audience Chamber situated high in the topmost levels of the Complex. He was afraid that his expeditions via ImXin had been discovered and had been rehearsing a defence if such was the case. His main concern, however, was for his creations whom he had come to view with a fatherly affection.

Vallon Spec occupied the central chair in the Chamber. Five other councillors sat in attendance upon her, including that prize idiot Kamon Drassec and the other toadies who formed the Inner Circle. All sat with disapproving looks directed at him. Discussions did not last long.

Vallon's voice was tinged with false sympathy; how she was enjoying every moment of his humiliation.

'So you see Garfun, your argument that your *pets* constitute a valid scientific experiment have been carefully assessed.' Here she nodded at each of her fellow councillors who in turn, with mock serious expressions, nodded in response.

'They have, as you are now aware, been unanimously rejected.'

Garfun longed to tell them exactly what he thought of their so-called deliberations but knew it would only make matters worse.

'The verdict of the Council is that these creatures cannot be allowed to breed. They must be euthanised; and that will be the end of this unfortunate episode. Quite clearly, this would have been avoidable had you sought approval via the usual channels.'

Vallon's voice was heavy with sarcasm. She knew full well that permission would never have been given even had the applications come to their attention. Such experimentation was a complete waste of time and resources. Resources better spent in thwarting their enemies.

'But surely…' Garfun's response was shut down.

'Euthanised,' Kamon's voice could not hide his satisfaction with the decision.

'Indeed,' echoed Vallon. 'But in consideration of your efforts, the Council has generously allowed you to oversee the process personally before reporting back to us that it has been accomplished. That will be all.'

Garfun gave each Councillor a withering look, abruptly turned, and headed for the exit. He would not give them the satisfaction of a response.

Vallon's voice interrupted his departure.

'You have two days Garfun. Two days. Or we ourselves will oversee their destruction.'

Garfun was proud that his footsteps did not break stride. Two days!

He stormed into his apartment in the fifth tower of the Complex. To say that he had built himself into a towering rage would be an understatement of the highest order. Garfun was beside himself with fury.

'Damn them all!' he yelled aloud in his frustration. 'Curse them to deepest pits of the seventh hell! I will be damned if I euthanise them! Do you hear, Vallon you cretin? You and all your lick-spittle councillors!'

Garfun fumed helplessly. Summoned to a meeting of the Council! Summoned! Not invited, not politely requested…summoned! As a senior scientist and Kareem Vastar's leading geneticist, he expected respect for both himself and his position. To be treated in such a way by that gang of buffoons. Truly, the City had fallen from its greatness with these dolts in control.

Garfun longed to have lived in the glory days of Kareem Vastar, when its culture and science were at their peak. He moaned aloud in frustration. Alas, wishing would never make it happen; he was consigned to live his days among lesser Kareems who looked to the glory of a distant past as a measure of their present-day greatness and (mostly imaginary) supremacy among the three cities. Now Palluvia and Paxal were seen as enemies and all research was focused on achieving ultimate victory over those the Kareems now distrusted to a level approaching outright hatred.

He poured himself a stiff measure of arrac, his own private brew, and sitting in his favourite chair pondered the course of action he would take.

There was no doubt in his mind that he would not obey the Council's ultimatum, but there was not much time to organise a swift departure for his creatures. It was many cycles since Garfun had travelled to the distant area of swampland once travel outside the city was banned. There he had found the puny humanoid amphibians which he judged to be on the verge of extinction and which he had manipulated in a series of genetic experiments. A grim smile touched his lips. Experiments that did things which, while not precisely against the law as the Kareems saw it, would have led to serious and possibly fatal consequences for him and his associates. Besides, surely it was his business if he manipulated his own DNA into that of the creatures? What boundaries should not be pushed in the name of scientific discovery? No, he had no qualms in that respect.

Of course, this meant that the current generation of the creatures were like children to him, now vastly transformed from the feeble humanoids they had been. Yes, they were *his* Graavens, and no power in Kareem Vastar would command him to destroy that which he had created. Garfun chuckled to himself. His fellow Kareems had initially used the word graaven as a joke term for his creatures, because even once he had refined their capacity for speech, they could not say his name properly. The closest approximation they could get was *'Graaven'* whenever they spoke to him and so what had started as a joke – and meant to be demeaning – had stuck. Even the creatures now thought of themselves as Graaven.

So, the questions then were how and more importantly when could he secrete them out of the city and where could they go?

Garfun pondered these questions and sat late into the night mulling over the options.

The lands to the west were vast, but even reaching them would be a challenge. Crossing the Caxaphalc was easy enough and he had the means to destroy the bridge to prevent any pursuit, but crossing the desert beyond the river on foot, would be a huge challenge. Even if successful, knowledge of the lands beyond the desert in recent times was limited to say the least. Certainly, they were inhabited by people and creatures who might take violent objection to the arrival of the Graaven… . But traveling further east was no option as this would take them too close to Paxal and Palluvia, not to mention the untamed forest tribes and the difficulties they represented to any folk travelling through their domain. They were a diminutive but dangerous people. No, it had to be west, but how?

Lost in thought and several beakers of arrac later, he drifted off into a doze. The effects of a long and frustrating day, grappling with the problem of getting his charges out of Kareem Vastar and the drinks he had consumed to calm himself, caught him unawares and he fell asleep in his chair.

A feeling of disorientation crept into his fitful slumber and brought him blearily awake. Within moments of opening his eyes, however, he sat bolt upright as he came to grips with his surroundings. Somehow, he was no longer in his apartment. As Garfun's eyes swept around, comprehension of where he now was, it had to be said, sent a shiver of fear straight through him.

This was a place he recognised from stories; to his knowledge no Kareem had actually accessed this location in living memory. Before him, reposing on what might be construed as a throne, sat a huge crystal pulsing with light. Connected to it, innumerable cables of varying thicknesses and different colours entered and left the room which, despite the overall dimensions of the huge space it sat in, was dominated by its presence. Here then was that which Menath had stolen and which was the central power source of the entire city. Since the unexplained disappearance of Menath a thousand cycles ago, this location had been inaccessible, shut off from intrusion by inexplicable means, despite the concerted efforts of generations of Kareems to enter it.

Now Garfun sat in the crystal's presence, almost within touching distance. He could not imagine why it was that he had been brought here because that was obviously what had happened. He felt a sensation within his head, like the gentle touch of a cool breeze against the skin and a voice spoke to him in his mind.

<Greetings Garfun. Put aside your fears, no harm will come to you here. You seek assistance with your Graaven creations. That assistance is already in motion.>

Understandably somewhat rattled, Garfun struggled to form a coherent response.

'Assistance? I'm sorry, but how could you know and, forgive me, what assistance can you provide?'

<The thoughts of all Kareems are open to me Garfun Bendax, including yours. Your experiments with your creations will have consequence far beyond your original intentions. Getting them out of the city is of paramount importance for what is to come.>

'What is to come?'

The voice which had seemed vaguely male changed its modulation and now sounded, to his mind, more female in tonality. There was a sense of sadness in it.

<That is for the future. Your Graaven people will be far away, and in time, may grow into a mighty nation. A fitting and lasting tribute to you.>

Garfun shied away from the implications behind the crystal's statement. He sensed a calamity approaching and his own involvement in it. Could this mean his own demise was part of that? He took a deep breath and shook off the feelings that had briefly arisen following the crystal's remarks.

'Well then. It seems that I am right to defy the orders of the Council. How do we proceed?'

Once again, the voice modulated, now more overtly masculine.

<You do not disappoint, Garfun Bendax. Attend now. Your Graavens have been prepared. Cloaked and shielded, they wait by the main gates. They are well supplied. Go to them and say your farewells. They must cross the bridge over the Caxaphalc and journey across the desert to a new land. Their leader, Grossa, carries two devices: these must be placed at each end of the bridge. Once the Graaven have safely crossed over the devices will activate and the bridge will be destroyed; your Council will not have the means to follow even if they wished to.>

Garfun breathed a sigh of relief and sat back. He had not realised till that moment the tension within him. Filled with a new determination and feeling lighter for it, he stood up.

'Thank you. I will make my way to them.'

<Stay. There is one more task for you to perform.>

Garfun's face crinkled in puzzlement; he could not conceive what else needed to be done. He sank back into the chair and waited in silence.

<Before you go to them you must take the Orb of Kalash; this you will give to them.>

Garfun gasped in surprise. 'The Orb of Kalash? But that is a relic of the older times, an artefact of incredible value.' He stuttered in his amazement. 'What possible use will they make of it?' He paused for a moment as he gathered his thoughts. 'You must know that it is locked in a sealed vault, so even if I wanted to, I cannot access it.'

<You will find the vault unlocked. No Kareem will bar your path. As to the why of it, the role the Orb will play in what is to come is critical. The consequence of your charges not having it are inestimable. In time the knowledge of its power and purpose will be revealed. Think Garfun, is it of any value locked away in a vault? No, its time is coming.>

Garfun contemplated the crystal's remarks. Was he seriously going to argue with this crystal whose knowledge and power were overwhelmingly great? It would be like a newborn babe arguing with an elder. There was so much here that was hinted at; he felt a great sense of frustration which he could not express, somehow tinged with deep regret.

<Do not despair, Garfun Bendax. You yourself have already played a mighty part in what is to come. Remember, part of your own essence is locked away in your Graavens. In that sense your heritage will live on as testament to your genius.>

He laughed out loud; it was true that he had more than a fair share of self-pride which did not endear him to some members of the Council.

'I never thought to be flattered by a living crystal. These are strange times indeed. Very well, if it is that important, then I will do what you ask. How shall I get out of this place?'

<Leave that to me. Good bye Garfun Bendax. We will not meet again.>

Even as a response was forming in Garfun's mind he felt his body go cold for the briefest moment and then he appeared directly outside the vault where the Orb of Kalash was located. All was quiet and he could neither see nor sense anyone in his vicinity. It was just as the crystal had said. Garfun pushed open the metal door of the vault and entered. It was not a large space and contained only one object, which sat on a pedestal in what should have been a sealed glass container. This too was open. Despite the crystal's assurances, he tiptoed forward, furtively reached out and lifted the Orb, half expecting alarms to sound and his presence to be quickly revealed to those whose role it was to secure the Complex. The Orb proved surprisingly light and cold to the touch. Deep in its heart he thought he could see colours swirling, but it may merely have been a trick of the lights which had illuminated upon his entry into the vault.

With the Orb firmly in his grasp, Garfun quietly left the vault expecting at every turn to meet with someone and trying to rehearse a plausible excuse for his presence, despite his implausible situation. As the crystal had promised, however, all remained quiet and he made his way to the exit without interference, his nerves jangling as he crept like a thief in the night. Punishment for stealing the Orb would be severe if discovered, not only for taking it but to whom he intended to give it. Eventually leaving the Complex behind, he breathed a sigh of relief as he walked over the Causeway Bridge and crept through the streets of the Upper City. In what must now be the earliest hours of the morning, though it was still dark, he at last came to the main gates, his way illuminated by the light of Orvasne which held its course across the night sky above the city.

The Graavens stood together in a silent group, their demeanour evidence that they too understood the gravity of what they were doing. It was clear that they were packed for a long journey; each carried a backpack and many had weapons clearly on display including the long bows for which they had developed an affinity. Garfun felt a tremor of emotion; these beings were ultimately his creation, he loved them and was caught between the sadness of seeing them depart and the elation that they would escape being euthanised.

Their leader Grossa, taller and more muscular than all the others, came forward and spoke quietly. 'The spirit voice said you would come to see us. Will you travel with us?'

Garfun lifted his voice so all could hear. 'No. My friends, I wish that I could come with you, but this is a journey you must make on your own. Your path lies far from here and you must not linger. Kareem Vastar can no longer be your home, though I wish it were otherwise.'

'So it has been said, though we do not understand why,' Grossa nodded. 'So be it, we will depart.'

He looked up into Garfun's face. 'We will miss you.'

'And I you. All of you.'

'I have one more thing for you,' said Garfun. 'Let us call it a parting gift.' He took the Orb from his deep pocket and presented it to Grossa, who stared at it intently. The faceted surface of the Orb glinted in the light of Orvasne arcing across the sky far above their heads.

'It is beautiful.' The other Graavens crowded around to get a glimpse of it. 'I shall make it an emblem of my House, all Graaven will cherish this gift that comes from you, Master.'

Garfun sighed. 'How many times, Grossa? I am not your Master, I never was. I shall always be your friend.' He reached out and briefly clasped Grossa's hand. Grossa did not pull back from the brief contact, even though touching was not something the Graavens were overly fond of.

Garfun made a shooing gesture. 'Now you must go, all of you. Take care. My blessing goes with you. Travel swiftly and with care. You know what you must do once you have crossed the bridge?'

Tarac, one of the Graaven females answered, 'The spirit has instructed us. We know what to do.'

For the briefest moment the Graavens lingered, but then began to take their leave, one by one coming close to Garfun and looking intently up into his face as if memorising his features. Without word or gesture they turned silently and walked away. It was perhaps the singularly most moving thing that Garfun had ever experienced and a silent tear tracked down his face as he watched them go.

Finally, only Grossa was left standing alone. Crossing both arms over his chest in the gesture Garfun recognised as the Graaven obeisance, he too strode away, the gate silently swinging closed behind him with a soft click. For some mysterious reason it felt to Garfun as if Kareem Vastar had suddenly become irrevocably shut off from the rest of the world.

For a long time he stood alone, overcome with emotion.

'Come, come Garfun, you are supposed to be a scientist, not some lovelorn poet.'

Turning, he made his slow and contemplative way back to the city where, deep within the Complex, final plans to activate the great weapon were reaching completion.

Three more days and it would be ready.

CHAPTER FIVE

As the blight that Apocris poured into the Threadway manifested, its effects on different worlds were many and varied. On some, civil wars erupted, or cataclysmic conflicts arose between opposing nations. On others, great natural disasters destroyed habitats and killed off entire species, leaving misery in the wake of their violence. In still others, great plagues swept the lands, incurable and deadly. Famine and disease walked hand in hand with crop blights and decay. Apocris exulted in the spread of its power and basked in the despair, terror, violence and hatred of millions that its actions engendered.

Tarvuli, even shielded as it was by Varnahrin, was not immune to the evil. Across the land a terrible sickness began. It spread rapidly. At first, its passage was made easier by the gateways that now connected the peoples of Tarvuli. By the time the seriousness of the contagion had been realised, closing the gateways completely was a waste of time. Despite this, in Ta'Morin all travel into the city was halted, its gateway only allowing outward travel. The Graavens however, did not isolate themselves and teams of them, endowed with medical skills learned from Grakh, departed to give aid to those who suffered, some never to return.

But there was no known cure and hundreds, then thousands, fell sick and died in great pain and suffering. The Graaven people, whose numbers had slowly increased since their occupation of Ta'Morin, faced the misery of unnecessary loss of life for the first time since the overthrow of the Empire. However, none suffered what others outside the city experienced, as Varnahrin suppressed the worst of it. Death itself could not be avoided. In consideration of this fatal disease, Varnahrin reached out in quest of an answer to halt the catastrophe.

At the end of a seemingly fruitless search, and in the unlikeliest of places, an answer was found.

ooooOooooo

Horven sat alone in a single chair placed upon a raised dais, in what was now referred to as the Great Council Chamber in the onetime Temple of Harkan that stood in the heart of the Ma'Vessick capital city of Gahrtok.

Other than the four tetran guards standing motionless alongside her, Horven was alone. She sat in silent thought, increasingly worried about the spread of the deadly contagion that had infected and killed so many and which, regardless of the precautions they had tried, seemed impervious to containment. Much around it was a mystery and various theories had been expounded: that its spread was aided by the winds, by the breath of others, by the water they drank or even by the birds and beasts of Tarvuli that appeared, in the main, unaffected by it.

Living as they did in close proximity to each other, the Ma'Vessick had suffered greatly and the sky around the city was constantly filled with the smoke of funeral pyres. Some few believed that this was the revenge of Harkan for betraying and abandoning the faith, but it was not held with any serious conviction. At the behest of Tishan Dar, Varnahrin had taken care of the zealots – all had mysteriously perished in their sleep – and these thoughts, irrational as they were, were merely a way of trying to explain the terrible calamity that faced them. There were no clandestine moves afoot to reestablish that hateful religion.

Horven's inward reveries were interrupted by the sound of the vast metallic doors at the entry to the hall being opened as a small group of Ma'Vessick were ushered in by Farelmy, the newly appointed Major Domo.

'Excellence, these four Ma'Vessick travellers claim to have news for your ears alone and would not be gainsaid. They have been checked for weapons and I took it upon myself to bring them to your presence.'

Horven sighed inwardly. It was clear that, despite her protestations, Farelmy was determined to treat her like some form of royalty, a concept she was entirely uncomfortable with. She realised that further discussion was going to be required with Farelmy to dissuade him of his notions; however, that time was not now.

'Thank you, Farelmy. You may go about your duties.'

Bowing several times, Farelmy backed his way down the hall toward the doors and Horven suppressed a smile as he shuffled out.

'Well, you have news for my ears alone? Who are you and what news is it that cannot be told to anyone else?'

One of the Ma'Vessick stepped forward and addressed her directly. Horven noted that there was no attempt by any of the group to bow to her and her brow creased in vague suspicion. Imperceptibly to any of the Ma'Vessick before her, her grip tightened on the arms of her chair and she leaned forward very slightly. Almost immediately and in response to that movement, as slight as it was, the eyes of her tetran guards turned red, the harbinger of immediate and deadly action.

While the individuals before her may not have noticed her faint movement, the reaction of the tetrans was unmistakable.

'We come in peace. We mean no harm to any here, including yourself Horven Var. Do we have your promise of safety?'

Horven stood very slowly, partly because any rapid movement would trigger a further response from her guards, but also to give herself additional time to frame an answer. Reaching her full height, she spoke: 'If indeed you have come in peace and mean no harm, then no harm shall come to you, in that you do indeed have my promise.

'But,' Horven paused a moment, 'I do not think that you are all that you seem, and if that is so then my promise is limited.'

The four Ma'Vessick exchanged looks with each other.

'Then it seems we must risk the limitation of your promise. We have travelled far to see you; I emphasise once again that we come in peace to you.'

No sooner had the words been spoken than the air around each figure shimmered to reveal four Hrv, their multifaceted eyes locked upon the dais on which Horven stood.

'Hold!' Her voice rapped out the moment the Hrv revealed themselves, as with one motion the tetrans went from a resting position to one where their energy weapons were pointed at the group which stood before them.

'State your business,' Horven's voice was edged with menace. 'Know that your lives hang in the balance and whether you walk out of this place alive will depend on what you say in the next few semmit.'

The leading Hrv spoke again, its voice slightly altered in timbre, now that the illusion had been cast aside. It spoke in sibilant tones, its mandibles shaping the words so that at times it was difficult to make them out.

'We have not lied. The deception was necessary; our kind could never move openly among warm-bloods for obvious reasons. You do not trust us and for reasons that are rooted in the past, we could never trust a warm-blood.'

Horven laughed derisively. 'Ha! Do not talk to me of trust, Hrv. Your kind threw that away when they corrupted the Ma'Vessick and caused the slaughter and enslavement of thousands. Speak! State your business. I will judge if what you say leads to your preservation.'

'Very well. You should know that the Hrv did not sanction what was done. The group led by Radek pursued their own ends. The Hrv seek only to live on our own lands as we have ever done and as far from warm-bloods as possible. In the long-ago days, we were driven from the lands upon which you stand. Harried and hunted, our nests destroyed and our eggs smashed. We fled until the remnants of the Hrv had diminished to just a few survivors. Our aversion to warm-bloods grew into hatred of all your kind. Beyond hope we found new lands, desolate and barren yes, but free from pursuit and so we began to rebuild.'

As the creature spoke and against Horven's will, the similarity of the plight of the Hrv and the destruction of the Graaven Empire resonated deep within her. Slowly she sat once again and the tetrans surrounding her lowered their weapons somewhat, in response.

'You seek to gain my sympathy with a tale that reflects the history of my own people?'

'I know nothing of your people, Horven Var, save what you did here. I speak the truth.'

'You claim to hate us and yet here you are. You claim to mistrust us, yet you have placed yourself in my power. To what end?'

'The Spirit of Ta'Morin has spoken to us and has asked for our aid in combating that which you face. So we have come to you, seeking guarantees that if we help you we will remain unmolested in our lands. You are powerful, quite capable of laying waste to my kind and repeating the terror of the before-times. We seek to bargain with you, to make a treaty between our Race and yours.'

Horven sat for long moments, her thoughts awhirl. That Varnahrin had been involved in this was a powerful indicator that these Hrv meant what they said. Horven gathered her thinking before she spoke.

'Even if I were so inclined to accept the aid you say you have for us, convincing the peoples who were the victims of the Hrv's deception and whose loved ones were consumed by your Race in sacrificial rites to the false god they created to enslave them, will be, let us say, *difficult*.'

As one, the Hrv drew back in alarm, turning to each other and communicating in high-pitched clicks, they moved their upper limbs in a deliberate manner that formed a necessary part of their vocal utterances.

It was clear that Horven's statement had caused great agitation. In response to this, the tetrans around Horven once again raised their weapons in instant preparation for potential attack.

After some frenetic moments, the Hrv turned and as one bowed down until their forelimbs brushed the ground. The lead Hrv spoke once again.

'What you have told us confirms our worst fears and exposes the real reason that Radek led his group away from our lands. You should know that all Hrv have an abhorrence to the eating of flesh. Our aversion to warm-bloods stems from this. We consume insects and drink the sap of plants that we grow for nourishment. I, all of us here, could no more eat the flesh of your people than we could eat each other. Now it is clear to us that Radek and his followers carry the taint. Our word for it would be impossible for you to pronounce. It is a rare defect in our Race. In the long-ago, years before even those who built the city of Paxal came to plague us, there was a civil war: two groups of Hrv in violent opposition to each other, one carried the taint, eaters of flesh and drinkers of blood. Eventually they were defeated and those who survived, eradicated. Still, once in a while the taint re-emerges. Such is the case here.'

As one, the group bowed again before Horven. 'We are sorry. Hatred of your kind is not based on the desire to destroy but rather on what was done to us as a Race. We did not seek conflict with those who came after, but they slaughtered our people and dispossessed us of our lands. Our technology, infinitely inferior to theirs, left us powerless to resist and so in terror, we fled.'

Horven sat back trying to assimilate the revelations that the Hrv had imparted. Their reaction to her statement had convinced her of the truth behind their words and she did not for a moment doubt that what had been said and the information provided, could perhaps change many things in time.

'What you have told me sheds new light on your people.' Horven paused. 'It seems you know my name, but what are yours? If we are to continue speaking with the possibility of forging the treaty you desire, then I should know who you are.'

The leading Hrv bowed its head in acknowledgement.

'Our names in Hrv speech would be impossible for you to vocalise. You may call me Trrz. These others are of my nest are Zekkr, Nedr and Sarrt.'

Even with simplification, Horven found the Hrv names difficult to pronounce, comprised as they were of clicks and hissing sounds, but the approximation was enough to individualise them and she no longer thought of them simply as Hrv.

'So, my accepting what you have said leads us to the *why* of your journey here.'

Without hesitation the leading Hrv spoke.

'Some few meh'chaal ago, as your people measure the weeks, we became aware of a presence in our minds. This presence identified itself as the Spirit of Ta'Morin and told us of the plague that sweeps your lands. The Spirit requested our aid on your behalf and told us that in return for this we might seek security for our Race.

Peace without fear of war. After much deliberation we agreed that we would use whatever skills we had to overcome the blight that sweeps your lands even though we were unaffected by it.'

In response to this, Horven leant back in her chair, her brow creased in thought and the Hrv paused in its speech. Horven lifted her hand. 'Say on, you have my attention.'

'We are cautious, Horven Var. In expectation of potential destruction some few of our race disguise themselves and visit warm-blood lands. We will not be caught by surprise in the event of an incursion into our lands and we know that the activities of Radek and his followers may well have led to a punitive expedition.'

'And now here you are, exposing yourself to the risk of death, seeking to bargain,' this was not a question from Horven, but a statement.

'Yes.'

All four Hrv stood silently, their forelimbs raised, but utterly still.

'With what do you wish to bargain?'

Trrz lowered his forelimbs. 'We bring you knowledge of a cure for the disease that infects your lands. In exchange for this, we seek a treaty to protect our homeland so that the Hrv may live in peace. We require nothing more from you.'

At the same moment that she waved her tetran guards down, Horven sat forward sharply in her chair. 'A cure?'

'Yes. We have already used it secretly on some of your kind and we know that it is effective. The formula requires the combination of the saps from different plants which we Hrv cultivate. In return for showing you how to make the cure, providing you with the seeds to these plants and the formula to ensure long term supply, we will agree to a treaty.'

Horven shook her head in wonder. 'Surely you must have assessed the risk that we could simply imprison you four and subject you to methods that would elicit the information we need – or that we would simply come to your lands and take it? You mistrust warm-bloods and yet you take this risk? Why?'

'We were never the aggressors that legend and the Paxals made us out to be. While we have an aversion to warm-bloods, the Hrv know that none now living had any part in what was done to our Race. The Hrv cannot sit back and watch those around them suffer and die needlessly. Without a cure, this contagion may mutate and then all life may die. So we come to you, not in friendship but in need. If any attempt is made to forcibly extract the information from us, we have the means upon us to terminate our existence. You may invade our lands, but the knowledge you seek is known only to a very few and they would all be dead by their own hands the moment your forces crossed into our lands. The Spirit of Ta'Morin reassured us that knowledge of the Hrv and our history would help to dispel the conclusions that many have made regarding our race.'

Horven smiled. 'You say that you have not come in friendship, but in need. The latter is certainly true. As a member of the Council, I give you my personal assurance that you need have no fear of harsh treatment nor would any under my command seek to invade your lands when what you offer and what you require in return is, to my mind, without issue. You may accompany me to Ta'Morin while I make contact with the other members of the Council. However, it would be best for you in the short term to resume your disguise for reasons that must be obvious to you. I will see to it that accommodations are made to meet your needs and I will expedite our deliberations on this matter.'

The four Hrv bowed deeply and, summoning Farelmy with the envoys in tow, it did not take long for Horven to settle her guests into accommodations with two tetrans guards to ensure their safety. She was not concerned about betrayal, for the voice of Varnahrin had reassured her.

Swiftly travelling to the gateway just outside of Gahrtok and utilising the device that allowed her passage, she crossed to Ta'Morin, advising the Council to prepare for a meeting. She forbore from giving too much detail in order to suppress any chance of rumours leaking out before the meeting had even taken place.

Having set these things in motion, she returned to Gahrtok and greeting the four Hrv once again accompanied them to the gateway.

'We have heard of these gateways but have never seen one or experienced travelling through one,' said Trrz. It was clear they had some misgivings about entering and Horven did her best to reassure them.

'You will feel a brief moment of coldness and some resistance which you must push through, but having journeyed once you will realise that there is little to fear. Come. I will go first and you will see me appear on the other side.'

The field outside of Ta'Morin could clearly be seen through the doorframe. Horven reflected that she was now so used to travelling this way, she no longer gave any thought to how strange and unsettling had been the first time she entered a gateway.

Smiling with reassurance she walked into the gateway and upon exiting in Ta'Morin, turned and beckoned to the four Hrv to come across. Their heads in close proximity, it was clear they were deciding who should go first. Horven was just debating whether or not she should go back when Nedr stepped forward; the other three following.

Without more delay the four stepped through to the other side, stumbling a little as all first time travellers seemed to do as they left the gateway.

'An interesting experience,' Sarrt's comment was directed to his fellow Hrv who all nodded in agreement.

Having overcome their trepidation at using the gateway, the four Hrv now stood in the fields outside the city proper. They exchanged surprised comments when they saw the extent of it in comparison to Gahrtok which was the only other city they had been in, so different to their nests which were largely underground and lacked the buildings that were a feature of warm-blood settlements.

'Welcome to Ta'Morin,' said Horven. 'Please follow me; the Council is waiting to greet you and you can explain to them in your own words the purpose of your journey. You have no need to fear, you are under my protection.'

Having delivered this reassurance, Horven led the way, the four Hrv following. Her step was light and, for the first time in many meh'chaal she felt a sense of hope blossoming inside her, in place of the despair that had so long resided there.

CHAPTER SIX

Grossa came to a halt and the other Graaven stopped be-hind him. For thirty dak'chaal they had been crossing what seemed to be a limitless waste. They were down to their last dregs of water and all were close to the limits of their endurance.

Tarac moved up and stood alongside. Without speaking, Grossa raised his right arm and pointed.

'Look there, Tarac. Do my eyes deceive me in the heat haze, or is that a line of trees I see in the distance?'

Tarac squinted her eyes and peered in the direction of Grossa's pointing finger. The heat shimmer made vision difficult but after some moments' consideration, she nodded.

'I believe you are right, Grossa. I think they are trees.'

He turned to the others standing behind him. They had all exceeded his expectations and grimly persevered through extremes of heat and thirst.

'One last effort will take us to the end of this part of our journey. Water and shade lie before us. Gather your last strength. Those with water, share it out so that all may have a mouthful to sustain us.'

Kalta, a male almost as big as Grossa, spoke.

'What if it is an illusion and more desert lies ahead? We will have used the last of our water.' Kalta's tone indicated opposition.

Grossa stepped close and he could see that Kalta fought the desire to take a step back.

He smiled into his face. 'Then we will all die together, Kalta.' He stepped towards the others and fixed them with a stern look. 'But I do not think that that will be our fate. We have not crossed the desert only to die at the last. Trust me in this, as you have done since we left the city.'

The Graavens nodded.

'You have led us well, Grossa. Let us journey towards our fate,' said Noram, a male Graaven who had proven to be a steady and resolute member of the band. Cries of assent came from the other members of the group as, Kalta's comments rejected, they each swigged a final mouthful of water, hefted their packs and trudged on.

Three chaal later and they could all clearly see that the terrain was changing. Scrubby grasses began to appear and in the distance, a herd of grazing animals could be seen, their features indistinct although they were large and many had great horns to fight off predators.

Soon enough the desert sand was well and truly left behind and they entered an area where the vegetation had transformed into pockets of cycads and other plants that were new and unfamiliar to them. Still there was no sign of water and the thirst that had plagued them all over the past days began to dominate their thoughts.

Later that same day, as the shadows began to lengthen, they saw smoke rising from a settlement ahead of them and they paused, considering their options.

'What happens if these people prove to be hostile?'

'Then we fight them, Tarac,' Grossa replied. 'This village crosses our path and we must find water. I do not wish for conflict with anyone, but it is beyond doubt that they will have water.'

'If they will share it with us,' added Noram.

'Standing here debating, will not answer the questions we have. We will approach. Make no move that could be misinterpreted as hostile, but be ready. Lotma, Verek and Xana hold twenty paces behind us and cover us if things go awry.'

Silently, the Graaven shifted their packs, giving their arms room to grab weapons. Bows were strung and arrows brought within easy reach. There was not one member of the group who was not apprehensive. They did not wish their first act in this new land to lead to bloodshed – but what would be, would be.'

Grossa looked around and smiled at each in turn. 'Come, we have journeyed far and left all that we know behind us; let us meet our fate with open arms, standing together.' As one they stepped forward.

Within the village of Tarata Kameha, the alarm was sounded. A group of individuals had been spotted approaching and while visitors were not unheard of, the fact that these appeared out of the east's vast and forbidding desert which the tribes who dwelt in the land of Crosh knew to be impassable, awoke a strange dread. Their fear was reinforced as the travellers drew closer and their features could be clearly distinguished; they looked nothing like any people the Kamehans had ever seen before.

Parana Noh Mello limped up alongside Bentono, the Village Elder. In the main, the Kamehans were simple farmers. They lived far enough away from other less friendly tribes on the very edges of fertile lands in a place prone to being swampy and difficult to farm, to avoid conflict. But they were few in number and had fled to these less hospitable lands so as to be left in peace. These new-comers may prove to be a new and unwelcome challenge. The Kamehans gathered together at the edge of their village, some one hundred adult individuals and any youngsters old enough to carry a weapon. These were mostly farming implements.

Bentono turned troubled eyes to Parana. Old and crippled, Parana was the village healer and their source of tribal wisdom and knowledge. He was respected and held in esteem by all the people.

'Look at the size of them, Parana! Have you ever seen creatures like them before. They look as if they could lift me up and break me over their knees with one arm! How do we defend against such as they?' Bentono's tone was fearful.

Parana nodded.

'Bentono, think for a moment. They make no hostile move, but stand still, waiting perhaps for us to make a move. I agree they look formidable but let us not leap to conclusions and instigate action that all may come to regret. If, as we think, they have come from the desert perhaps they are thirsty and hungry? Why don't we offer them water and try to treat them like any other guest?'

'Are you serious, Parana? Who will have the courage to approach them?'

'Give me a gourd of water, Bentono. I am the least threatening individual here. I will approach them and offer them food and fire. Come now, if they strike me down then you will know their intent and the village will have only lost a cripple.'

Bentono sighed in frustration. 'You know full well you are much more than that. But have it your own way, you have been right so often before I have not the wit to argue with you.'

He reached out and gripped Parana's hand in his own. 'Be careful, my dear friend.'

Parana patted Bentono's hand. 'I am the soul of caution.'

Taking up a large gourd of water that one of the villagers passed to him, Parana limped out to meet the strangers leaving a palpable feeling of fear behind him emanating from each one of them.

Grossa's eyes squinted with effort as a small, shuffling figure emerged from the crowd of individuals who stood looking at them from the edge of settlement.

'We could sweep through these people like a storm wind through the grass, Grossa,' said Noram.

'That may be true, Noram, but we know nothing of this land or how many others there may be; we cannot afford war. We will exercise caution and I will go and meet this person.'

Grossa placed his pack on the ground and taking off his belt, laid aside the mace and knife he carried. He considered the limping individual who approached and whose height barely reached his waist. If he was scared, he did not show it; Grossa admired his courage.

He stepped forward towards the approaching figure, hands by his sides, as the stranger came to a stop three steps away. Grossa crossed his arms in the Graaven way of greeting and smiled. A mild look of surprise briefly passed over the cripple's face, to be replaced also by a smile and a nodding of the head. This was immediately followed by an unintelligible flow of words and the lifting up of a gourd full of water. Cautiously reaching out, Grossa accepted the gourd nodding his head in thanks. It was a large container to the creature but diminutive in the hands of Grossa, who despite a raging thirst, sipped the water which proved to be cold and sweet tasting.

As Parana hobbled out towards the strangers the features of the one who awaited him sharpened into focus. It was only by a complete effort of willpower that he kept moving forward and if he slightly missed a step then this was hidden by his limp and the crutch which he clamped securely under his left arm. It was not simply the fact that this individual towered over him, his body (Parana assumed it was male), displayed a muscular torso with a barrel chest and broad, powerful shoulders.

Everything about him was so different and alien in aspect compared to Parana's people. There were two things in particular: the creature's skin had a faint iridescent sheen, unlike any skin he had seen before and also bore markings, striations with waves and swirls of muted blue, yellow and a dusky red, that were clearly distinguishable. The patterning covered the visage and arms of the creature, and presumably the rest of its body hidden beneath its clothing. But it was the face that really set him apart. A strong smooth brow sat above large round eyes that were of a deep and impenetrable black, save for the bright yellow irises. A nose that was small and well-formed had large, almost vertical nostrils set above a thin-lipped mouth filled with many regular and even teeth.

His hair, if such it could be called, rose in long spike-like quills over the crown of his head and disappeared into the collar of his tunic. On each side of the head were set rounded ears, small in proportion to the large face. Even his clothes and boots were made of materials and fabrics that Parana had never seen, certainly not made from the skin of any animal he recognised.

The creature's eyes calmly observed his approach and assessed him; it made no move but stood silently.

Having handed over the water gourd, which appeared to be gratefully received, the creature held it behind him and another figure approached. In size somewhat smaller, it moved with a sinuous grace and now Parana thought this could be female. The biggest difference at first glance was its hair, so different to the male's. It looked more flesh-like but was long and plaited with brightly coloured stones held back by a metallic band over ears that were somewhat larger and shapelier than those of the male. The same black eyes observed him with obvious curiosity and accepting the gourd, the female took a sip of the water. She then smiled at Parana, spoke a few words to her companion, her eyes never leaving Parana's, and returned to the group, passing the gourd around. With as many mouths as there were, Parana thought it wouldn't amount to much more than a tiny mouthful each.

Grossa kept his face blank in response to Borka's comment of, 'Ugly little runt, isn't he? But he has courage, I will give him that.'

Returning his attention to the male standing before him, Parana licked his lips nervously and smiled up into the stranger's face. He tapped his chest and said 'Parana' in as clear a voice as he could muster. The giant in front of him tilted its head to one side, eyes crinkled in thought. Parana repeated the gesture and his name.

'Porarnna,' came the response in a voice that was deep and well-modulated. Grossa pointed at Parana with a very large finger; three fingers and a thumb that he noted were webbed. Parana nodded, smiling at the strange inflection to the word.

Then Grossa tapped his chest and said 'Grossa'.

Now it was Parana's turn to narrow his eyes in concentration.

'Gersha,' he said. Grossa nodded and smiled.

'Close enough,' he said, nodding again. Graaven words which Parana correctly interpreted.

Parana rubbed his stomach and pointed to his mouth. 'Kehsa?' he asked.

'If you mean hungry, then yes.' Grossa nodded and smiled, rubbing his stomach in response.

Parana nodded back.

'This could be the biggest mistake of my life,' Parana said out loud but in a tone that he hoped sounded welcoming. Grossa's nodding took Parana to the verge of hysterical laughter but once again he maintained control over his emotions.

He beckoned Grossa in a gesture large enough to include all the gigantic, alien looking people standing further back.

'Come, eat with us.'

Grossa in his turn looked over his shoulder. 'It seems we are welcome and if I interpret correctly, they offer us food and drink. Be mindful that to them we are as giants and we must appear as strange to them as they do to us. So, watch how you act and cause them no concerns; we do not want bloodshed in this new land. It's allies and friends we need, not enemies, at least not yet.' Picking up their packs the Graaven followed Grossa quietly, observing the village and these strange small people with genuine curiosity and passing remarks to each other.

With the hollow between his shoulder blades twitching, Parana turned his back on the giant called Gersha in what he hoped was a sign of trust and limped back towards the village, where his people still clustered to await the outcome of Parana's welcome, some openly fearful of what might eventuate.

As Parana drew near to the village, Bentono walked out to meet him.

'Well?'

'We have guests for a meal, Bentono. I believe these people are friendly. Huge and strange looking to be sure, but friendly I think, so tell everyone to relax and let us prepare food for us to share with them and perhaps this may be the start of a mutually agreeable friendship.'

'That will depend on their intentions, Parana. But you are the Hakimsa, our Holy Man, so let us hope that Bekkor is feeling benevolent.'

'Well, we have avoided bloodshed so far and standing close to the one named Gersha, who I assume is their leader, I cannot help but think that offering the hand of peace is something we will be thankful for in time to come.'

Bentono turned towards the gathered villagers and spoke words which virtually mirrored those which Grossa had spoken to his people. A hum of discussion was heard in response to these words, curiosity mixed with trepidation.

Tarata Moka tilted her head towards her old friend K'lane with one eye on the approaching strangers.

'We don't even know if they can eat or will even like our food.'

'Nonsense, Tarata. I defy any creature not to enjoy my terrax cake. Bekkor himself would feast heartily and clear his plate.'

Tarata shook her head at K'lane's blasphemy then nodded with a smile. 'I have no doubt that you are right, old friend.' They hurried off to help prepare food for their unexpected guests.

Over the coming days and weeks, Parana was proved to be correct. Admittedly, there were some tense moments when the language barrier led to difficulties, but between Grossa and Parana these were smoothed over and, as the two peoples began to learn each other's languages, the incidents lessened.

The Graaven learned that Parana's people lived in a region they called Crosh and while they referred to themselves as Kamehans they were actually part of a broader tribal group called the Hagala. The Kamehans were mostly farmers and being peaceable, had been driven to the area that lay near the desert by their more aggressive neighbours who had left them alone now for some time. But they lived in fear that they would be attacked and driven off even from these lands.

For their part, the Kamehans learned that the Graaven were also very few in number and had fled, for reasons unclear, across the great wasteland. The fact that there were fertile lands lying on the other side of the desert was a revelation to them and led to much discussion and conjecture.

There was one other thing that was particularly fortuitous for the Graaven. The land to the north of the village was a swampy expanse of fens and giant reeds, totally unsuitable and uninhabitable as far as the Kamehans were concerned, but perfect for their new Graaven friends, descended as they were from amphibious forebears who had thrived in a semi-aquatic environment.

After several meh'chaal, having reached an agreement with their new friends, the Graavens left the village and travelled northwards to adopt the swampy and unclaimed lands as their own.

Here they built canoes from woven reeds and explored the waterways, constructing dwellings from the same materials. They fished and hunted the abundant wildlife and even the giant Kazarla, the savage and many-toothed predators which inhabited the swamp, were no match for their cunning. The Kazarla skins provided a tough and durable leather which the Kamehans valued highly, so amid all this plenty they traded often with these people whom they gradually came to view as firm friends and allies.

In the safety of their new home, the Graaven set about breeding. Their numbers rapidly swelled. Graaven females could produce multiple eggs when the need required and both male and female saw it as their duty to increase their peoples' numbers, so that within a short time they had doubled and then tripled the size of their group.

The Graaven people were flourishing.

Garfun Bendax would have been overjoyed, had he been alive to see it.

ooooOooooo

Horven made her way to the Council Chamber with her Hrv guests. The Council awaited their arrival in one of the refectory buildings, Varnahrin having already communicated their imminent arrival to them.

The four Hrv shuffled in nervously behind her; as Horven's eyes swept over the Graaven councillors there present, one was noticeable by his absence.

'I see that Majek is not with us. Is he delayed?' Horven asked of no one in particular. After an exchange of looks which boded ill, it was Borta who answered.

'I am so sorry to advise you Horven, but just in the last chaal, Majek succumbed to the disease. We mourn yet another loss.'

Horven stood silently in remembrance of Majek whose dry wit and wise counsel would be sorely missed. Menkh, Horven thought, would be very sorry to hear of Majek's passing and the circumstances that led to it, as they had formed a close bond in the years that he had been Menkh's steward.

Taking a deep breath, she nodded. 'Then perhaps this meeting is timely.' Turning, she swept out an arm. 'I introduce to you Trrz, Zekkr, Nedr and Sarrt. They have exposed themselves to great hazard to reach us and they have promise of a cure.'

'A cure!' exclaimed Borta, and the five councillors exchanged looks and comments.

'Then you are most welcome,' said Harma to the Hrv.

'Perhaps,' said Horven. Turning to the four in question she spoke to them: 'I think now is the time to show your true form.'

Again, Horven witnessed the same shimmering effect in the air and in the blink of an eye the four Hrv were revealed.

If the initial reaction of the Council was amazement and a sense of relief at the news of a possible cure, it was nothing to their reaction at seeing four Hrv in their midst. A babble of conversation started which took some moments to quell.

Horven waved her arms in a calming gesture.

'I can assure you all that they mean us no harm – quite the reverse in fact. I further believe that if they had any evil intent, the Spirit of Ta'Morin would never have allowed them access to the city. Come councillors, resume your seats and listen to what they have to say.'

'We will listen,' said Lanak, 'but you Hrv must understand that our experience with your kind leads us to deep mistrust.'

Trrz bowed. 'We acknowledge what has gone before, but let us tell you what we have conveyed to Horven Var and you may make your own decision.'

As the councillors settled, the Hrv once again related their tale and the information they had. During this time Varnahrin spoke into Horven's mind:

<Preparations have been made to expedite the production of the cure. The resources of the city have been deployed. But you must leave here now. I fear that Mareen and Halika have sickened. Lerma is with them and you should join him.>

Horven felt the blood drain from her face and a wave of emotions swept through her.

<Go child. I will convey the news to the Council. They will understand your departure. All will be well here>.

Horven abruptly turned on her heel and left the meeting. The confusion of the councillors was replaced with immediate empathy as Varnahrin's words entered their minds. Their gaze followed Horven's departing figure before returning to the four Hrv who stood before them.

With the influence of Varnahrin, the meeting and the details of an agreement were concluded verbally in short order.

Borta, one of the senior councillors, now spoke:

'You have said you come not in friendship, but in need. I think I speak for all of us here when I say that your actions speak more loudly of friendship than of necessity. In thanks for the cure you offer, and on behalf of all Graavens, we pledge to hold true to our words this day. Your lands will be preserved. May you grow in peace and prosperity.' The other councillors smiled, nodding in agreement at this statement. All four Hrv bowed in acknowledgement of what was said.

'Then let us make haste to prepare the cure as we have agreed,' said Zekkr. 'We carry seeds of the plants and dried ingredients to make the first batch. These plants grow rapidly in the right circumstances. We will teach you how to harvest them and distil and blend the essence of each one.'

Talak, another of the councillors, spoke in agreement:

'The Spirit of Ta'Morin has placed the resources of the city at our disposal. If you will accompany me, we shall attend Grakh's surgery. He and his assistants will be best placed to learn your techniques and I believe he has the knowledge and understanding to produce what is required. Come.'

In company with the Council led by Talak, a tall Graaven who Chaired meetings in Horven's absence, the Hrv delegation set out to begin the task of preparation.

ooooOoooo

Horven left the Council meeting in a highly emotional state. She had faced life or death in combat, fighting a combination of fear and excitement, but here there was only fear and she fought to control the feeling of panic that threatened to overwhelm her. She pushed these thoughts down deep inside and refused to think about the many 'what ifs' that arose in her mind.

She arrived breathless at the dwelling that she and Lerma shared whenever they were in Ta'Morin. While their duties often took them away from the city, when they were together with Mareen and Halika, they felt truly like a family. Lerma in particular doted on their two spawnlings who were rapidly growing to maturity. Graaven childhoods, if they could be described as such, were all too brief and therefore to be particularly cherished.

To reach their home, Horven had to cross two of the many bridges that crisscrossed the seven rivers as they flowed towards the Complex. Now, Horven could not remember her passage home, so deeply preoccupied was she. The door opened soundlessly before her and she took the steps two at a time to the second-floor sleeping compartments.

Lerma had carried Mareen and Halika into the largest room and made beds upon the floor. At first, Horven thought that Lerma too had succumbed as he made no move to greet her but sat still upon the ground holding the hands of both spawnlings in his own. Nervous tension and lack of sleep had however, stolen upon him and Horven saw that he had dropped into a fitful doze, his back

87

propped against the wall. On their respective beds both spawnlings lay in a deep slumber, their green skin pale to the point that the markings stood out in sharp definition, a sure sign they were unwell.

As she looked at them, unbidden tears clouded Horven's eyes, and a sense of helplessness before this terrible and unnatural disease descended on her; the disease that so many on Tarvuli had succumbed to. Some died quickly. Others lingered in terrible pain while still others, only a rare few, eventually recovered albeit with physical scars from their harrowing experience.

<They have been placed in deep sleep, Horven Var. This will slow the spread of the disease and perhaps give the Hrv time to prepare the first batch of their cure,> Varnahrin spoke in her mind.

'Is there nothing more you can do?' Horven's voice was loud and anguished.

<Child, all that can be done is being done. Hold on to hope. All is not yet lost.>

Horven drew in a deep breath and turned to mind-speech.

<I am sorry Varnahrin. The fear of losing them is overwhelming.>

<Apology is not required, Horven Var. You must live for them and you must ensure that the Hrv receive whatever they need to expedite this cure.>

As Horven stood in silent communication, Lerma stirred and upon seeing Horven attempted to rise.

Horven lifted an arm to stop him.

'Stay, Lerma.' Without further speech she sat down beside him, placing her right hand on top of his left which clung to Halika's. Draping the other arm around his shoulder, she leaned in close.

'How long have they been like this?' she asked quietly.

Lerma swallowed and fought down his own feelings of despair. 'Only a few chaal. At one moment they were both fine, laughing over our evening meal and then they exchanged a look, one I will never forget, and took a deep breath; their eyes rolled up in their heads and they fell, lifeless to the ground. It was then that these lesions appeared on their skin.'

'Lesions?'

Releasing Mareen's hand he lifted the light sheet off Mareen to expose her upper torso. Great sores could be seen, leaking a milky fluid. The skin surrounding each lesion was blackened, and this blackness appeared to be spreading in raised welts that looked for all the world like the fingers of some creature of nightmare reaching out to other areas of infection.

Horven was sickened and repulsed by the sight and her feeling of helpless frustration was now supplemented by a hatred of the malevolent force that created this blight.

Gently she replaced the sheet and hid the noisome infection from view.

'And how are you? Are you feeling alright?'

'Do not concern yourself over me Horven Var, it is our spawnlings that matter. But I fear for them, Horven. I cannot imagine our life without them.'

Horven gripped his hand and quietly told him of the news brought by the Hrv, and of their plans to concoct a cure.

'That is the best news possible. I only hope that it will not be too late for us.'

'We will not give in to despair, Lerma. While there is life, hope lingers.'

'Then go,' said Lerma. 'Help these Hrv where you can, so that the production of this cure is achieved as quickly as possible. We are not the only ones to be suffering in fear and doubt.'

Horven nodded, she squeezed Lerma's hand and pressed her forehead against his in the Graaven manner of affection.

'I will sit with you for a short while. The Council are quite capable of dealing with things.'

Lerma looked as if he might argue the point but then weariness overcame him and his eyes closed as he fell into a deep slumber.

Horven felt a tear creep down her face as her eyes alighted on Halika and Mareen. Unbidden her thoughts turned to her long dead sibling Mareen and to happier times long ago.

ooooOoooo

Horven shook herself out of her reverie. She was not sure how long she had dozed beside Lerma, but realised that she had indulged herself enough; there was work to do and perhaps a brighter future to come.

Checking to see that Halika and Mareen had not stirred, she left Lerma in slumber and quietly exited the room pushing her fears to one side and hanging on to Varnahrin's words. If hope was to triumph over despair, then every effort must be made to support the Hrv and overcome the logistics that would be necessary in transporting the cure to their friends and allies.

CHAPTER SEVEN

It seemed to Tishan that they had been walking along the seemingly endless corridor for a very long time. After much discussion regarding the challenges to come, she had fallen into a companionable silence with Thatras and had become used to the strangeness of her surroundings. She was fascinated by the changing views on her left side as she walked along. The fact, as Thatras had informed her, that each new opening led to another world had thrown her into a state of deep contemplation. So much had happened to Tishan, indeed to all the Graaven people, that her concept of who she was, and of what reality itself actually was, had fundamentally altered; she now found herself in a fluid process of adaptation to the ever-changing events she experienced. She reminded herself that this whole place was a construct, but she shied away from the contemplation of who or what had the capacity and ability to create such a place.

She had walked several steps further, before she realised that Thatras had stopped directly in front of a set of windows, indistinguishable from every other of the hundreds they had passed by. Silently Tishan retraced her steps and stood alongside Thatras, looking out at the space beyond.

As Tishan focused her attention on what was contained within the window frame, she saw a panorama unlike any she had observed before. At first, she thought it was a vast plain composed of some black, oil-like substance, but upon seeing a ripple move across its vast surface she revised her initial view; perhaps it was in fact a lake of black liquid. Above the lake the sky was a pale, washed-out pink suffused with a dull light that did little to illuminate the planet's surface; rather the overall effect was depressing and dreary. There were no other animals or plants nor any other features such as mountains or hills to relieve the oily blackness. She took an instinctive step back as a vast portion of the 'lake' suddenly rose upwards, lifting into the air above. It slowly took shape, re-forming itself until it resembled the leg of some huge insect. In the distance beyond, dozens of other similar shapes now appeared, stretching ever upwards, each appendage ended in a vast claw until finally – having perhaps reached the limit of movement – the claws opened and closed before the peculiar shapes began to descend. Slowly they disappeared into the black fluid until the surface of the lake was once again still, but for an occasional ripple that disturbed its surface.

'Behold the Enemy, Tishan Dar,' said Thatras.

Tishan's gaze lingered on the loathsome sight before her, then slowly she turned her head towards Thatras; when she spoke her tone was incredulous. 'Is there nothing left of the planet bar this creature? It does not seem possible.'

'After thousands of cycles, this thing has entirely absorbed everything around it; even the living force of the planets within its own system have been consumed. Only the energy it receives from its offspring keep it alive. As you know, through them it also absorbs knowledge and now we are aware that, somehow, an alter ego of itself has emerged which, unlike its parent, is free to roam the Universe. The Balance is now at the tipping point and we are on the cusp of a new equilibrium. If this creature and its offspring are not destroyed, chaos will eventually rule. Even destroying this thing is only a partial step on the way to resetting the Balance.'

'But surely once we have taken care of its offspring our task is done?'

'Taking care of this creature and its loathsome progeny is no simple feat, Tishan Dar. But even if this is achieved, there is no guarantee that Balance will be restored as it was originally conceived, and universal chaos avoided. There will still be work needed to limit the effect on reality that these creatures have had and to maintain equilibrium in the way the Intelligence intended. We should not forget that we must also contend with this creature's alter ego and that may prove an even greater challenge.'

'I don't understand.' Tishan's mind reeled. 'I thought that once, if and when we had achieved our plans, we could then return home. You know, assume our lives as they were.' Even to herself, Tishan thought she sounded like a small and confused child.

'The fact that the threat here may be eradicated does not end or reverse the evil they have started. It will take many cycles to offset this and to help ensure that the ripples left by their actions are managed. As Agents of Balance, you and Menkh will have a role to play in that, along with others like you. Remember, once you achieve success here, you must face the second challenge, as your triumph would have a direct impact on the Enemy's clone. While there are several possible scenarios, in my view an attack directly upon Tarvuli is the most likely result. It will be a titanic struggle and will require every bit of available power to overcome it. *That* is the final challenge.'

'But why would Tarvuli be the particular focus of its wrath?'

Thatras's voice was empathetic. 'Because Tishan Dar, it has already battled with Menkh and Crixac. The knowledge it gained led to its first assault which, to its chagrin, led to its defeat. It knows that a mighty power protects Tarvuli and your success in destroying the parent must lead to the strongest suspicion that, of all places, Tarvuli must be directly involved in that act. Child, you have not thought beyond the moment and I cannot blame you for that. Knowing all this, how can you then return to your old life as you are now? You, like Menkh, have transformed. You have become so much more than what you were before. In your heart you will always be Graaven, but your life span will be hundreds, perhaps even thousands of cycles more than a normal one of your Race. You and Menkh will have each other, and if you wish, you can keep watch on your home world, indeed that will be one of your roles. For a short time, you can return and rest, no one would deprive you of that recompense if we are successful, but ultimately there is more for you both to achieve.'

Tishan's thoughts and emotions were in a whirl. The enormity of the imminent task ahead had completely overshadowed any thought of what lay beyond that. Her mind shied away from the understanding that she would outlive her offspring and all those she called friends on Tarvuli. A deep sadness welled up inside her and threatened to overwhelm her senses. But then her Graaven training asserted itself. In her previous life within the Empire, she had buried friends after battles too many to recall, and had seen many come to an untimely end. As she was now, she and Menkh could at least work towards achieving a future of prosperity and happiness not only for their Graaven people and for all those who called the world of Tarvuli home, but to countless races on other remote worlds too. Surely that was a purpose worth the sacrifice?

Taking a deep breath, she nodded. 'Yes, you are right, Thatras. I see that now.'

Now it was Thatras who shook her head in wonder. 'What a remarkable creature you are, Tishan Dar. You receive news that would have sent some creatures mad ,and yet within moments, you assimilated that knowledge, rationalised your thoughts and reordered your mind. Quite remarkable. It is no wonder that Varnahrin invested you with power. I do look forward to working with you and Menkh in time to come.'

'Well Thatras, if that is to occur, we must first eradicate this *thing*. Do you have some further plan in mind?'

Thatras placed an arm on Tishan's shoulders. 'Oh yes child; I think you will like it.'

'As I have already told you, all these windows are in fact gateways,' said Thatras. 'By utilising this one, you avoid having to travel by the Threadway or by any other means to the Enemy's location. The first warning that it will have of an alien presence, is when you appear.'

'Yes, that does sound like a significant tactical advantage; however, I can see one flaw.'

'Which is?'

'All these windows take you to the surface of the world they are connected to. In this case, however, there is no surface. It would seem to me that as soon as I exit the gateway, I will emerge directly onto the creature itself. Possibly even sinking inside it, if that rippling surface is as liquid as it appears from here.'

'I do not see the flaw, child. In your new form you do not need to breathe and your body will be impervious to whatever immediate environment you find yourself in. As it is, you can utilise the Rod of Klemish to shield you. You can drop the Orb and depart, using the Threadway to speed your escape.'

'You make it sound simple, but I foresee any number of issues. Nor do I believe that the Enemy will not have some sort of defensive reaction to my presence. As to the Orb, how much time will I have between depositing it and escaping?'

'Ah well. Now that *is* a potential issue,' said Thatras. 'It is impossible to know how long. As I told you, being here has suppressed the Orb's expansion. Although highly unlikely, it may be that once through the gateway, it will immediately disrupt. Much more likely, is that the expansion process will continue till it reaches a critical point. This should allow you time to get a safe distance away.'

'Wonderful. So, can you at least tell me how far away I need to be when the Orb disrupts?

'Put it this way, Tishan Dar. When the Orb disrupts, its energy discharge will also fatally impact all the planets and anything else that currently forms the system the enemy world occupies. That includes that System's star. The initial energy release from the Orb will therefore be magnified as the star too tears itself apart. All this material will be expelled far out into space where one of three things may happen: the debris will continue to expand outwards until the energy force dissipates; or, it will all collapse back in on itself in a reverse shock and, in time, a new body will form. There is also the third possibility that the disruption of the Orb, composed as it is of alien matter, will culminate in a gigantic rift as the fabric of space itself opens up, creating an immense field of gravitational force. This will mean that much of the expelled debris and unleashed energy, and all of the alien matter, will be violently drawn back into this void before the rift slams shut.'

Tishan nodded her head. 'So, a long way away, then,' she said drily.

'Didn't I just say that?' said Thatras. 'Ten million persangh, to use your Graaven measurement, should get you safely away; the energy pulse will take a little time to reach you at that distance and you can continue to retreat before it as it dissipates or reverses. But I wouldn't linger. That goes for exiting the planet as well. When the Orb disrupts, the initial blast will take but a moment.'

Tishan nodded her head. 'We are sure that no living creatures will be killed as a result of this?'

'On that score you need have no concern. The surrounding planets have long been drained of any life-force.'

'Very well.' Tishan sat on the floor as the immensity of the task manifested in her mind. It was all very well saying that her body had been transformed, but deep inside she was still Tishan Dar and she was filled with doubt and trepidation. Her thoughts turned inwards to a time long ago when she had felt equally overwhelmed, and doubtful of her capacity to overcome the challenges before her.

ooooOooooo

The battle was not going well. Tishan's Praka had been reduced from five hundred effectives to less than one hundred. With her own eyes, she had seen their Kalvak isolated and beaten to a bloody pulp under the maces of the enemy. Now they were being pushed back. Having lost contact with the other elements of their impisch, Tishan and those of her unit had no idea if the same was happening across the field of battle. All was confusion; occasional flights of arrows passed overhead sounding for all the world like some huge flock of birds flying low, and there was the usual metallic sound of weapons punctuated by screams of the wounded on both sides, along with shouted cries of command and the blowing of horns.

For a moment there was a lull in the fighting and a burly hoplex turned towards her. 'Shu Mut. What are you orders?' Tishan swallowed, her mouth was parched.

'What of Shu Lan Garn?'

'Dead. Struck down moments ago. Only you are left, Shu Mut.'

Tishan Dar nodded. Newly promoted, she was uncertain and disoriented. Clearing her mind, she swiftly scanned the terrain. Before them, what she could see of the plain was covered in bodies, some piled in heaps of dead too many to count, in testament to the savagery of the killing. Somehow their praka had been pushed into a bowl-like depression so that her view was limited, but rapidly scanning her surrounds, she saw that immediately behind their position a rocky outcrop offered possibilities. A narrow gap appeared to open into a small space. If she could get the remnants of the praka into it, their flanks would be protected and their shields could offer more effective defence. Less than a spear-cast away, the lull in the fighting might give them just enough time to reach the site.

Taking a deep breath, she called out: 'Fifth praka withdraw! Withdraw to the rocks behind us.'

Her call was echoed by the hoplex who stood alongside her and whose voice carried even further.

'Withdraw to the rocks!'

Despite their fearful casualties, discipline was still strong. Turning abruptly, Tishan jogged toward what she hoped was the protection of the rocks that now reared up before her.

Reaching the narrow opening she had seen, she turned and beckoned to those remaining hoplex who still ran towards her. Her heart filled with pride at the determination she saw. They were a pitiful remnant, many carrying wounds, but perhaps they might be able to survive if the rest of the impisch was still on the field.

'Shields up! Form a wall. The burly hoplex who had first spoken to her was not of her praka, but had taken station alongside her.

'What is your name?'

'I am called Takla. I was of the third.'

'All dead?'

Takla nodded. 'Only me left. Perhaps a few wounded might be found.'

'Well then Takla, see if anyone else has water. Here, take my flask, share it out.'

'You first, Shu Mut. Without you we have no command.'

Tishan nodded and after taking a few grateful sips, she passed her flask to Taka who moved off down the line.

They stood now in the opening of a small cave, her hoplex forming two ranks, their flanks and rear protected by the rock walls. There was enough room for some badly wounded who had managed to get to them to lie in the shade. That was another blessing; they stood out of the fierce heat. It was Carminac Gar, the Season of Abundance and the temperature could become high, especially out on the plains.

Discerning movement, she saw a body of enemy warriors, many times the number of her hoplex, approaching their new position.

'I see these vermin want to share our shade!' she called out. 'What do you say?'

Ninety Graaven voices called out as one. 'Piss off!'

Tishan laughed. 'Spears! Let's give them a warm Graaven welcome they will not forget!'

In what seemed like moments their foe had formed a line and with a crash struck home against the Graavens, the enemy lines seriously compacted by the narrow entrance. Tishan saw that whoever commanded them had failed to organise the assault so that their attack was not impeded by the tightness of the opening, thus squeezing them together in such a way as to block each other's path. The Graaven spears took a fearful toll. The enemy dead piled up, forming a barricade that added to their difficulties and they finally drew back. Now ninety Graaven had become seventy. Tishan shook her head, her new promotion looked certain to be her last.

Takla had sustained a head wound which bled profusely, but he stood alongside her once more. Turning, she looked him in the eye. 'I am Tishan Dar. It has been a pleasure, Takla. I hope we meet in the afterlife.'

Takla wiped a smear of blood away with a torn piece of kit and smiled grimly. 'We may not be summoned by Slax Ar Terrun just yet,' he said, naming the Graaven Goddess of death. 'Look there!'

Tishan's eyes followed his outstretched arm. She could see that beyond the lip of the depression there was some kind of disturbance. The enemy were turning away, pushing their way back up the slope in what must be a response to whatever it was that had caused their attack to be abandoned so precipitately. It was then she heard voices chanting. Faint at first, the sound gradually grew in strength as they drew closer and she could make out the words, in response to which the tendrils in her neck flared out. She realised who were coming to their aid.

'Who are we?'

'We are Baran Mec!'

'What are we?'

'The right arm of the Empire!'

'Who stands before us?'

'The enemy!'

'How many?'

'Not enough!'

With each cry and response, a crashing sound followed by the screams of wounded and dying was a counterpoint to the rhythmic chant she could clearly hear and then the first elements of Baran Mec cleared the lip of the depression and began to descend.

'I don't think I have ever been so happy to see the guard approaching. Their maces make a particularly satisfying sound, Shu Mut,' said Takla.

'Not just any Baran Mec, Takla,' said Tishan. 'The markings on their shields are those of the Pohlan Harac.'

'You are right,' said Takla. 'If the Pohlan Harac is on the field then surely the day is ours?'

Tishan nodded. 'At what cost, I wonder?'

In any event, Tishan knew at that point that she and what remained of her command would live to see another day though many friends had been lost. She had faced the challenges and had risen to meet them in leading her praka.

It was some while later that Tishan Dar was summoned to the presence of the Pohlan Harac himself. Apparently, her actions had been noted, as amid the terrible slaughter there had been few Graaven actions of note albeit they had held the field and the enemy had retreated into their mountain stronghold. Once again, Tishan was filled with doubt concerning her orders: perhaps she was being summoned to be made an example of. Her nerves getting the better of her, she breathed deeply as she was led past the two Baran Mec who stood guard at the entrance to the royal tent. Finally, she was brought to a standstill among many senior commanders whose talking stilled as she stood, anxiously awaiting her fate.

On a raised dais in the centre of the tent a figure dressed in bright mail rose from his ornate chair and stepped down to meet her. In itself that was surprising, but then Menkh Ab Dur had a reputation for being very different from just about all other Graaven.

Tishan crossed her arms and bowed in the formal Graaven salute. Tishan had never seen the Pohlan Harac up close, and when she dared to look into his eyes, she saw a frank expression softened by a smile. Menkh Ab Dur had the ability to make you feel as if you were the only person present who mattered. Even before he said anything, Tishan felt a strange connection. Here was a person worth knowing.

'I have heard reports of your action on the field. Your quick thinking separates you from many. Would you not agree, Stragosh Sem?'

A tall female similarly clad in mail, nodded in agreement. 'Indeed, I would, Pohlan Harac. Most commendable.'

'My thoughts exactly. So Shu Mut, what is your name?'

'I am Tishan Dar, Polan Harac.'

Menkh's brow crinkled in thought. 'Dar? You are spawn of Herpec Dar?'

Tishan nodded. 'The same, highness.' A brief image of her mother flashed into Tishan's mind.

'Well, if my mind wasn't made up before, it is now. She was an outstanding Kalvak with a great future, taken too soon.'

'I remember her well, Pohlan Harac. A most excellent sagit and cool, under fire,' an unidentified voice called out.

'It seems that the spawn of Herpec Dar is made of similar stuff. Tishan Dar, will you consent to join the Baran Mec in my personal guard? The Empire has need of good commanders.'

Tishan felt as if she were in a dream and hoped that she would not wake too soon. She could only stammer out her thanks and numbly accept a promotion which was the goal of any Graaven warrior.

'Very good. I am pleased.' With these words and – unusually for a Graaven and unheard of for royalty – he reached out and gave Tishan's shoulder a brief squeeze.

In that moment, Tishan knew that fate had taken her to a cross-roads in her life and, such was the impression that the Pohlan Harac made upon her, that she would happily give up her own life in defence of his.

ooooOoooo

Tishan came out of her reverie to see Thatras looking curiously at her.

'Lost in thought, child?'

'Remembering a time long ago when I doubted myself. On re-flection I have always had some degree of doubt but I have always pushed through. Ultimately, I have always done the best I could.'

'That is all anyone can do, Tishan Dar. One thing I do know, if you and Menkh cannot achieve the task set before you, then no one can.'

Tishan smiled. 'In which case, we should set about saving the Universe.'

Thatras laughed aloud. 'I do like you so very much, Tishan Dar. I must take a stronger interest in your Race, if they are all like you.'

'You will have to judge for yourself. Come then, tell me how I activate this gateway.'

Thatras nodded. 'It is easy enough. Walk closer to the frame; as you draw nearer to it, it will begin to glow, you will know when it is fully activated as the view from the frame will disappear and you will feel a pulling sensation. After that, you simply step into the opening. You will find it a strange sensation and while the initial activation pulls you in, you must continue to walk though it will require both sustained effort and concentration.'

'I have been through a gateway before; we have several on Tarvuli.'

'Yes. But that is like comparing climbing a flight of stairs to scaling a mountain. It will require all your will. The Rod of Klemish will help you and in any event, it is better to shield yourself now than try to do this when you emerge.'

Thatras held up an arm and the Orb appeared floating above it. In Tishan's imagination it seemed filled with a menace she had never attributed to it before, but then she hadn't fully appreciated what it was. From her other hand Thatras produced a bag made of metallic-looking material, which shimmered even in the dull light of the corridor. Deftly Thatras place the Orb inside it and the bag sealed itself shut. Handing the bag to Tishan, she spoke:

'This bag will make it easier for you to carry the Orb. The material it is composed of will also disguise its presence and may help to slow down the approach to critical mass.

'You mean it will keep it from disrupting too quickly?' said Tishan.

Thatras patted Tishan's shoulder. 'That's what I just said, child. Do try and keep up.' Before Tishan could respond, the Acclydian suddenly seemed to lose focus and a low-pitched humming noise issued from the form of Thatras.

Tishan became alarmed and spoke aloud. 'Thatras, are you alright?'

For some moments there was no response, but then the strange sound ceased and the Acclydian once again looked directly at Tishan.

'My apologies. The Adept Frzath whom you know, has made contact. They seek to aid your efforts and so I have agreed that we will wait for a signal from them before you enter the gateway.'

'Aid? Did they say how and in what form this assistance would occur?'

'They did not, but I am sure that any assistance they can provide will be welcome. Even now they are coordinating something, so we must trust them on this.'

'Then while we wait, tell me more about your people, the Acclydians,' said Tishan.

The form of Thatras seemed to ebb and flow, losing its humanoid features momentarily before resuming the shape it manifested earlier.

'We are an ancient Race and we were never prolific as a people; it took a long time between conception and birth and we were already long-lived. You are to me as a blade of grass is to a mountain in terms of age. We were once quite different to look upon but over time we have changed. Largely through scientific experimentation we sought to adapt to a form that could react to the environment it found itself in. While we were ultimately successful there were unforeseen consequences and our numbers drastically diminished. There are now few Acclydians and ultimately there will be none. We lost our ability to procreate, you see, and all attempts to artificially recreate ourselves proved fruitless. Add to this the fact that we have journeyed far beyond our home world. I can't recall the last time I actually met with another Acclydian and my memories of my planet of origin are so vague now as to be beyond specific recall.'

Tishan felt a wave of sadness wash over her. 'Do you not get lonely?'

'An interesting question. The short answer is – no. You see, when we altered ourselves thus losing our ability to breed, we also lost certain emotions and feelings. I do not miss seeing others of my Race and meeting other beings like yourself is endlessly fascinating. I am not subject to the emotions that you are and this is both a strength and a weakness. I have not lost my ability to empathise nor have I lost my curiosity to see new places and meet other beings. This has become the prime focus of my existence and so will I continue until I am no more.'

Tishan nodded her head. 'Do you have regrets? Do you think that there was a time in the long-ago when your people might have considered that, just because you had the knowledge and ability to change yourselves, that it was *not* necessarily something you should do?'

'You do ask the most fascinating questions,' Tishan Dar. Thatras paused for several long moments. 'Perhaps there was just such consideration. But of course, once we had embarked upon these changes, what we then became precluded such thoughts. It was, in any event, far too late. We became travellers and teachers. We soaked up knowledge and imparted it to others. Hence my being here with you in this place.'

'Yes, this place. I still haven't got my head around it although I stand within it.'

'Give it another ten thousand years child, and you will begin to form a better understanding of the nature of the Universe.'

Tishan laughed loudly. 'Yes, I am sure you are right, Thatras.'

A smile formed on the features of Thatras in response to Tishan's' laughter. 'You really are a breath of fresh air. I do hope we meet again when this is all over, there is much I would like to share with you.'

'I should like that too, Thatras.'

'Try not to get yourself killed Tishan Dar, the present reality would be the poorer for it.'

'Is that a compliment, Thatras?'

'Compliment? Perhaps. Not something I indulge in often, when you are as old as I am.'

The form of Thatras melted and reformed and Tishan once again heard the strange sound and vibration she had experienced earlier. She could not tell how long she had been in the Construct. While it seemed brief enough within, there was no way of telling how much time had elapsed in the reality that existed outside of it.

'Come, child. Our discussions must await a future time. The moment has come for you to depart.'

CHAPTER EIGHT

Mendikar entered the inner sanctum of the Grand Temple.

Located in X'cotl, the chief city of the Chosen, the temple itself was a brooding presence which dominated X'cotl and all who resided within it. As a High Priest of the Fifth Circle, he was one of very few permitted to enter the Presence, though it was a privilege that few envied. Contact with the Chosen deity was problematical at best and death a miscalculated answer away. It was not without a high degree of trepidation that Mendikar made his way through a labyrinth of passages descending deep into the bowels of the temple. At last he reached the long passage that led to its very core wherein resided their God. The passageway inclined gradually upwards, illuminated by lights that gave off a sickly red glow.

Reaching the end of the passageway he strode up the several gilded steps that ended in front of a vast and elaborately carved doorway. Rapping his staff three times upon the ground before it, he stood with a steadily increasing pulse rate as the doors swung open before him. To step into the Presence could lead to several unpredictably unpleasant outcomes – including his own demise.

While the Chosen were paramount in the arrogant belief of their superiority to all other forms of life, they worshipped their God in fear of the ever-present possibility that they may be called on to make the ultimate sacrifice. While any of the Chosen happily consigned others to torture and death, they were not enamoured of having the same experience thrust upon them.

In Mendikar's long life he had personally witnessed thousands of sacrifices. The Chamber of Devotion was located one floor above where he stood. The Chosen herded their captives through a lofty hallway, its walls made of a black stone which absorbed all light, so that the lamps held aloft by the guards barely gave enough illumination to prevent stumbles. Tortured and starved, their prisoners were held in bonds which were themselves capable of inflicting torment upon any who might think to struggle and avoid their fate. To add to their misery, they were goaded by whips which bristled with energy like strands of lightning, leaving terrible scorch marks on the flesh.

Ultimately, as the hallway grew darker still, they came to the end where, milling in terror, they were violently shoved into a great hole in the floor and plunged down into darkness. It had been constructed in such a way that even in that dim light it looked like nothing so much as a huge, gaping mouth, its circumference marked by carved stones resembling pointed fangs. The victims' screams echoed as they disappeared into an unguessable end. Occasionally, prompted by sheer despair and hopelessness, a group of captives would overpower a guard and they would all fall into the darkness. Mendikar held nothing but contempt for those Chosen who were stupid enough to allow themselves to fall prey to the desperation of their captives.

Walking forward the obligatory twenty paces, Mendikar heard the doors seal shut behind him . He gripped his staff tightly and stood still, vainly endeavouring to control his fear. Here in the Inner Sanctum, it was totally dark. Not even the faintest glimmer of light gave any indication as to the size of the room he stood in or indeed what form the Presence actually had. Rather he heard a grating, slithering sound of something vast that drew towards him. Then silence descended once again and despite his best efforts Mendikar's heartbeat increased to such a rate that it felt as if the organ would erupt out of his chest, its frantic thudding seeming to echo within that dread darkness.

Mendikar managed not to flinch as he felt a slimy substance touch his face. Whether the fingers of a hand or some kind of tentacle, it stroked his skin in an almost intimate gesture leaving a cold, wet, yet oddly burning sensation behind. He resisted the temptation to reach up and touch it. He knew from experience that this would leave a red and blistered welt that would take days to heal. A vast presence entered Mendikar's mind, probing his thoughts and leaving him feeling, as ever, naked and vulnerable.

The voice which echoed in his head was high pitched and overtly female, as if the owner of that voice were an ancient crone.

<Aah. Mendikar. How sweet the taste of your flesh. How exquisite the terror that you so desperately try to conceal from me. Rest easy. You are still my favourite.> The voice was lascivious, the words spoken as if in the middle of mating, like an unwanted lover's smooth talk. Then, within a heartbeat, it changed to something harsh and threatening, so that Mendikar squirmed.

<Of course, that may change if you displease me. You wouldn't do that would you, Mendikar? No of course you wouldn't. I am your God and you worship me and bask in the light of my benevolence. But Mendikar, I hunger. Where are the additional sacrifices you promised? My appetite grows!>

A silence ensued, there was no need for Mendikar to answer, the Presence knew all his thoughts.

Once again the voice changed, now it was like a mother comforting a hurt child

<Yes, yes I see. There have been reversals. How unfortunate. Despite the advances in technology I have given you. Despite your conquests and power, your people are still being challenged quite successfully, it would seem, by these other creatures. How…. unfortunate.>

Suddenly the voice became a screeching wall of sound that took him to the edge of insanity.

<You pathetic fool! I will give you one last chance. I told you what would happen. I gave you the means to defeat them and yet you have not! And don't seek to blame the incompetence of those beneath you. You Mendikar, you alone, carry the guilt of failure!>

Despite himself, Mendikar stood sobbing. Drawing in great breaths he regained some semblance of control and for several long moments, he stood silently in a puddle of his own body fluids, until the voice came again, accompanied by a further slimy touch upon his face. He could hardly form a coherent thought and any words he tried to utter would merely sound like poor excuses. He thought it better to stay silent.

<Yes, dear Mendikar you have understood perfectly; after all, what point is there in speaking when I already know your thoughts?>

Several moments passed in silence as he mentally held his breath, sure, that this time his end was at hand.

<Oh dear, I have unmanned you. Poor Mendikar. Do not despair. Yes, I am angry but I will give you one last chance. You are still one of my favourites. Even now I have formulated a revised plan in answer to your failures and placed it in the minds of your new subordinates. Yes, yes. Your new sub-commanders will be much better and Mendikar, you will enjoy slaughtering those who have so disappointed me. You can even taste their flesh, provided they come to me alive. It will be my pleasure to show them how deeply disappointed I am in them. Yes, yes it will take them some

time to learn.> The Deity paused while it considered the punishment and enjoyment to come before at last resuming.

<Even now the enemy approach this System with intent to attack. They actually think to threaten me! Me! How I look forward to partaking of their flesh and wallowing in their terror.> The voice seemed to purr in anticipation.

<You need to be ready to welcome them when they get here.>

Mendikar sensed a shift in movement away from him and the slithering sound diminished in volume.

<Go now.>

A pause.

<All is prepared. It would be most unfortunate if you were to disappoint me again, Mendikar.>

The slithering sound drew further away until he could no longer hear it or detect a presence. Still, he waited for several long moments reassuring himself that the Deity had truly gone. It would not surprise him if this was a trick with unpleasant consequences for him if he moved too soon. He shivered, took a steadying breath, turned around and departed through the door which opened silently once more for him.

Once safely away from the Grand Temple, he issued commands as to his departure from the home world when he would take overall control of the Deity's plan. His excitement grew as to the fate that awaited his erstwhile commanders. Obviously, it was their incompetence that had led to earlier failures, despite the recent rebuke he had received. Mendikar was sure that, once he had washed and donned fresh robes, he could arrange a satisfactory and pleasantly painful entertainment for himself that would keep his erstwhile subordinates alive prior to their delivery into the Presence, thus satisfying his own humiliation and fulfilling the directions given to him.

He licked his lips in pleasurable anticipation.

ooooOooooo

The Chosen System comprised fifteen planets of varying sizes and compositions, and dozens of moons. A large number of these had long been colonised by the Chosen, either as secondary settlements or as mines and other installations for the extraction of various ores, metals and minerals. These rich deposits added to the power and strength of the Chosen, supplemented and augmented by the knowledge imparted to them by their Dorath Mar 'deity'.

Menkh and Crixac floated in silent invisibility on the very edges of Chosen space, the Chosen home world visible as a reddish speck almost lost in the myriad of stars that could be seen around them. Like the Allroians, the Chosen had colonised a number of planets within their system, but unlike the Allroians who used their AI technology to establish settlements, the Chosen colonies were built by flesh and blood utilising the expendable slave labour of conquered races. The Chosen had been fortunate in that their world occupied a part of space where other populated worlds were relatively close by, including another within their very own system, and whose technological advancements and aggressive instincts were no match for theirs.

It was difficult to gauge the passage of time as they waited, but in what seemed a relatively short period since their materialisation from the Threadway, the Allroian battle fleet appeared out of the nothingness of space. In arriving so precipitately, the Allroians had anticipated the advantage of complete surprise and had crafted their plans accordingly. Their main objective being the obliteration of the monstrosity that over the years of their mutual enmity and conflict, they had come to learn was the real source of malevolent power behind the Chosen. While the Allroian possessed the capability to destroy all life on the enemy home world, such an action was anathema to their Race who, at the core of their being, abhorred violence.

Dozens of Allroian vessels, instantaneously decelerating from speeds many times faster than light, emerged from hyperspace.

With the exception of the central command ship in each formation, Menkh knew that each vessel was crewed by artificial intelligence, their Allroian controllers interfacing with each ship via a sophisticated network of controls. Highly trained, an individual Allroian could simultaneously command and direct several vessels at once. At the same time, they were both physically and mentally connected to their fellow Allroians in each command ship so that communication between them was seamless. Situated at the heart of each formation as they were, they were shielded by the immense power of several surrounding craft whose main role was to protect and preserve the living Allroians inside. Conversely, the outer ships carried the main armament of the fleet whose primary role was the destruction of the enemy formations.

Within an inner chamber in each central vessel, up to twenty Allroians floated in a viscous fluid in suspended animation, their tentacles intertwined so that, if it were possible for an outsider to peer into the chamber, they would resemble a single entity with dozens of component parts rather than individuals. The liquid provided some protection during travel and also comprised nutrients and other elements which helped sustain the bodies that were contained within it. While no physical movement of the intertwined bodies could be discerned, this belied the intense mental activity that was taking place. Around each individual a complex tracery of fine hairlike threads was attached, and it was through this interface that control of the fleet vessels was achieved.

The interaction between the individual Allroians was such that, not only did their physical arrangement mimic a single entity, but so also did their mental acuity. In reality they thought as a single being whose power was supplemented by all.

Within moments of their appearance, each formation had rearranged itself to maximum effect and they entered into phase two of their plans. Here, however, a weakness was revealed. Even though careful surveillance of Chosen defences had been undertaken, the Allroians had made some fundamental miscalculations, based on inaccurate intelligence and flawed predictions of the Chosen capacity to retaliate. In large part this was due to the power of the Dorath Mar who had cloaked and hidden much of what they had previously observed and which now proved to be a source of grave concern.

As the Allroian formations passed in close proximity to a world thought to be uninhabited but for several small mining colonies, the Dorath Mar's capacity to shield the Chosen from prying eyes was now illustrated. The mining colonies themselves were not only more extensive in size and scale than intelligence had led the Allroians to believe, they also housed hundreds of attack vessels which now began to rapidly ascend from the planet's surface. In addition to this, and impacting further on the Allroian battle plan, planetary-wide shielding was activated to protect Chosen installations from external attack.

Inside their command vessels, the Allroians now swiftly revised their plan. Of panic or consternation there was none. The combined superintelligence of the Allroian 'commanders' calmly reassessed the situation and reacted accordingly. Reorganising their formations to meet the newly revealed threat, longer range probes searched for enemy vessels approaching from previously unobserved locations to supplement the Chosen surprise counterattack.

In a smooth and finely tuned manoeuvre, each battle group was thus adjusted to reflect a defensive posture rather than an offensive one. Vessels whose primary function was protection, rotated to the outer layers of each school, activating their shielding to cover the entirety of the formation. In the heart of this new configuration, attack vessels recalibrated their firepower so that their armament could pass through their defensive shielding to target enemy craft without disrupting the shield's effectiveness.

The Chosen craft, seemingly without number, albeit much smaller than the Allroian vessels nevertheless demonstrated powerful weaponry which now began to assault the enemy fleet that had dared to enter Chosen space. Unlike the Allroians' battleplan, the Chosen onslaught seemed to lack coordination and a series of violent attacks began to take place from multiple directions and at different points around each separate battle group. Where concentrated firepower might have secured a breach, instead different vectors were subject to sorties which achieved little success.

Allroian shielding flared violently as it deflected the energy beams and projectiles from Chosen attack craft. This was interspersed with pulses of virulent purple light that shot from inside the Allroian ships' formations with bewildering speed and flawless accuracy, destroying Chosen vessels en masse in a burst of energy. As Menkh watched, he saw that as one Chosen vessel was hit, the energy force seemed to be magnified, and forks like those of a lightning storm lanced out, crippling or destroying any enemy vessels close to that which had been struck.

The frenzied attack lasted an indefinable time. Disabled Chosen vessels, fragments of destroyed ships and other matter floated around them while, in the silent vacuum of space, the battle raged on. The Allroian shield showed no discernible weakness and at last, after realising that their attack would not succeed, the Chosen ships drew off, momentarily.

<It looks like they have finally realised they need a new attack plan,> said Crixac.

<Yes. I would estimate their losses at around thirty percent. Quite significant, I would have thought.> Menkh responded.

<You aren't Chosen, and I suspect at least some of their ships have slave crews on them.>

<You may be right Crixac; even so they should have broken off their attack earlier. I see the Allroian fleet has been steadily

progressing towards their target so this assault has not resulted in anything yet but Chosen losses.>

On board the Chosen command vessel, High Priest Mendikar ground his teeth in frustration at their losses and turned viciously on the ship's Commander.

'I should have your guts pulled out and burned in front of your eyes. Can you not see that the attack was uncoordinated? Piecemeal assaults by glory hunting fools whose only interest is their own self-aggrandisement? You stupid worm! Coordinate the next attack and concentrate it. If you can punch a hole in their defensive shielding, we can pour in among them and take down their command.'

'But you saw for yourself that they could not be controlled; what else can I do?'

Mendikar nodded his head in consideration, his eyes never leaving that of the commander's.

'Yes indeed, what else can you do?'

Larmic, the Chosen commander, barely registered the jewelled dagger that Mendikar produced with surprising speed from under his cloak. The first blow of the blade entered Larmic's neck, his eyes opening in shock. By the seventh vicious stroke commander was dead, his body falling to the deck leaking green ichor.

Mendikar turned a malevolent stare on the crew standing motionless on the command deck. 'Open fleet communications. I am assuming total command!'

The threats that he subsequently issued were gruesome enough to quell the most ambitious among the Chosen. It was not just the fate each individual would suffer which held them in check, but by extension the horrific sacrifice of all those connected in any way to all who dared to defy orders, before they too were killed in the most dreadful and protracted manner.

The Chosen losses as significant as they were, were rapidly replaced and this time the attack was coordinated with deadly efficiency. Simultaneous and concentrated attacks were now aimed at a single vessel in each Allroian formation. Though dozens of Chosen craft were destroyed others continued a vicious and unrelenting assault.

The Allroian fleet was designed to engage opposing fleet formations, they were not adapted to withstand attacks from hundreds of smaller attack craft. At last, the defences of one battle fleet were pierced and dozens of Chosen ships sped through the gap. Fast and manoeuvrable, they played havoc inside the fleet formation and although the Allroian battle ships had defensive capacity, they were now proved vulnerable. With further coordinated attacks by a swarm of Chosen craft, the individual Allroian ship defences proved inadequate. All along the outer hull of targeted vessels, bright flashes of light showed evidence of successful strikes against them. First one, then another blew up in a blinding flash as internal systems disrupted. The terrible energy waves emanating from the destroyed ships caused immense damage to surrounding vessels and these too became ever more vulnerable to attack.

Finally, several Chosen attack vessels penetrated to the very centre of one formation. Inside it the Allroians, realising their impending fate touched each other's minds in a final mental embrace of farewell. Within moments the ship that carried them disappeared in an explosion of total destruction.

The annihilation of the control ship and the mental farewell of its living crew touched every Allroian mind and had a profound effect on the other two battle schools. Following the eradication of their command vessel, all surviving craft in the first fleet formation began to withdraw as per their programming and rapidly disappeared as they accelerated away. The robotic crews of several ships, so closely under attack that they could not disengage, self-destructed, taking many Chosen vessels with them in the maelstrom of released energies.

In triumph, the Chosen redoubled their efforts against the remaining battle fleets whose defensive shields, while weakening against the sustained onslaught, still resisted.

<Crixac, it galls me to stand back and watch this battle unfolding. It seems clear to me that the Chosen now have the best of this engagement. Their capabilities were grossly underestimated by the Allroians.>

<I agree. As we have discussed, the destruction of their deity should indeed have a profound effect on the Chosen, but is the time yet right? We have not heard from Frzath.>

No sooner had Crixac formed the thought than the voice of Frzath echoed in Menkh's mind.

<We too are watching, Menkh and Crixac. Go now and launch your attack and may the Intelligence guide you in this task.>

With one accord and in the knowledge that time was against the Allroians, Menkh and Crixac drew on the power of the staff and, summoning the Threadway, focused their combined will on Katlun, the Chosen home world, travelling there in a moment of time.

CHAPTER NINE

Grossa held his hand up and the Graaven trading party behind him came to a halt. There were forty of them in the group, the males and females roughly even in number. As one, they lowered their packs laden with items and goods intended for trade with their friends the Kamehans, and stared expectantly past the figure of Grossa, wondering what had caused him to stop their progress along the now well-worn path that led to the village. A few looks were exchanged but not one word was spoken. Tension filled the air and the tendrils on their necks flared in response, their skin markings engorging and deepening in colour. To an outsider it would be a fearsome and alien sight and one that might well presage violence.

Ahead they could see a villager running towards them pursued by three others who the Graaven immediately saw by their dress were not Kamehan. These waved weapons in the air and called out loudly in pursuit. Their intent was obvious and as the running figure drew nearer it was clear that whoever it was, was reaching the edge of exhaustion, clothing torn and smeared with what might be blood.

Grossa turned his head.

'Borka, Marpon. Bows. Kill this carrion who would harm our friends.'

Wordlessly the two Graaven stepped forward. The pursuers were some five hundred paces away and approaching rapidly. If they had seen the Graaven before them they did not alter their pace and bore down on the rapidly tiring villager who the Graaven now could see was Priona, a daughter of Bentono.

With a final burst of speed, no doubt prompted by seeing the waiting Graaven before her and the promise of aid, Priona managed to reach them before her pursuers could catch her. Grossa stepped forward, gathered Priona in his arms and bore her upwards as she fell, at last. Gasping for breath she looked up into Grossa's face.

'Please help us. The village….' She said no more but passed into unconsciousness.

At last her attackers shuffled to a halt some two hundred paces away from where Grossa had caught their erstwhile prey. They had never seen anything like the Graaven before and their confusion and indecision ensured their doom.

The first attacker had only just raised a spear in defiance when the initial arrow, travelling at tremendous speed, slashed clear through his heart and slapped, quivering, into the ground behind him. Death was instantaneous. A second arrow slammed into the head of his companion to the left, lodging in his skull with such force that he was thrown backwards. The third attacker barely had time to turn away from the unexpected assault when two more arrows struck him simultaneously; as with the first shaft, the arrows passed through his body, penetrating the ground as he fell heavily upon the path.

Borka looked at Marpon. 'Not bad shooting for a spawnling,' she said.

Marpon smiled back and replied with just a hint of smugness, 'Thank you Borka. You are a fine teacher.'

'What now, Grossa?' she asked.

'Down packs. Talita and Geht you stay here with our friend and watch over her. She doesn't appear to be hurt badly, just some scratches and bruises; she will wake up soon enough. And watch the packs, you are responsible.'

The youngest spawnlings in the group, Talita and Geht drew themselves up proudly. 'Don't worry Grossa, we will do as you say,' said Talita.

Grossa almost smiled but kept his face stern and gave a curt nod.

'The rest of you – with me, at the run.'

For a race of people standing over eight feet tall Graavens could move at speed and with surprising stealth. It was pure luck that they were very close to the village and in a position to help, if not too late. They had set out when the moon glow of Orvasne was just disappearing below the horizon as Avlar lifted its face above the horizon, promising another fine day. The hour was still early.

As they approached the village they could hear shouts and screams and Grossa felt a terrible rage building inside him. Who-ever these attackers were, they were going to pay dearly for harming their friends, the people whose aid and support had en-sured that the Graaven people could prosper in this strange new land.

They reached the stone wall that now surrounded the village and which the Graaven had largely helped to build. To allay Kamehan fears of attack, they had transported stones and rocks from the desert and, with a skill that they did not know they pos-sessed until the need required, had constructed this sturdy dry-stone barrier that would aid in blunting any attack giving their friends time to prepare, or so it had been hoped.

Peering over the wall they saw that the surviving Kamehan had formed a circle at the heart of the village, sheltering within which were the defenceless aged and small children. Bodies, mostly of their friends, lay scattered on the ground, some still moving but being despatched by their enemies. In every sense the Kamehans were being hard-pressed and on the verge of a savage defeat by a large number of warriors who surged up to the defenders like a wave.

'You have a plan, Grossa?' asked Borka.

Grossa turned to Borka. It was clear to them all that he was in a fighting rage, his skin markings fully engorged and the tendrils on his neck flaring redly.

In a voice devoid of all emotion he said, 'Kill them all. Protect our friends. Show no mercy.'

'Works for me,' said Borka.

'Follow me!' yelled Grossa as he vaulted the wall at the same time freeing the huge club he carried and hefting it in his right hand.

Borka prepared to follow him but called out to Marpon: 'You, Kallet and Gortho hold back and pick off any you can safely kill. If you see anyone that looks like a leader kill them.'

Marpon nodded and deftly restrung his bow. In moments the Graaven had vaulted the wall. They swept down upon the enemy like a storm wind. It was not just the surprise, but the sheer savagery and strength of the Graaven that made them seem like monsters from nightmare to the attacking force. In short order they were proven to be no match for the giant Graaven. In moments, the hunters became the hunted as in confusion they tried to flee back from whence they had come. Many threw their weapons down in surrender, to no avail. The Graaven had seen the bodies of their friends strewn upon the ground and as one they were filled, like their leader, with a killing rage. Those of the enemy who threw down their weapons were smashed off their feet or shot down with arrows. With the striated markings of their skin en-gorged and glowing with colour, the Graaven were of alien and terrifying aspect.

Within the circle of villagers, Bentono felt himself relax and closed his eyes in relief. They had been close to a terrible defeat and death. Parana had been struck with a spear and Bentono held him in his arms. He prayed to Bekkor that it was not a death blow; he looked down at Parana who was still conscious and aware of his surroundings.

'I think that you were right. Our Graaven friends would have made mincemeat of us,' Bentono said, wryly.

Parana smiled through the pain of his wound. 'Told you so.'

Finally, all the enemy had been killed, but one. A snivelling youngster, quaking with fear, was hauled before Grossa, who held in one hand the gory head of the war chief who had led the assault. Grimly the head was held out and delivered into his shaking hands.

Grossa pointed beyond the wall. 'Go,' he said in the Kamehan tongue, in a tone that made the hapless captive shudder. 'Do not return here.' Without turning his head and with piercing and mer-ciless eyes fixed on the cringing captive, he addressed a Graaven standing to one side.

'Marpon, trail him, if he drops the head kill him.'

The young captive may not have understood the words but the meaning was fully comprehended. He looked up fearfully at the alien and the implacable expressions on the faces of the beings that surrounded him, fearful that this was some kind of trick and that death awaited him. Silently the Graaven drew apart, giving an opening for the youth to pass. He took tentative steps towards the promise of escape, at first looking back over his shoulder in fear, and then he ran as fast as he could, away from the scene of horror, gripping his grisly charge tightly in his hands. Only the one named Marpon followed him at an easy jog, his immense bow in his hands, the intent clear.

In the aftermath of the attack, Bentono was overjoyed to find that his youngest daughter Priona was alive and well. The Kamehans mourned many of their people, but were mindful that, without the aid of their friends, the death toll would have been far, far greater, the consequences of their defeat unthinkable.

In contrast to the savagery displayed by the Graaven during their assault against the Kamehan foe, their treatment of the wounded was of the gentlest care and concern. Their knowledge of the treatment of wounds, and of the use of healing plants that grew in the swampy environment they inhabited, saved many lives. If there had been any lingering doubt in the minds of the Kamehans as to the intentions of the Graaven, it was completely dispelled after the attack.

In the days that followed, the Graaven discovered that the attackers were distantly related to the Kamehan people. They too were of the Hagalan Nation and the relocation of the Kamehans to their new lands had been prompted by the hostilities with this tribe, known to them as the Takama. Many times greater in number and overtly more aggressive than the Kamehans, they hoped that their settling far from them would result in peace. In the knowledge of this now forlorn hope, the Graaven counselled that a scouting expedition should set out to assess the likelihood of further attack and, as peaceable as their friends were, there were many who agreed they could not now simply sit back and hope to be left alone. It was generally believed that the Hakama would seek revenge for their humiliating defeat.

After long deliberation, a consensus was reached and a party of fifty Graaven and twenty Kamehan set out for the enemy lands, travelling with care and stealth. Marpon had tracked the released captive until the boy met with a small party of his people who were camped a long day's march from the Kamehan village, perhaps to await news there of the successful attack. They had set off hurriedly, Marpon tracking them all the way back to their own village.

Now, after some twenty dak'chaal the Graaven finally saw smoke rising ahead from the village that Marpon had noted. Spreading out and using the cover of fern trees that grew in abundance around them, they quietly observed the enemy settlement. It was a large village with many hundreds of huts surrounded by a log palisade. Four massive gates pierced the walls allowing passage by roadways that led to the heart of the site, in which stood a great hall, many times bigger than any other discernible building. It was clear that preparations were being made for a foray. Many warriors were gathering there, while weapons and equipment were being stockpiled.

'What do you think of this, Bentono?' Grossa asked.

'I have only one thought. They are planning another attack in vengeance and this time they are making sure they have the numbers to achieve their goal.'

'I agree. Borka?'

'I too agree. What do we do?'

Grossa smiled. 'It is a large village, made of wood with thatch for roofs. The weather is hot and dry. I wonder how good their people are at fighting fire?'

Bentono turned a surprised expression on Grossa. 'You are proposing we attack? Now?'

'We await nightfall. As Halidar rises, we will rain fire down upon them and sweep through their village killing as we may in the confusion; then we withdraw.'

The attack was a complete surprise and brutally efficient. The Takama were so confident in their overwhelming numbers and so arrogant in their belief that any attack against them was an impossibility, that only a few guards were in place to raise an alarm; those that were, were quickly dealt with. The first indication of any disturbance were the flaming arrows that flew like comets across the night sky, lodging with deadly accuracy in the thatch of the dwellings, their fire quickly taking hold. By the time any alarm was raised, it was already too late.

The enemy, swarming in confusion, were cut down as the attackers swept with silent savagery into their undefended village. Unable to understand the nature of the attack, other than a vague sense of giants of terrible aspect dealing out death in the smoke, their panic was such that they completely failed to provide an effective effort to fight the fires. The flames leapt with frightening ease from one building to the next, resulting in a conflagration of epic proportions. So successful was the assault that almost the entire village was burnt to the ground, hundreds of Hakaman people perishing in the flames along with all their belongings.

The agreed horn call sounded and the Kamehan and Graaven fighters withdrew. Two Kamehan casualties had fallen, borne away by their comrades, and the Graaven warrior Marova had sustained a serious wound that might prove fatal. However, the enemy force had been decimated, dying in the battle with their implacable foe or burnt to death in the flames. Many more had been incapacitated by terrible burns.

From the cover of the fern woods above the smouldering ruins of the village, Bentono looked down at what they had done. While he felt justified in the aftermath of their attack on his people, he yet could not look at the destruction and loss without feeling great sadness.

'I think your village is now safe from these people. They are vulnerable and must be feeling as your people once did,' said Grossa.

Bentono nodded in agreement.

'You are right of course. But I cannot revel in their pain and loss; it was to leave such things behind that we fled to lands we believed no one else would want.'

Grossa turned to look at him.

'You are related one to the other, share the same gods and the same culture and yet remain separate tribes warring and killing each other for land and domination. There is much here that is good, but as long as your petty jealousies prevail you will not truly thrive. No. You need a unifying power that cements and draws you all together.'

Bentono looked at the Graaven and turned his eyes back to the remnants of the Takama village. There was no argument he could put up to refute Grossa's words; he was right.

Grossa looked at Bentono for several moments before his gaze turned to his people who were gathered around him. Tall, strong, unmatched.

'Yes,' he mused. 'A unifying power.'

Bentono, hearing these quiet and introspective words looked up into Grossa's face and shuddered at the expression he saw there. Once again, he was glad that the Graaven saw his people as friends. He would hate to be their enemy.

ooooOoooo

Menkh plunged down through the Chosen planet's atmosphere, his concentration so intent on the ballooning energy he and Crixac channelled into the staff, that they were oblivious of their speed.

When the surface of that world drew into focus, Menkh came to an abrupt halt. As far as the eye could see, were buildings and in between the buildings, every surface was covered in what appeared to be stone paving. Not one tree, plant or green thing was visible. For many persangh in every direction, it was one vast cityscape. The buildings were uniformly constructed of some drab grey material that absorbed light, the only visible variation being in the height of the buildings. Strange vehicles moved along roadways or flew through the skies. Few Chosen could be seen walking the pathways and Menkh assumed that the city must be connected by tunnels or covered walkways, reducing the need for passage outside. There was no colour, save for that drab grey; even the sky appeared overcast. The whole effect, from the height where Menkh hovered above, was depressing, and he couldn't begin to imagine its impact on those who dwelt there.

<In all my travels I have never seen such a wearyingly depressing place,> Crixac's voice echoed in Menkh's mind.

<I agree, my friend. I wonder what this world looked like before it was covered by stone. This whole vista leaves me drained of all happiness.>

Menkh's words were more pertinent than he knew; there was more to the city's effect than merely a disheartening spectacle. The resolve that Menkh and Crixac had formed to destroy the Dorath Mar seemed to crumble away. They felt both hopeless and powerless and as the insidious feeling grew, so too did a mounting sense that their objective to exact retribution was pointless, doomed to failure. So overwhelmed with hopelessness were they, that they lost all direction. Where before there was certainty, now there was only doubt, accompanied by the creeping sense that something sought them out, a presence that hunted them with evil intent.

<Menkh! We must regroup, leave this place before we are totally overcome and our presence discovered.>

Menkh did not respond, albeit his innermost thoughts were in complete agreement, his body was sluggish, while trying to move was an exercise in sheer willpower. He exerted every effort, but each time he did so the feeling of resistance and antipathy overwhelmed him. Finally, in a titanic effort of will, Menkh focused into his staff and with tentative initial movement he at last advanced, gradually increasing speed across the surface of the planet.

Somehow, the act of moving helped to dampen their sense of despair and they started their search for any break in or relief from the monotony of the buildings and that sense of hopelessness. At last, they came to a vast ocean, whose grey waters lapped a shore devoid of any natural beach or coastline, presenting only a continuation of the great walls and buttresses of stone and metal. The waters of the ocean seemed to have receded, revealing a sterile stretch of sea floor that, while not built upon, was devoid of any plant life. It seemed as if the sea itself drew away from the artificial shoreline in revulsion.

Beyond hope, far out across the waters and well away from the land itself, they saw a vast island in the midst of the seas. It drew them like a magnet. Here at least, was plant life of many colours that was a balm to the soul. Like two travellers dying of thirst in a desert and coming across an oasis, Menkh and Crixac descended onto the island. For a time Menkh simply stood there devoid of conscious thought and filled with wonder. While the land mass they had traversed was the singular most depressing place he had ever seen, here was its utter opposite. Menkh was transfixed by the beauty and colours of the plants, trees and flowers surrounding him. Huge multi-coloured insects flitted from plant to plant and for reasons Menkh could not discern he felt tears flowing down his face.

Many different species of majestic trees towered above them, so stunning in their overall effect that the eye became bewildered. Leaves and flowers of every colour imaginable could be seen and the air was filled with the heady perfumes of flowers and spices. The very ground they stood upon was a rich loam where smaller plants and grasses grew in abundance.

Crixac's voice in Menkh's mind was hushed and filled with horror.

<If the rest of the planet was once like this, what the Chosen have done is an utter abomination!>

Menkh could only nod.

<The Chosen, or the Dorath Mar? To have done what they have done to their own world…!> Menkh left his thoughts unfinished. Like him, Crixac could not formulate a clear response.

After what seemed an age standing in that place of wonder, Menkh felt the return of his resolve to destroy the Dorath Mar, reinforced by the unalloyed beauty of his surroundings.

<Not by chance were we drawn to this place, Menkh. I feel the hand of the Intelligence in this. There is no feeling here of despair.>

Menkh nodded his head in agreement. Their sense of urgency and resolve was once again in focus.

<Come Crixac, we have a job to do. Let us hope that in destroying the evil that the Chosen worship, this place at least will be preserved.>

Without further thought Menkh ascended high into the air and, not without some regret and sadness, left the island far below as they sped off to complete the mission he and Crixac had embarked upon.

On returning to the mainland, Menkh began to see that while every surface was covered by buildings, they occasionally flew across areas where there was an even denser concentration of construction. Here the buildings rose much higher than their surrounds and there was much more traffic both at ground level and in the air.

The Eye of Malavak had shown them the massive temple that dominated the Chosen city of X'cotl and housed their Dorath Mar deity. Its grounds spread for hundreds of persangh and in size and scale dwarfed what had been the temple of Harkan in Gahrtok. It was in fact, a city within a city. The Chosen priesthood who lived there governed every facet of everyday life and over years the religion they practised had virtually eradicated all emotions akin to kindness, compassion or mercy.

Menkh came to a halt far above the temple complex. Black and forbidding, its brooding presence lay like a well of darkness, a place of nightmare. An almost palpable sense of malevolence emanated from it, feeding and strengthening the source of despair that permeated everywhere.

<It's a miracle that the island we saw has survived, but I think even there I could sense the beginnings of a taint in the air.>

<Yes, now I think on it, I believe my reaction was partly a sense of impending loss,> said Menkh. <Time, I think to deliver justice.>

<Yes, let us be about this, my friend.>

Concentrating their thoughts, gripping the staff in both hands and surrounding themselves in a mental aura of protection, Menkh and Crixac focused all their will upon the staff until it thrummed with energy. Intense blue light built and built until it seemed it could take no more and then at last, Menkh plunged down like a veritable comet until, in a pulse of energy, his translucent form penetrated the very fabric of the temple going from incalculable speed to a complete stop in a heartbeat. In that instant, the Dorath Mar within, became aware of intruders in its domain and before it could react, Menkh and Crixac released the pent-up force of the staff.

It was akin to being present at the birth of a sun. Everything within several hundred persangh was vapourised. Every vestige of the temple at every level above and below the earth was extinguished in a single moment. And in a single moment, every living thing within that vast complex ceased to exist. Long lines of starved and beaten captives were spared the gruesome fate their chained and weary steps took them inexorably towards. Menkh had no time for regret, it was impossible to save so many. Both he and Crixac took comfort that they, at least, had been spared the horrific and gruesome death that so many before them had suffered in the clutches of the Dorath Mar.

It was perhaps the purest coincidence that the annual convocation of priests was taking place within the temple at that time. Hundreds of them – from the lowliest acolyte to the most exalted of princes – were assembled from all parts of Katlun and from a number of worlds under Chosen domination. Within that single heartbeat of time, they joined their hideous god in death. The discharge of force, however, was not yet fully exhausted. Incandescent energy was transmitted along the tendril of power that connected the Chosen Dorath Mar to its loathsome Mother and delivered to that monstrosity a degree of pain such that it had never experienced.

Beyond the borders of what had once been X'cotl, individual Chosen experienced a huge mental jolt akin to burning one's hand on a hot pan except that, instead of pain they felt an intense loss. Like having part of oneself ripped away and a void left behind.

Everywhere, no matter what they were doing, Chosen mentally stumbled, lost focus and stopped what they were doing. Some screamed in anguish and threw themselves mindlessly from buildings to their deaths, others were violently sick or became completely disoriented, moving as if blinded. A feeling of indescribable sadness, akin to the aftermath of the death of a parent, overcame them. Those few who had not killed themselves, slowly recovered their wits. As rational thought returned it was replaced by something else: a terrible guilt began to manifest at the enormity of what they had done, both individually and collectively, and of what they had become. Many simply sat down where they were and wept inconsolably.

Then, at first difficult to quantify, there was a collective reaching out towards something that hovered on the edge of perception. A mind-altering and tentative stretching out towards something different, something whole and clean, followed by a feeling of mental release. Chosen everywhere looked at each other, at their surroundings and at themselves in a new light and realised that they had emerged from a nightmare of horror. New possibilities opened before them. It was the very beginning of a transformation which would ultimately change the Chosen forever.

On the edges of Chosen space, the attack against the Allroian stuttered to a stop. Chosen craft disengaged and fled back to whence they had come, no less confused and disoriented than those who lived on their home world.

Menkh floated within the vast crater that had once been the temple. Far below him the ground glowed with an intense heat.

<Did we overdo it?> Crixac asked.

Menkh had to work hard not to laugh at the tone Crixac used.

<Considering that the effects seem to be mostly limited to the temple complex and there was no planet-wide explosion, I think we have done rather well. Let's hope that the little shock we sent to Mother has given Tishan the opportunity to make a permanent change there.>

<Indeed.> Crixac responded. <Well, no use hanging about here. We must make all haste to join Varnahrin. If our Adept friends were right then we can expect an imminent assault on Tarvuli itself.>

Menkh mentally agreed.

<Let us see first if this act has also had the desired effect on the Chosen attack and if the Allroians have managed to withdraw.>

They summoned the Threadway and returned to the location of the great battle.

ooooOoooo

At the moment of its destruction, Mendikar had collapsed into unconsciousness such was the impact of the Dorath Mar's demise. It was a sleep from which he never awoke. Freed from servile fear, several crew members nearby plunged jewelled daggers into his comatose body. With his demise and without his iron will, along with their new and unanticipated sense of release, the Chosen attack lost all cohesion. Of their own accord, units began to break off action and return to their home base.

The Allroians sensed that some great and profound event had occurred and in consideration of their own losses withdrew in good order. Finally reaching a safe distance and assured that their adversaries had indeed withdrawn, they accelerated as one and disappeared from Chosen space.

All this had been observed by Menkh and Crixac, floating on their own, unobserved.

Menkh was in the process of formulating a thought to Crixac when he was overwhelmed with a sudden and intense feeling, a reaction to some as yet unexplained event, the impact of which had been relayed through the Threadway. Crixac too was affected by this wave of emotion.

As one they shared the same thought <Tishan!>

<Yes> said Menkh. <I can think of no other explanation. I believe that Tishan has achieved the destruction of the Enemy.>

<One of the Enemy, Menkh. We must not forget its alter ego and while the demise of the Mother may have led to the destruction of its offspring, I do not believe that it will have had such an effect on that which trapped you and I.>

Crixac had no sooner formed his thought than they were both impacted by a further reaction transmitted through the Threadway. This one had such an adverse effect that their senses were nearly overwhelmed. A malevolent focus of hatred so intense it too transmitted itself through the Threadway.

<There can be no other possible target for this creature, except Tarvuli. It will speed to Tarvuli and endeavour to achieve what it failed to before,> said Crixac.

<Then let us waste not a moment longer.>

No sooner had Menkh's mental response formed, than in mutual accord they ascended the Threadway and disappeared, directing their focus with all haste back to Tarvuli.

CHAPTER TEN

Within two Graaven dak'chaal, the first batch of cures had been created, much faster than anticipated and due in no small part to Varnahrin's influence and Horven's organisational flair.

The Complex boasted a number of well-equipped laboratories and it was a reasonably straightforward matter to recommission one that was suitable for distilling the saps of the numerous plants the Hrv had brought with them. The Hrv, true to their word, proved to be expert in the botanical uses of the plants they knew and the knowledge they shared was of immense value. The facilities were adapted to propagate the seeds in order to provide a regular harvest of seedlings that could be transplanted in conditions ideal for boosting growth.

Grakh and his small team of healers had, with the Hrv, worked with little sleep or food, so urgent was the need. In the meantime, the first seedlings cultivated in the laboratory had been planted out. With a sense of rightness, the atmospheric conditions within the structure where Graaven eggs were incubated, proved the ideal environment and already the first plants were thriving, reaching a point where their sap could be harvested.

During this short time, the malodorous lesions and blackness on the bodies of Mareen and Halika had spread slowly but inexorably. While many in Ta'Morin were sick, the Council knew from Grakh that Horven's spawnlings were the only ones to exhibit the spreading blackness.

Waking on the third day from a restless slumber alongside Lerma, Horven became aware that someone stood outside their dwelling seeking access. Rising quietly and only after making sure that Mareen and Halika still breathed, she made her way down the stairs to the door.

Upon its opening she saw that Councillor Borta and one of the Hrv stood outside. Having worked in close proximity to the Hrv over the last days Horven had begun to recognise subtle differences in the markings on the Hrv carapaces and she thought that this particular individual was Trrz, confirmed a moment later when Borta spoke.

'Trrz and I have come straight from Grakh. The Council has agreed that Mareen and Halika shall be two of the first Graaven in Ta'Morin to take the cure. Here are two doses.' Trrz then offered up two small vials of a dark red liquid.

Overcome with emotion, Horven took Borta in an embrace and tears flowed freely down her face.

'I thank you Borta, you and the Council and of course you also Trrz and your fellow Hrv.'

Trrz bobbed his head and clicked mandibles to acknowledge Horven's gratitude.

'Go now, Horven,' said Borta. 'You must get your spawnlings to swallow the mixture. Let us pray that it is not too late.'

Holding the two vials as if they could break at the slightest touch, Horven bowed her head, and turning without a word climbed back up the stairs. Conflicting emotions, hopes and fears, exhilaration and depression warred within her. Lerma stirred as she entered the room.

Holding up the two vials so that Lerma could see them she could only manage a few choked words: 'The Council. Cures. They must swallow them.'

Passing one to Lerma who ministered to Halika, she herself tenderly lifted Mareen's head and slowly began to drip the liquid into her mouth. After what seemed an age, the vial was empty and both she and Lerma sat back, their hands gripped tightly in mutual hope and longing.

'Now we wait,' said Lerma.

'Yes,' Horven drew close to Lerma where they sat on the floor and rested her head on his shoulder. 'We wait.'

Despite their mutual fear and longing, keeping silent vigil over their two spawnlings and the strain of the last days, their exhaustion overcame their resolve and they both fell into a deep slumber. Horven slipped into a vivid dream of the past.

ooooOoooo

Horven and Mareen were standing guard duty. Ordinarily, Horven found this requirement to be boring to the point of distraction and focusing attention a supreme test of her powers of concentration. However, this was not the case whenever she was posted at the K'num Prashar or Great Market.

This huge area at the centre of Tarmech, capital city of the Graaven Empire, was dominated by the soaring Temple of Bekkor. At this hour of the day the temple cast its great shadow across much of the square.

Beneath a cloudless violet sky Avlar and Colunda, the twin suns of Tarvuli, could be seen. Avlar sat almost directly overhead while Colunda had begun its descent toward the horizon. Their combined heat was somewhat dissipated both by the shade of the temple and the great awnings that reached out to cover the perimeter of the market square where hundreds of stalls were set up.

Not only was every kind of foodstuff available for purchase but every possible item too; tools, clothing, weaponry, cloth or a myriad of others – could be bought at the Great Market. Three full praka of Baran Mec kept watch while teams of Graaven cleaners, composed of individuals from the lowest clans, were kept constantly busy sweeping the flagstones and removing the detritus of thousands.

Horven and Mareen continuously swept their eyes across the crowds. Individuals from every corner of the Empire were present. Not only were there people from the vassal states of the Empire but also from the provinces. Percassians with their dark skin were garbed in bright robes of yellow and red, tall hats made of felt perched upon their heads. Horven was always surprised that they did not fall off in the milling crowds. No doubt the elongated skulls of the Percassians ensured that, however it looked, they sat securely.

Interspersed among these brightly coloured individuals wove small groups of Voenians. Much shorter in stature, the males sported long and intricately braided beards providing a contrast to their shaved skulls which were tattooed with swirling geometric designs. The females had long hair which swept down almost to their ankles, and, like their menfolk, this too was braided with brightly coloured beads and other items woven into the whole. Their faces displayed the same whirling tattoos as the males.

The diminutive tribal people from Crosh, clad in cured and embroidered hides, slipped through the crowd with the grace of dancers executing intricate movements that kept them from the crush while golden-skinned Kassarins, their bodies almost completely covered in long white robes which shimmered in the sunlight, strode with long legs that seemed out of proportion to their upper bodies.

Horven was endlessly fascinated by this moving panoply of colour and the noise was something else again. While Graaven speech was the common tongue used by all comers, nevertheless the language and dialects of these disparate peoples, unified under the Empire, created a maelstrom of sound that confounded the ear.

Mareen and Horven exchanged a look. With such a volume of sound, somehow magnified by the stones of the alcove in which they stood, speech between them was difficult but as siblings a single expression often conveyed more than mere words could. Talking was kept to a minimum to avoid having to shout to be heard.

Horven mused over the power of the Empire. The Graaven people, once few and viewed with suspicion, had risen to pre-eminence over hundreds of sem'chaal, as her people recorded the passing years. The Graaven had a natural proclivity for war and the power of their military and the discipline of their troops was a key factor in their ability to conquer the lands which surrounded them. However, the Graaven also showed a remarkable forbearance towards those peoples who fell within their power. Provided that these conquered races gave their allegiance and yearly tribute, they were largely left alone. The Graaven did not interfere in their way of life and, apart from a garrison of troops to oversee Graaven interests, life continued much as it has before. Unless of course there was any attempt at rebellion, which on occasion had occurred from time to time, due no doubt to the light hand that the Graaven exercised over those subjugated.

It was then that those who rose up in rebellion were treated with ruthless retaliation. Throughout the Empire, a series of strategically placed fortress towns had been established. Connected by well-made roads, the Graaven could rapidly field thousands of troops to crush any uprising before it even got fully underway.

Horven nodded her head to herself; yes, these were the two keys that held the Empire together: tolerance and strength. Except for the Perduvians, of course. The Graaven had been at war with them for many sem'chaal, even now the heir to the throne, Menkh ab Dur and the Pohlan Kar himself, Dur ab Shemma, were preparing for an expedition to finally subdue these Perduvians. Horven wished that she too was part of this effort rather than stuck on what seemed to be endless guard duty.

A sudden nudge from Mareen broke into her reverie. As if in answer to her thoughts there was a swirl in the crowd. A knot of Baran Mec could be seen clearing space around a central figure who shimmered in flowing robes of Phalandrel silk, from one of the Empire's vassal states prized for its cloth. Horven drew herself up as she saw that it was Menkh ab Dur the Pohlan Harac himself. As he progressed, so the tumult from the crowd diminished around him in that vast area. Unhurriedly he made his way around some of the stalls, engaging the stallholders in discussion and eyeing their wares. If the Baran Mec were perturbed by this behaviour and Menkh's exposure to risk, they nonetheless appeared composed. Behind Menkh, a coterie of palace servants paid for his purchases and hefted the various packages.

Horven and Mareen looked at each other in wonder. No member of the nobility had ever walked among the marketgoers, let alone purchased items from the stalls. It would seem the rumours that this noble was different from all others, barring his sibling Pershiva al Dur, might indeed be true.

Horven's internal ruminations abruptly ceased when she saw that Menkh was heading directly for where she and Mareen stood guard. As he came before them, they stood to attention and clashed their arms across their chests in the salute of the Baran Mec.

Menkh pointed behind him to a tall and grizzled Baran Mec warrior who had fixed them both with a look that had terrified many a raw recruit. 'Shu Lan Cars informs me that you are Horven and Mareen Var?'

Horven's mouth had quite dried up and it was Mareen who responded.

'That is quite right, my Prince,' she said.

'He also tells me, and believe me when I say that he does not often heap praise on anyone, that both you and your sibling Horven display some prowess in your combat skills.'

'The Shu Lan is most complimentary. It is true that both Horven and I won the recent tourney.'

Nodding his head, Menkh looked at each of them in turn. It was the first time Horven witnessed his capacity to focus on an individual in such a way that his entire attention seemed on you alone and all else faded into the background.

'I take only the best in my personal guard. I would be pleased if you would consider joining it?'

Horven felt like a spawnling at her first fair. She could not contain the grin that came to her face, upon which the expression on Cars' face became even more grim, nor could she avoid a fleeting look at Mareen who displayed exactly the same expression.

They both stammered out a grateful acceptance in such a way that Menkh gave them a warm smile. 'Good, very good. I am most pleased. Report to Shu Lan Cars at first watch in the morning. He will explain your duties.'

As he turned to leave, they both spoke at the same time. 'Thank you, Pohlan Harac!'

Menkh stopped momentarily and turning back said *thank you* in a tone that to their ears, conveyed some degree of humour.

Cars gave them a frozen look devoid of amusement, which effectively removed the smiles from Horven and Mareen's faces.

'Seventh Gate, first watch, be early.'

His voice was like gravel scraping over metal. Horven and Mareen gave him their best salute and watched him leave, followed by the other Baran Mec who exchanged curious glances with them both.

The grins they exchanged once the Pohlan Harac and his party moved on, dimmed the light of Avlar in intensity and the peal of laughter made several marketgoers turn in alarm.

ooooOoooo

When Horven's eyes opened after several chaal, she was at first disoriented and then filled with guilt that she should sleep while her offspring suffered and may have died while she slumbered. Instantly, her attention snapped to Halika and Mareen.

She reached across and shook her sleeping partner's shoulder.

'Wake up Lerma! We both fell asleep.'

Horven quickly leant over the still form of Mareen, terrified that during her weakness of exhausted sleep the worst may have happened. It was not until she saw that Mareen was still breathing quietly she realised she was holding her own breath. Tentatively lifting the coverlet, she looked at the lesions on Mareen's body. Fearing the worst she thought at first that she was imagining what she saw: the ulcerations were no longer leaking pus and it was clear that, while still visible, the threads of blackness had noticeably retreated. Looking across to Lerma who likewise was checking Halika they exchanged a look of profound relief, gripping each other's hands and smiling. For the first time since their spawnlings had succumbed, she felt a sense that things would now be alright.

As the days passed, both Halika and Mareen continued to rapidly improve. The lesions on their bodies dried and healed and the blackness disappeared as if it had never been. Horven could not remember a time when she had been so happy, a feeling compounded by the fact that all across Ta'Morin the effect of the cure was similarly being experienced by others, so that there was a general sense of euphoria. As to the Hrv, the Graaven collectively felt a deep and profound gratitude towards them and a formal treaty was drawn up, unanimously endorsed and signed by the Council.

Preparation of the cure became more intense and the logistics of disseminating it were tried and tested over many days. Here the gateways that had been established proved critical in the rapid delivery of the medicines and both Pershivon and Drenyk, the spawn of Tishan and Menkh, took an active role in their delivery. As the Graaven became more practiced at propagation and preparation of the treatment, so the Hrv accompanied the visits via the gateway, providing their expert knowledge on questions regarding dosages and expected timeframes for the cure to take effect. Soon the Hrv, undisguised and in their normal appearance, were being welcomed wherever they went and this change in attitude towards them began to influence the way that they too, previously thought about those they referred to as warm-bloods.

ooooOoooo

Tlkcha's poctech sped over the great plains, the steady wind from the east driving them onwards.

Tlkcha's close friend Gremma kept watch as they steered a steady path through the grasses that grew as far as the eye could see in every direction.

The Xotic had sailed over their lands for generations and from their earliest years all Xotic were taught how to safely handle and repair the craft that traversed the great plains. In their training they also learned of the various routes that their people had employed since the elder days, to journey from one scattered settlement to another. These paths, unrecognisable to any but the Xotic, were not only safe from obstructions but provided the most direct ways from village to village.

Since the arrival of the blight in their lands, Tlkcha's role had been to journey far and wide maintaining contact with their people, albeit from a distance, leaving such medicines and food as they had for the afflicted. Now she travelled with renewed hope, for the cure made by the Hrv had arrived, carried through the gateway from Ta'Morin by Drenyk and Pershivon.

Gremma's voice called out from the bow of the poctech, drawing her from her thoughts. In the distance, but rapidly coming closer, was a single poctech almost identical to their own, standing motionless in their path, its sail flapping desultorily in the wind.

'Shorten sail!' Tlkcha called and her crew swarmed over the rigging, lowering the single mainsail with practised efficiency. The poctech slowed to a stop some fifty paces upwind from the other Xotic craft. Their arrival had not disturbed the dozens of small, winged carrion hunters, called macroa, that were swarming over the dead bodies that lay exposed on the vessel.

'Do we search for survivors?' Chalayla asked.

Tlkcha shook her head sadly. 'No point. Even if only one of the people was alive when they stopped their craft, these flesh eaters would have killed them. Gather the crew; we shall say a prayer to the Sky Father and leave them here.'

It was Xotic practise to leave their dead on the prairie exposed to the elements, so that they returned to the sky and the earth from whence they came. Leaving the bodies thus, did not overly concern Tlkcha and her crew, though they were saddened that more of their people had died so horribly from the affliction.

Being semi-nomadic, the disease had had less impact on the Xotic than it had on those peoples who dwelt in large townships and cities. When it did take hold in a village, however, its effects were devastating. The Xotic had quickly learned that staying isolated and communicating from afar was the best way to manage the contagion, though several villages had been decimated before they understood this. Now at last, thanks to an unlikely source, they had an effective cure and with it had come renewed hope.

When the prayer was over, Tlkcha ordered the sail hoisted and as it bellied in the wind, she closed to thirty paces to see if they could discern markings on the craft which would tell them which village it had come from.

Although still upwind the stench of decay reached their nostrils as the seething mass of carrion eaters continued their ghastly feast.

'They are from Lakana!' Gremma called back from her post in the bow. 'Let us hope that the village survives.'

Tlkcha hoped so too. Lakana was one of the most isolated villages and their next destination. It was a mystery how the disease could have travelled this far, but the poctech told a different story. Perhaps they had had contact with another infected village; it was impossible to tell if the vessel had been returning to or travelling from Lakana. Perhaps the village itself would hold clues to this tragedy.

As they journeyed on, they began to come across great herds of kakesh, a long-necked herbivore that could run with great speed when needed, and other grass eating animals. The poctech was not seen as a threat, indeed few grazing herbivores of any kind were unduly disturbed by the vessels of the Xotic except for the lumbering four-horned beasts the Benshin referred to as 'mursk vek' and which the Xotic called 'dasheka', that were often easily spooked. However, where you found herbivores there too you would find the beasts that fed on them. Among them were Gravosh which resembled the Gonverdeem in size and strength and hunted in packs; also the Mellax, terrifying giant lizards with razor-like teeth and claws that fortunately were most often solitary predators.

A vast herd of dasheka currently occupied the path that Tlkcha needed to take, so, reducing sail they journeyed carefully through them. Fortunately, the beasts obligingly moved out of their way as they approached and it was only occasionally that they needed to manoeuvre around a stubborn bull or cow.

The horned heads of the creatures came up level with the sides of the poctech but the dasheka were more interested in the grasses they consumed than the strange animal that passed through their herd. All was progressing smoothly and Tlkcha's craft was finally approaching the outer edges of the herd, when things rapidly changed for the worst.

At first it was barely noticeable, given that their craft had increased its speed and was vibrating as its mainsail bellied out in the strong breeze. Then they noticed that the dasheka, as one, had ceased eating and their heads were up, sniffing the air. In moments, the beasts went from stillness to rapid movement. At the same time Gremma called out 'Earthshake!'

Alarmed, the dasheka now veered across the craft's bow as they sped in fright and desperation.

Tlkcha ran to the tiller bar located amidship and threw her weight at it.

'Turn with them! Turn!'

They followed the retreating herd with the poctech braced hard-around. Two smaller four-horns crashed into their craft which shuddered with the impact but sustained little damage. Still on the outer edge of the stampeding herd, the vessel now ran in the same direction as the terrified animals. The bearing they headed had the wind coming across them from the right and their pettak-skin sail caught it and drove them at a speed which easily matched the dasheka, now running at their top speed. Surreptitiously, Tlkcha, aided by Kamra, who was manning the tiller prior to the earthshake, steered a delicate course to get beyond the herd.

They had nearly achieved this when the earthshake intensified in power. The poctech, still barrelling along at speed, began to move erratically and around them some dasheka collapsed, unable to maintain their footing on the heaving ground.

Sailing over the terrain at near top speed, the earth ahead of the poctech suddenly rose up before them, forming a cliff of disturbed soil and rocks. There was nothing that could be done. Their ship, continuing with undiminished speed, raced up the vast slope of agitated ground. Miraculously, its wheels did not sink into the soil and cause them to crash, which would doubtless have led to fatal consequences for the crew. Hanging on with grim determination and expecting catastrophe at any moment, they reached the summit of the wall of earth and saw that beyond it, a deep and jagged trench had been torn in the earth. Hundreds of dasheka disappeared into the cavernous crevasse, their forlorn cries echoing as the remains of the herd scrambled madly to turn away from it.

'Hold on!' Tlkcha yelled. She and Kamra braced their legs and wrapped their arms around the tiller bar as the poctech flew into the air. For heart-stopping moments the poctech sailed through space, still pushed by the wind. Then dropping rapidly, it slammed hard into the ground with such force that the Xotic crew were flung around like dolls. With a despairing cry, Marla was thrown backwards off the vessel. Striking the ground with a sickening impact she rolled into the maw of the trench.

The two rearmost wheels of the vessel had slammed into the lip of the crevasse and for a moment it was touch and go as to whether the ship itself would fall back into the gaping trench, but against all odds, the sail and mast remained intact and the wind continued to push the craft forward. The front four wheels gripped the earth and the poctech heaved forward with a mighty lurch.

Behind them the trench groaned shut with terrible finality as the remnant herd of dasheka continued their panicked flight into the east. The vibration in the earth stilled; the stunned Xotic allowed the wind to spill from the sail and the vessel to come to a halt. All on board carried bruises and two of the crew had broken bones. It was the hand of fate that only poor Marla had perished.

'Den Har the Sky Father be praised!' Chalayla said. 'I thought that was the end of us all.'

Each of the Xotic said a silent prayer of thanks while Tlkcha ordered the crew, organising aid for those badly hurt and checking on the damage to the vessel. Although the song of the wind continued in its steady power, after the noise of the herd and terror of the past hour all seemed quiet and peaceful in contrast.

As Avlar neared the horizon, and Halidar, the first of Tarvuli's three moons began to rise, the Xotic prepared a meal. Joining hands around their campfire they spoke a prayer and shed a tear for their friend and crewmate, Marla.

'Tlkcha,' Chalayla asked, 'Marla has fallen into the earth to her death, do you think that her spirit will reach Den Har?'

Many of the crew had held the same thought and listened closely to Tlkcha's response. She considered her answer carefully before replying.

'We of the Xotic leave our loved ones under the sky but eventually all flesh and bone returns to the earth from which we came. The spirit of Marla will have sprung from her body and sped towards Den Har. I believe that she rests with the Sky Father and, one day, we will see her spirit return to us.'

There was much nodding of heads and the mood with the crew was quietly reflective, taking comfort from Tlkcha's words. In her mind she wasn't sure if Marla's life had been in exchange for theirs and their miraculous escape. Whatever it was, they were still alive and safe – for now.

The night passed without incident, though in the early hours of the morning the coughing grunt and roars of gravosh could be heard in the distance. As the first light of Colunda lit the horizon, the Xotic completed all checks of their vessel, climbed aboard and continued on.

As they settled into their journey, Sapek, one of the older crew members came up to Tlkcha as she stood at the front of the vessel peering ahead in the dawn light.

'What are your thoughts on Lakana?'

'Meaning?' asked Tlkcha.

'Meaning, do we think any there are still living? It has been in my mind ever since we came across that ship that perhaps those on board were trying to flee but had the sickness among them already, poor souls.'

Tlkcha placed an arm on Sapek's shoulders. 'I have the same fear, Sapek. But all we can do is get there and see for ourselves.'

Nodding, Sapek returned to his duties leaving Tlkcha to her thoughts. She prayed that they would find the villagers safe and well.

Once they had navigated their way through the earth disturbed by the earthshake and returned to the path they recognised, they were able to maintain a steady speed throughout the long day. At one point they passed near to where a pack of gravosh lazed in the light of Avlar and Colunda. A huge carcass lay in close proximity to them, evidence they had been feasting and so gave the poctech little attention other than a twitching of ears and a look in their direction as they passed by.

So like gonverdeem in many ways, they were savage and highly effective hunters, but lacked the sentient self-awareness of the gonverdeem. Tlkcha's thoughts went to Fendrax and wondered how she and her litters were faring and whether they too had been affected by the disease which stalked the land.

Colunda had sunk beneath the horizon and Avlar was low in the sky when at last Lakana appeared in the distance as the ship crossed some gentle hills. Like most Xotic villages it was constructed of stone gathered over generations, as the people cleared the plains of obstructions that would hinder the passage of their craft. With roofs made from the woven stems of the prairie grasses weighted down by stones, they were snug dwellings made to withstand the winds that ever blew out of the east.

Silently the Xotic stood, manning the sides of their craft, and watched as their poctech, its sail dropped, came to a slow stop.

Only the sound of the wind sighing over the plains and the plaintive call of the batak, a small and brightly coloured bird that made its nest from mud and which inhabited most Xotic villages, could be heard.

The Xotic exchanged looks.

'Lower the ladder. We shall look for survivors. Touch nothing. Call out if you find anything,' Tlkcha ordered.

Their voices hushed, the Xotic disembarked and moved in pairs towards the village, mouths and noses covered against the stench of decay that immediately assaulted their senses as they drew close to the village's outer wall. The gates stood open, moving and creaking slightly on their leather hinges in the ceaseless wind. Several poctech were drawn up near the walls ready for journeys that would now never happen.

It took courage to look into the scattered dwellings; in one after another they found the decaying bodies of inhabitants. The Xotic were not an abundant people. Semi-nomadic, they gathered each year for a great festival where marriages were made and friendships renewed. There was not one Xotic who did not think of those, now in the embrace of death, as friends and relatives; tears of sadness and loss dampened the cloth that covered their lower faces.

It was then that they were surprised by an intense euphoria: Chalayla and Gremma found a baby clinging to life in that place of death. By some miracle, the baby was still clutched in the arms of its dead mother and unaffected by the disease, its cries drawing them into the largest building. Here, many bodies lay together in what appeared was a last and desperate refuge, and here they had died, comfortless and despairing in each other's arms.

Making soft and comforting sounds, Gremma gently lifted the child and turning to Chalayla said, 'We passed by a pen of pateka; they will give us some milk for the child. I will see to that while you take the baby out of here.'

'I will wait by our poctech. Try not to be too long, the poor thing is starving.'

'Wait Gremma. We have to consider that the child may be infected. If we take it, we may all die and worse, spread it to others.'

Gremma drew herself up and stood before Tlkcha. 'If that is true then we are all dead already Tlkcha. Just entering the village may have killed us all. But I cannot abandon this child here in this place of sorrow. I could never live with myself, even if it leads to my death.'

Sapek nodded in agreement. 'Gremma has the right of it Tlkcha; to leave this poor child lessens us. We must take our chances. Of all here this little one has lived, surely this is a sign from Den Har?'

Tlkcha looked at the Xotic who stood by; all nodded with one accord.

'So be it. Let us pray that Den Har has led us here for this purpose.'

Gremma passed the child to Chalayla before hurrying off. Tlkcha called after her: 'You should release them all, once you have enough milk. Then they can at least graze on the plains, otherwise they will die here too once their feed is exhausted.'

Pateka were hardy, goatlike creatures, domesticated by the Xotic and kept for their meat and milk. Fortunately, they had had plenty of fodder and water and so till now, had survived the calamity that had befallen the village.

Though they were all buoyed to some extent by the rescuing of the baby, who fed greedily on the pateka milk, the question now arose of what to do with the many bodies.

'We cannot leave them as they are. We must carry them out onto the plains and give them up to Den Har, in the way of our people,' said Sapek reflecting the general feeling of them all.

'It will be neither any easy nor a pleasant task. Their bodies are decaying and we need to be mindful of infection,' said Chalayla.

Murna spoke. 'There are several poctech here. Why not use the winch and load them with the bodies? That way, we can lift several at one time and then hoist sail and let the winds and the will of Den Har carry them where they will. To the north lie only empty lands and then the mountains. Let the Sky Father determine where their last voyage takes them.'

Murna's words were greeted with much nodding of heads and Tlkcha, observing the group, also nodded her agreement.

'It is a good plan, Murna. We will drag the poctechs to the gates, load each one and then set them running on the winds.'

Even so, it took three full days to accomplish the task. The Xotic did not stay within the village but camped on the plain well outside and upwind, keeping watch fires burning brightly lest night predators should draw close attracted by the smell of the bodies. The crew washed themselves thoroughly in hot water infused with barnma, a grass with pungent juices used by the Xotic as an antiseptic.

In the end, the bodies took up the space of five poctech. On the fourth day, Tlkcha's crew gathered together and said a prayer to Den Har for the spirits of those who had died and gave thanks for the baby they had named Lakana in memory of the villagers. Not one of the crew had fallen sick and the baby flourished, looking none the worse for its ordeal.

Now they fixed the tiller bar of the vessels, hoisted sail and released them to the wind. Silently they stood and watched as, one by one, the five poctech disappeared from view with their sad cargo, carried onwards into the empty lands beneath the sky, running northwards towards the distant mountains.

The Xotic stood quietly for a long time after the last of the poctech had disappeared. Not a few shed tears and many held each other close.

Finally, Tlkcha clapped her hands. 'Come friends. We have done all that we could. We shall wash ourselves in the river and clean the stink of this place from our bodies; then we will eat and drink to the memories of our kin. Let the wind cleanse this place. Tomorrow we will begin the journey home.'

Smiles began to replace the sad looks, as the thought of returning home to a warm hearth and their loved ones cheered them. Gathering soap and drying cloths, they walked down to the clear and sparkling waters of the nearby river and washed themselves clean.

ooooOoooo

Draachnull sat cross legged rocking back and forth on his haunches while softly crooning to the small child he held in his arms.

Like so many of the Benshin, his granddaughter Tleaa Do Pakana, Laughing Eyes, was at death's door. Yesterday, Pershivon, daughter of Tishan Dar had arrived with two others who revealed themselves as Hrv. They had come with what they promised was a cure and in desperation the Benshin had allowed all the people to be dosed. The children first.

Draachnull, like so many of his people, had lost loved ones to the terrible disease. Miraculously, old as he was, he had remained free of infection. This had been more a curse than a blessing, as one by one those nearest and dearest to him, his wife, daughter and her children had all succumbed until only little Tleaa was left.

His son, long estranged to him, might still be alive. He hoped so, but it had been many a long year since they had quarrelled over some stupid thing he could no longer recall, and he'd left to live with the Thunder Water Clan.

In his arms the small child stirred, her first movement in some hours, yawned prodigiously, opened her eyes and smiled. Draachnull burst into tears. Tears of joy that Tleaa had come back from the brink of death and tears of relief, bittersweet tears that Tleaa would never know her mother Npath, or her grandmother Satarna.

153

In that moment, Draachnull determined that in all his remaining years he would tell Tleaa about them and show her the places that were special to them. In his mind, he gave his thanks to Varthansh Mek, the Keeper of the Forest and the Lightning Clan's chief deity.

Around him Draachnull heard other voices calling out in joy, as happy tears and laughter replaced the wailing of grief that had been constant over many days. Tleaa had fallen back into a deep sleep, the sleep of rest and recuperation rather than of death. Gently Draachnull lay her down on furs and went in search of food for her and himself, returning to wait by her side until she awoke.

A week later the Lightning Clan, much reduced in numbers though they were, organised a feast day of thanksgiving. The feast was also held in tribute to their friends from Ta'Morin, Pershivon and Drenyk, and the two Hrv, Trrz and Zekkr who had arrived with Pershivon with the cure.

As the evening drew on and the three moons rode the night sky, the Benshin sat around a huge fire passing gourds of tek beer, singing to the sounds of flute and drum.

They had prevailed on the two Hrv to drop the disguise they habitually employed amongst strangers when travelling outside their lands. If the Benshin held any reservations about their true appearance they were all too grateful to the Hrv to let it show. The Benshin had gathered baskets of insects and choice forest flowers and plants for their guests which the Hrv, either out of politeness to their hosts or in genuine appreciation, ate surreptitiously. They also seemed to have developed a fondness for tek beer sharing a gourd between the two of them.

Draachnull sat near their guests. Little Tleaa in his arms was nodding sleepily but determined to keep awake. A battle she was losing. Draachnull shook his head. Life was strange. These Hrv looked so alien and yet, as one got to know them, so their appearance grew less strange. Just a very large insect at the end of the day, and surely the Benshin and Graaven must appear as strange and alien to their eyes. Given the history that Draachnull had come to learn of the Hrv it had taken not only courage to come to the lands of those they saw as enemies, but also some degree of compassion. Even if they sought some undertakings from the Graaven to safeguard their lands, was this not something that any Race might do in their place? After all, they could simply have let the disease run its course, but had chosen not to.

Draachnull was drawn from his reverie by a disturbance beyond the light of the fires that blazed brightly, and for a time he could not see what was happening. Then several members of the Thunder Water clan walked into the crowd and calls of welcome were heard from all the Benshin. They had heard that the Hrv were in the village and had set out to travel to the Lightning Clan as they also wished to express their profound gratitude for their work with the cure. No less than all the other clans, they had suffered great loss. Among those who had travelled was Draachnull's long-lost son.

Setting the now sleeping Tleaa down gently Draachnull stood with care. Strong emotions flowed through him and his eyes filled with tears. Seeing him, Mateka walked forward and stood silently before him looking deep into Draachnull's eyes.

'Word came that Npath and Satarna had succumbed. Surrounded by death, I came to deeply regret the angry words and the lost years; will you welcome my return, Father?'

Draachnull stepped forward and took Mateka in his arms holding him tightly, overcome with emotion. Tears rolled down his face and he could feel Mateka sobbing also.

Eventually he had enough control of himself to speak.

'My dearest son. I too am filled with regret. How happy I am to see you. I was too proud to say sorry, too stupid to reach out to you. How Npath and Satarna would have rejoiced to see you come home.'

Smiling, Mateka pushed Draachnull back a little way staring into his father's eyes but still grasping his shoulders. 'My heart tells me they are rejoicing with us from the spirit world.'

Draachnull nodded, the pain of the last weeks replaced by joy.

'I am sure you are right, my son. Come and meet your niece Tleaa. By grace of our new friends and their cure, she has returned to the world of the living. You will see she looks so like her mother. Then you must tell me all that has happened to you.'

They sat together long into the night.

Mateka related all that had happened since he left. He had not married, although many had been willing. He had made friends, many of whom had succumbed to the terrible disease, but like Draachnull he had been untouched. The finality of death and the sadness left in its wake by those who grieved had led Mateka to reassess the events that caused him to leave the Lightning Clan. Only through the lens of loss could he finally see the stupidity of the argument and so it was that he determined to return and to seek forgiveness.

'There is nothing to forgive, my son. Let us acknowledge that both of us are at fault. It is past and done. We shall go forward together and now Tleaa will have an uncle who will help nurture and protect her.'

Mateka looked down at the small child who had climbed sleepily into his arms as he sat by the fire. It was a wondrous thing to him and he felt the spirits of Npath and Satarna with him. Smiling he looked at Draachnull. 'Let it be so,' he said.

CHAPTER ELEVEN

Tishan turned to face the gateway. Now that the moment was here, she fought down her fear and trepidation. She felt a weight on her shoulder as one of Thatras's arms rested upon it in reassurance.

<Young as you are to me Tishan Dar, I have great faith in your ability. You truly are a singular individual. Push through the gateway, deposit the Orb and leave as quickly as you can.>

Thatras looked deeply into Tishan's eyes for a brief moment and spoke aloud in a voice whose timbre reflected genuine caring.

'May the Intelligence guide you all your days. The Balance is all.'

Before Tishan, the form of Thatras began to melt away.

'I hope we meet again, Thatras,' she said.

A sibilant whisper answered her parting call before the form of Thatras disappeared.

'As do I.'

Tishan stood alone in the vast corridor. Closing her eyes, she summoned the Rod of Klemish which coalesced in her hand. Focussing her will upon it, a blue aura of protection surrounded her.

She stepped forward till she was but a single pace from the frame and stood still, waiting for activation.

In moments, strange glowing symbols began to appear around the frame, pulsing with a red light that grew bright and then dimmed until the flickering ceased and a steady red glow stabilised. A hissing sound could be heard from within the frame and abruptly the view of the black lake disappeared and was replaced by nothingness. Now it was like standing before the entrance to a cave and a gentle movement of air seemed to draw her towards the opening. Tishan stepped up onto the bottom of the frame, the pulling sensation increased markedly and in Tishan's imagination she felt that she stood before the maw of some terrifying and inimical creature. Clearing her mind and with a concentrated effort, she pushed such thoughts away, took a deep breath and stepped into the blackness.

At first there was a falling sensation which was also disorienting as her eyes could discern nothing on which to focus, but which abruptly ceased as she felt her feet come into contact with a floor of some kind. Even the blue radiance from her protective aura did little to lighten the inky blackness that surrounded her and it was cold, icy cold. Far ahead she saw a single pinpoint of light and without any other point of reference she pushed towards it. Push was the operative term because there was resistance to forward movement. While she felt she was standing on solid ground it was impossible to see it or assess what it was made of, indeed the uniform blackness meant she could have been walking upside down but she suppressed that thought as it led to an immediate feeling of dizziness. With dogged determination and steady and sustained effort, what she felt initially as slow progress became easier as she adjusted to the movement required.

It seemed that the point of light before her grew bigger with infinite slowness. Tishan felt she would like to rest, but, fearful of the consequences of stopping her forward movement she pushed on resolutely. Finally, her thoughts turned to the Rod of Klemish and at first, more as an experiment, she channelled additional will into it with the single goal of making progress easier. The radiance around her turned from a cool blue to a bright, and more intense whiteness and Tishan felt much of the resistance to her progress recede.

Her thoughts echoed her relief.

<Tishan Dar, you were always a slow learner!>

Now that the effort required to push through was significantly reduced it felt no more than akin to walking through ankle deep mud, a clinging resistance that sucked at her feet but did not require the physical exertion that had gone before. Perhaps it was only her imagination but the light she was heading towards now grew visibly and rapidly larger in aspect.

Finally, after what seemed a terribly long time, she judged that only a few steps separated her from the light source that had directed her steps. As she had drawn closer its opaque whiteness had resolved and she could now see a similar view to that which she had observed in the corridor with Thatras. Mentally she prepared for her exit through the gateway. It was a challenge emerging from those on Tarvuli, and she expected that exiting from this one would be significantly more difficult.

The light from the Rod of Klemish had returned to the cool blue luminescence of earlier and now that she had reached the exit point, she took a mental deep breath and pushed through the gateway. Here she met strong but not unexpected resistance to her efforts, whatever the doorway was composed of seemed to bow outwards as her body leaned into it until with an unexpected snap, all resistance suddenly ceased and she lurched out of the gateway, which disappeared abruptly. She stumbled forward several steps, sinking somewhat into the viscous black slime that surrounded her and which stretched unrelieved in every direction. In consistency it was like sticky mud and she felt herself slowly sinking deeper until the Rod of Klemish halted her descent into the slime.

Above her, a clear sky of washed-out pink was illuminated by a dull light which added to an overall depressing effect. She had expected to feel revulsion, but instead for some inexplicable reason only a terrible sadness stole over her. For some moments she stood non-plussed. Should she simply drop the Orb here and exit? Somehow that did not feel right and as she pondered her move, unobserved behind her, the vast pool of oily liquid began to rise up silently, rearing into the sky and forming a body of titanic proportions and nightmare aspect.

With a feeling of alarm, the tendrils on Tishan's neck flared, and she spun around to look behind. Towering above her manifested a being so grotesque that her mind had difficulty comprehending what it was she saw. Several multi-faceted eyes sat above a set of mandibles positioned in front of a mouth that she could see was armed with countless serrated teeth.

On Tarvuli there was a giant species of insect that to her eyes this creature resembled. Many-legged and covered in poisonous spines, its multiple eyes sat above pincers that fed its prey into its mouth. The Graavens called it the 'Axarta'. A deadly predator, its sting could quickly paralyse animals many times its size and once paralysed the axarta would feast, or worse still if that were possible, lay its eggs on its still living, helpless prey so that its hatchlings could feed. Full grown axarta were large enough to take down prey five times their size and an unwary Graaven had been known to die a particularly horrible death in its claws. If threatened, the Axarta gave off a putrid smell in its defence and the Graavens carefully avoided those areas on Tarvuli where they could be found, as killing one was a risky business that required careful planning. As the Enemy rose up before her it was this image that leapt into her mind, though the Dorath Mar was infinitely more repulsive to the eye and its stench overpowering.

Now all around her other shapes arose from the black liquid. Multi limbed appendages followed by another head whose black and soulless eyes fixed on her with hypnotic effect. Before Tishan could react, the arms came crashing down upon her and she was swept upwards, held inside clawlike fingers and carried towards a cavernous mouth which opened to receive her.

The Rod of Klemish flared into incandescent whiteness and as it did so a primal scream, unlike anything she had ever heard was emitted by the creature. The hand – if such it could be called – that held her, burst into flame and was consumed in a flash. Tishan fell from its grasp striking the liquid surface with a huge splash and penetrating deep into the fetid slime that stretched in all directions, but was otherwise shielded from harm by the Rod.

Then a voice entered her mind, the anguished cry of which was so powerful that she felt her head would burst.

<It burns, it burns! Find it! Whatever it is we will make it twist in agony, living death will be its final days!>

For a few moments Tishan was undetected as she reoriented herself within the fluid into which she had plunged. Her senses focused on her immediate surroundings and, enhanced by the Rod, told her that the liquid surrounding her was not mud but some other kind of organic material. It took only a moment more to realise that in fact she was floating inside the Dorath Mar.

Reaching a decision, she retrieved the metallic bag that Thatras had given her. The mere thought of retrieving the Orb caused the bag to open and she quickly took the Orb out. No sooner had she done so than two things happened at once. Firstly, on release from the bag, the Orb's expansion was so rapid that it slipped from her grasp and, before she could catch it, sank rapidly down into the liquid beyond any hope of recovery even had she wanted to.

<So be it,> thought Tishan.

Forcing herself to calmness and suppressing the Dorath Mar's voice which still screamed in anger and frustration as it sought out her whereabouts, she summoned the Threadway. At first nothing happened and in consternation Tishan wondered whether the lack of life force within the planetary system the Dorath Mar world occupied, meant that the Threadway here was non-existent.

Immediately following that disturbing thought a yell of triumph entered her mind.

<We have you! We have you!>

Once again, powerful arms grasped hold of her body and with frightening strength dragged her out of the liquid and threw her high into the air. Dozens of appendages and multiple heads rose up beneath her as she plummeted back down towards claws eager to grasp hold of her. Closing her eyes in her last moments, time seemed to slow and images of her life flashed in her mind. How strange to die here on a remote world in the grip of this loathsome creature, so far from her friends and her home. A profound sadness overcame her and then a state of resolve and acceptance. If nothing else, the destruction of this thing was worth her own life.

<The Balance is All,> she thought.

Then, the Rod of Klemish having been thrown from her grasp, and at the very moment when Tishan was powerless to resist and about to be torn apart, the Dorath Mar released its hold and Tishan plunged back once more into the slimy liquid that covered the planet. There followed almost immediately a scream of pain whose volume and intensity again smashed into Tishan's brain like some great tsunami and left her reeling.

Something unknown and remote from her had struck the enemy, causing it intense pain and distracting it for several vital moments. This only served to increase its fury, once the initial shock wore off.

Oblivious to the destruction of the Dorath Mar on the Chosen home-world that had occurred in that moment, and whose terrible end sent shock waves of energy into its loathsome parent, Tishan fought through her confusion as to what could possibly have caused such an effect and tried to regather her thoughts.

In reaction to the shock, the fluid around Tishan became even more agitated and a huge claw slashed into the liquid close alongside her, frantic to grasp her once again.

In intense desperation Tishan reached out mentally for the Rod of Klemish. Upon its coalescing in her hand, and with its combined power once more in her grasp, the Threadway at last manifested itself mere seconds before she was drawn into another massive claw enveloping the space that she had floated in just moments before, passing through her body without effect as she rapidly ascended.

Yet another titanic scream of rage erupted from the Dorath Mar as its prey escaped. Her departure not swift enough to prevent that terrible voice entering her mind.

<Flee pathetic creature, flee! I perceive who you are! Your world is doomed, Tishan Dar! You and the rest of your Graaven filth! We are coming and you and all your kind will endure in pain and torment for a thousand cycles!>

Far below and unnoticed deep inside the creature, so intent was its focus on Tishan, the Orb had now reached a critical mass; its disruption imminent.

<What did you hope to achieve? You are an insignificant nothing!>

Suddenly the voice changed in timbre, a note of incredulity edged with fear.

<What is this? What have you done?>

High above the planet's surface and moving rapidly away, Tishan failed to hear what was the last utterance of the creature the Graavens had dubbed the Dorath Mar.

A brilliant white light of glaring intensity erupted far behind her. The lonely world, now totally consumed by the Enemy, was

vapourised in a single moment and an explosion of cosmic proportions sent an irresistible shock wave of deadly energy flashing
outwards in all directions. Forks of what appeared to be lightning,
too numerous to count, arced off into space as three other worlds,
now merely desolate chunks of rock orbiting that system's ancient
sun, were also vapourised as the shock wave struck them with prodigious force.

The unleashed energy powered outward at tremendous speed.
The impact of the force as it struck that system's star seemed for
some moments only to flow around it. But the power of the Orb's
disruption was such that, what should have taken ten million cycles
to occur, happened in an instant as the star tore itself apart, its
obliteration magnifying even further the terrible effect of the orig-
inal detonation. Several lifeless worlds had formed that forlorn
system; now in moments every one of them disintegrated so that
a giant cloud of debris was created, expanding rapidly outwards
into space.

As Tishan sped away, even her astonishing speed kept her
barely ahead of the unleashed power of the disruption. Gradually
however, she left behind the swirling maelstrom of heat and light
that had threatened to overtake her. She was overcome by the awe-
inspiring spectacle she could see and at the overwhelming power
of the Orb's ignition. Finally, after what seemed an age of rapid
movement away and judging her position to be beyond the last
edge of the expanding wave of destruction, she slowed to a stop.
It was only then that she felt a new and sudden force manifest,
now pulling her backward towards the source of the explosion.
Despite the vast distance she had travelled, the pull was strong
enough that she had to exert all her will in resisting it. Slowly, her
efforts reduced the drag in strength and with extreme caution, she
journeyed back towards the source of the detonation, curious to
see with her own eyes what was eventuating.

From all directions the debris which had blasted out into space was being drawn back faster and faster and as the speed increased so too did the force of attraction, becoming more and more powerful and irresistible.

Still far beyond what had been the outer limits of the system wherein the home planet of the Dorath Mar was located, there came an enormous pulse of white light which briefly flared and then faded into nothing. The force that had exerted such potency abruptly ceased, leaving an enormous field of debris and dust that still moved back at great speed with residual energy.

Tishan continued her journey backwards until she arrived at a point where she felt a sudden sense of alarm causing her to come to an abrupt stop. Around her the cloud of material had come to a point where it appeared to slide around an invisible wall of energy. Beyond that wall there was utter blackness which appeared to be devoid of all matter, like a veritable hole in space. Tishan had no idea what this blackness was, only that it gave her a feeling that to approach any closer to this unknown phenomenon would be the height of foolishness, particularly as she had survived and stood witness to a cataclysmic event of titanic proportions.

Determining her course of action and concluding her thoughts, she turned and ascended the Threadway once more. Her mind conjured an image of Thatras which made her smile.

<I am not sure that the word 'disruption' fully illustrates what just happened,> she mused to herself.

Tishan's thoughts were more accurate than she knew, however: the forks of energy that had initially been discharged into space were linked to all of the Dorath Mar's ghastly offspring which, like lightning rods, drew the destructive and searing power of the Orb's detonation to themselves. On countless worlds dominated by their evil, their screams of agony could be heard as they were incinerated. Their obliteration left those races who had become their disciples in evil, bereft, and in turn fearful that their own existence might now also come to an untimely and horrific end at the hands of whatever terrible power had been unleashed.

Far away, the entity that had sprung from the Dorath Mar and which now called itself Apocris, had felt the ripples of destructive energy which resulted from the disruption of the Orb. Unlike the other offspring however, Apocris fed off its parent, drawing energy from it, and while the connection to it withered and died, it did not suffer the same fate. For a moment there was searing pain as the connection was destroyed followed by a period of disorientation, but Apocris recovered rapidly.

In an instant, it knew what had occurred, even as to the effect on the offspring which had so recently fed their power to the parent. Now all were utterly consumed in flame.

In overwhelming reaction to this event, it released the Threads into which it had been pouring its malice and instead, an all-consuming rage manifested itself to the exclusion of all else. It knew from where this destructive power had emanated and in moments had decided it would obliterate that world and absorb the strange presence that protected it. Apocris had grown in power and knowledge and while the source of its nourishment had been destroyed, this inexplicable presence offered a new source, perhaps greater still; with it, Apocris, who even now hovered on the verge of immortality, would become an invincible and terrible force for evil and imbalance throughout the cosmos.

In mere moments it turned its focus on Tarvuli and disappeared.

CHAPTER TWELVE

The strange disease had ravaged many of the Gonverdeem; some died quickly in terrible agony while others were overcome by a strange mental disturbance. Lingering for many days until starvation or thirst finally ended their suffering, they were a danger to themselves and others of their litters who they failed to recognise. Deaf to any pleas, they would attack and rend with a strength completely out of proportion to their bodily weakness, as if possessed by some terrible and malignant power.

Kuhltar had tracked Haran for several days. Far to the north-west of Xotic lands, it was rugged terrain. Kuhltar knew there was no plausible explanation for Haran's behaviour except as a symptom of illness or some form of mental derangement.

Other than to collapse in a heap at the setting of the suns and rise again at first light, Haran had stopped for neither food nor drink. It was clear to Kuhltar that he was suffering from some strange and baffling affliction, nor was he the only Gonverdeem so affected, although Kuhltar had observed that only males seemed to succumb in this way.

Unlike Haran, Kuhltar had to periodically stop to hunt game and also drink from the muddy streams she occasionally happened upon. Water was scarce in the desolate lands through which Haran now travelled, driven in madness to an untimely end.

Kuhltar had sent out her thoughts and knew that Fendrax was tracking them both, though what she and her dam could do even together was a conundrum which she had been wrestling with these past days. Always keeping him in sight, Kuhltar had not approached Haran as yet, but that time was drawing very near as he must be reaching the extremities of his strength through lack of nourishment and water.

It was as she mused over these thoughts, that Haran suddenly stopped and turned in her direction.

Now motionless, Kuhltar could see that the journey had impacted Haran terribly. One of the larger of his kind, his ribs showed through a coat matted with filth, lacking the sheen that indicated good health.

Kuhltar drew closer and stopped, far enough away that she could turn and elude him if he became violent.

<Brother, you are sick. You need to stop, to rest. Where are you going? What purpose is there in this journey of yours?>

Haran swayed slightly on his legs. His six eyes were glazed over and he gave no response. Except for the fact that he was standing upright under the strength of his limbs, he could have been dead. Kuhltar sensed nothing. Then in a single terrifying moment he launched himself at Kuhltar with impossible speed. She was caught utterly by surprise, as one sweep of a massive claw raked her face, instantly blinding her in one eye and opening up a deep wound in her neck. It was only that the power of the blow unexpectedly knocked her down which foiled Haran's attempt to deliver the killing bite and he overshot his target, stumbling slightly.

It was enough time for Kuhltar to leap to her feet and run as fast as she could away from Haran and to higher ground, leaping over boulders before turning, in her pain and shock, to see if Haran had attempted to follow her.

It was as if nothing had happened. Haran stood motionless and silent as before. Snuffling the air, his head lifted in Kuhltar's direction and after few more moments he moved off once more, seemingly oblivious to all around him.

Kuhltar sat in pain and grief for the brother she knew was lost. Whatever he had now become, Haran as she had known him was no more. In her anguish, she howled into the lonely sky, her cries echoing off the rocks and dissipating into the air.

Far away, Fendrax heard those cries. Her hackles rose in alarm as she read all the despair within them. She Who Hunts gathered herself and leapt away, following the echoes of Kuhltar's lonely call.

Before Avlar tipped the horizon at the waxing of that same day, Fendrax reached Kuhltar. Nuzzling each other in deep affection, Fendrax saw that one of Kuhltar's eyes was damaged beyond hope of recovery. The wound inflicted by Haran was in a place where Kuhltar could not reach. Surreptitiously, in the way of the Gonverdeem, Fendrax licked the wound, cleaning it of dirt and debris.

<Daughter, you must go south. Find a Xotic village. Your wound needs closing and the Xotic have the skill to do this.>

<But what of Haran? We cannot leave him to die alone in the wilderness, we must do something.>

Kuhltar's thoughts were desperate.

<He would have killed you, daughter. I am not sure we can do anything.>

<That was not Haran. Haran is dead, only his body contains life, yet still I cannot bear the thought of him going on and on until......> Kuhltar's thoughts trickled out to be replaced by grief.

<I will follow him, Kuhltar. I will do what I can, little though it may be. It is bad enough to lose Haran, I will not stand to lose you also, daughter. Find that Xotic village and see to your wound. As to your eye, I am afraid that nothing can be done.>

Kuhltar stood shakily.

<And as to that I have five others. I will do well enough. It will be as you say.>

Kuhltar licked Fendrax's face in affection.

<Be careful,> warned Kuhltar. <His speed and strength were like nothing I have ever experienced before. How this can be so when he has neither eaten nor drunk over many days, I do not know.>

Despite the pain of her wounds Kuhltar moved away quickly while Fendrax watched her form dwindle into the distance.

Turning, Fendrax set off to follow the trail left by Haran, tracking him discreetly for several more days. In the back of her mind she reflected on his affliction; she had no idea how he kept going, in any other case he would have died long days ago yet still he kept on and now Fendrax herself began to suffer from deprivation. They had entered a mountainous and arid region which lay so far to the north of Xotic lands that they were unexplored by any Gonverdeem. She knew however, that some days' journey to the south of where Fendrax now picked her way over rocky outcrops in the tracks of Haran, lay the Gap of Crethic.

She had no idea what drew Haran on and on, or where he could possibly be going, if indeed there was any objective in his mind.

Finally, Haran stopped and stood motionless. Fendrax, now weaker from lack of food and water, approached cautiously to within a few wary paces of where he stood.

Turning around he stood and faced her.

He spoke in a voice tinged with madness.

'You should not have followed me; it was bad enough that Kuhltar did so. It was as much as I could do to control the impulse to kill her. I have journeyed to remove myself and this infection from any possibility of contact with others – and yet here you are.'

'I could not leave you to die alone, my son,' said Fendrax. 'It is not right that any Gonverdeem should perish far from their kin.'

'You should go, Mother. Even now the last strands of control are melting away, soon insanity will replace the last reserves of reason and you will be its target.'

The voice of Haran had lifted an octave and now dropped to just a whisper.

'Go. Please go.'

Fendrax sighed. She realised that there was nothing she could do and the hope she had nurtured that she might be able to help was a forlorn one. In sadness, her voice echoing a depth of loss and regret, she began to turn away.

'So be it Haran. Know that Kuhltar and I will always love you.'

It was too late. As Fendrax began to retrace her steps a huge roar echoed behind her. What had once been Haran was no more and in its place a ravening and mindless beast had taken hold.

Even with Fendrax's speed of movement she was too slow to avoid the crashing impact of Haran's body slamming into hers or to deflect a vicious slash of his right paw, claws unsheathed, that opened up a huge wound along her flank.

Fendrax roared in pain and shock. The impact of the charge had bowled her over and with great agility she sprang to her feet as Haran, his face a mask of savage ferocity leapt upon her for a killing blow.

Rearing up, and using her greater body strength she managed to throw Haran to one side, exposing his belly as he fell. He was ripe for a killing stroke but Fendrax could not do it. Even though he had changed he was still of her blood, neither could she prevent the memories of teaching him to hunt, or of journeys made in happier times when he and Kuhltar were but cubs.

Haran got to his feet; the eyes that focused on her held no vestige of reason or recognition. He would not stop till either she was dead – or he was.

Behind her was a vertical drop into a cleft between two pillars of rock which towered above her high into the air. At the base of the cleft, jagged fragments of stone reared like fangs.

Haran gathered himself and with a mighty roar sprang once again with the intent of bearing Fendrax down. Fendrax could not begin to imagine where his strength and power came from after so many days of privation.

As Haran's body flew towards her Fendrax rolled onto her back and, employing her powerful hind legs, used the momentum of Haran's leap to catapult him over the edge. A bellow of fury ended abruptly as he struck the jagged outcrop far below.

Fendrax stood at the edge of the chasm and gave out a great roar filled with sadness and loss. It echoed among the rocks and continued on for several moments so that it sounded like many voices in counterpoint.

Fendrax felt the weight of her years and now the terrible wound she had suffered along with other cuts and bruises, caused her to close her eyes in pain.

Turning her head, she looked up into the violet sky. 'Rest well my son. Know that you were loved till the very end.'

She turned her mind from Haran to her own plight. Here in this desolate place, wounded as she was and depleted from days without food or water, she knew her position to be perilous. She recalled that Menkh had spoken of a gateway located in the Gap of Crethic which was much closer to where she stood than any Xotic village. If she could reach it, if it worked, it could take her to Ta'Morin. It was a big 'if' but some hope was better than no hope. Wearily and with her wounds throbbing and stiffening, she turned southwards. It would take at least four days in her current state to reach the Gap of Crethic and her condition would only get worse; the possibility that she might encounter trouble from other creatures on the journey did not bear thinking about.

With dogged determination she set out.

For two days she dragged herself southwards. By pure good fortune she discovered a small puddle of water in a shaded overhang, the last vestiges of a rain shower at some recent time in the past. Muddy and brackish as it was, it renewed her strength and after falling into a troubled and pain-wracked sleep she pushed on.

It was on the morning of the third day that the trouble she had feared, manifested in the form of a lone Mellax. It leapt out of the shadows of some rocks with all the savage fury of its kind, yet it was young, not fully grown. At any other time, Fendrax would never have been caught by surprise in this way, but the pain of her wounds and lack of food had severely weakened her, and robbed her of her keen hunting sense. Ultimately it was only desperation and luck that enabled Fendrax to rip open the Mellax's body and kill it. Ironically, she could not even gorge herself on its flesh, as an eater of carrion, its meat was tainted and inedible.

Fendrax lay a long time gasping for air and unable to move. Drawing on her last reserves of strength she clawed her way upright and continued on. The Gap of Crethic was in sight, it was the worst misfortune that she had been attacked so close to her goal. Now all her focus was on moving one paw after another, limping slowly onward. Her only chance was to find the gateway and then hope that it would activate for her. She knew that if the gate could not be opened she would not last another day, but at this last extremity it was the only option left to her.

ooooOoooo

One morning shortly after the formal signing of the treaty with the Hrv, Horven was passing near to the gateway that had been established just outside of Ta'Morin. When the terrible illness was at its height, journeys through it had been restricted, such had been the fear of spreading the infection further, but now travel both into and out of Ta'Morin had almost returned to levels prior to the coming of the plague, increasing rapidly as the Hrv cure was delivered to far-flung areas.

Now, Horven detected the movement of someone coming through the gate and she paused momentarily to greet whoever it was arriving. Time seemed to slow as the form of Fendrax stumbled forward several steps before collapsing to the ground. In stunned surprise, Horven ran forward and kneeling alongside the great head of the Gonverdeem placed a hand on Fendrax's massive shoulder.

The once beautiful giant predator was matted with dirt and her emaciated form revealed several deep cuts and one huge wound that stank of infection. Of her six eyes only the two largest opened and these were filmed over. Horven felt tears rolling down her face and memories of riding upon Fendrax's back as they swept like the wind across the great grass plains of Tarvuli came sharply to mind.

One great eye focused with difficulty on Horven.

'Do not speak, Fendrax,' Horven said as she stroked the matted hair. 'Rest now, you are among friends.'

Several Graaven had gathered quietly around Horven and she issued rapid commands.

'Fetch Grakh. Tell him that Fendrax lies here with a terrible wound and I suspect the illness may also have hold of her. We will set up a shelter here, the weather is mild and we dare not try to move her.'

The Graaven moved with alacrity and soon enough Grakh came bustling along with two assistants in tow.

'Varnahrin alerted me to Fendrax's arrival and condition. I knew it had to be something bad for her to have used the gateway.'

'Can you save her?' asked Horven.

'As to that, I can administer the Hrv cure and treat the wound and infection but she is extremely weak. Our medical knowledge is vastly superior compared to when we arrived. We can get drip lines set up and take other measures, but I fear the worst.'

Horven nodded her head. 'I know you will do the best you can.'
Standing up she moved to one side while Grakh got to work.

'I can only guess the dosage for a Gonverdeem and cannot speculate on any side effects, but there is always hope.'

For several chaal, Grakh and his assistants Torme and Hvaal worked tirelessly, disinfecting and stitching the great wound and doing the best they could to clean the matted hair. During this time a shelter was rigged and everything that could be done was completed.

The voice of Varnahrin came into the minds of both Grakh and Horven.

<You have done what you can. Her spirit runs far from here. You must talk to her every day, Horven, and remind her that she has friends who love her and wish her to return. Ultimately, if her will is strong enough her body will rally.>

<What happened to her?> Horven asked.

<The disease affected the Gonverdeem differently to those like you, driving the males who were infected into a violent and irrational madness, but causing the females to fall into a deep coma. At first, Fendrax was resistant to illness while several of her litters succumbed to it. Haran was overcome and, in an effort to isolate himself, travelled far into the wild. Fendrax and Kuhltar followed. Haran wounded Kuhltar in his madness and finally Fendrax fought him in his last extremity and to Fendrax's grief she killed Haran, but in doing so she sustained the deep wound and other injuries you can see.

Now falling gravely ill, a terrible thirst overcame Fendrax and in desperation for water she was attacked by a Mellax while drinking. She managed to fight it off, no mean feat in her weakened state. She continued in pain until before dawn on the twentieth day after the attack, she reached the gateway in the Gap of Crethic which opened for her and so, at the very end of her prodigious strength, she came to Ta'Morin and to her friends.>

Horven dried her tears and took a deep breath.

<I will do as you say. I will speak to her every day and I will tell her that her friends love her and remind her of our journeys together.>

<Then you will have done all you can, Horven Var. The Balance is All.>

The tone of Varnahrin's voice was sad, which Horven assumed was a reflection of Fendrax's condition. So, for several dak'chaal, she came and sat by the unconscious form of Fendrax and spoke to her.

Horven's preoccupation with the organisation of the Hrv cure and her concern over Fendrax distracted her from other matters that usually took up much of her time. Halika and Mareen were almost completely restored to full health, while Lerma, who had been like a rock upon which she could anchor in times of worry, had seemed to withdraw into himself which Horven put down to tiredness. Lerma, in Horven's mind, had become her right arm, steady and always reliable in a crisis. He, more than any other Graaven, had brought her back from despair after the passing of her sibling Mareen in the battle against the Dorath Mar.

ooooOoooo

She Who Hunts crept silently through the tall grass of the prairie. Around her, several of her pack, widely spread out and completely invisible, moved stealthily towards their prey in the half light of an early dawn.

This was the latest of many such hunts that had occurred over past dak'chaal. She Who Hunts stopped in confusion and wrestled with the origin of the word that had come into her mind. It was an alien word and yet somehow familiar to her: 'dak'chaal', where had that come from?

Silently shaking her head in frustration, she continued, the scent of the prey getting stronger. Suddenly a snarling roar shattered the stillness of the fading night as Death in Shadow leapt from his place of concealment and threw himself on the quietly grazing herbivore that was their collective target. Echoing his roar, the several members of the hunting pack also leapt forth, their combined weight bringing the massive creature down, its plaintive calls enough to cause a stampede of panic in the giant herd that stretched without limit to the far horizon and that heretofore had grazed silently on the tall grass. The drumming of their feet as they rapidly departed could be felt through the earth and their cries of alarm gradually faded into the distance.

She Who Hunts remained motionless, battling the conflicting thoughts that assailed her mind. For days she had hunted, although in truth she was not now certain that each hunt was different or whether it was the same hunt repeated over and over. Until now, she had not questioned the presence of her pack but as she focused her thoughts, she realised that Death in Shadow was her great, great grandsire. This realisation caused her no consternation, but rather felt right and natural. Indeed, the others of her pack comprised her immediate parents and others of her ancestry that stretched back through time.

Then again, there was that annoying buzzing sound, that of late seemed to follow her everywhere. Like a night insect that constantly drew close to her ears and kept her awake, she wasn't sure now if the buzzing sound was in fact actual words and the more she thought about it, the more the buzzing began to take on shape and meaning. The sound called to her with an annoying insistence.

Breath On the Water drew close to her.

'You did not join us in the hunt, child.'

'I am sorry Mother. I was distracted.'

She nodded her head and turned her green eyes toward her daughter. 'You are not yet ready to join us. Clearly there is that which keeps you on the other side.'

She Who Hunts felt a momentary sadness. 'I am sorry.'

Breath On the Water laughed and it was a sound of gladness and deep affection. 'Foolish child. We will always be here for you. We will await your return and then you will journey across with us.'

Somehow a deep understanding of Breath's words manifested in her mind and no further explanation was needed.

'Come child. Say your farewells to us. I think that whatever it is that calls you has great meaning and perhaps a great love for you to hold you back.'

'You may be right, Mother. It is certainly most annoying!'

Breath laughed again and knocked her head into She Who Hunt's shoulder.

'Come.'

She Who Hunts sat quietly following the farewells and watched as her pack moved off. She continued her vigil until one by one they disappeared from her sight into a bright light that her eyes could not pierce, until at last, on the very edge of her vision the massive form of her mother turned and a great coughing roar issued forth.

She Who Hunts stood and answered the call, her own roar throbbing out so that the very air seemed to pulse with it.

As the sound died away Breath on the Water turned and disappeared from sight.

She Who Hunts was left in silent thought. She had expected to feel a sense of loss but was surprised that in fact she rather felt a sense of anticipation. The annoying buzzing sound had finally transformed itself into words, a plaintive call for her to come back. She knew now who made that call and she knew also whence the word 'dak'chaal' had come.

Fendrax stood and followed the sound of the words that led her away. She was going to give Horven Var and also her two spawnlings who had joined the call, a piece of her mind, pulling her back from death like this. Fendrax laughed aloud and began to run faster and faster towards the sound of their voices.

CHAPTER THIRTEEN

Lerma did not feel right. He wasn't ill exactly, but he knew that something was wrong. It didn't seem serious enough to worry Horven about, who had enough concerns with the Council, the ongoing despatch of the Hrv cure and now also with the treatment of Fendrax. Although watching Halika and Mareen recover was a blessing that always revived his spirits, he nevertheless couldn't shake the feeling.

Several dak'chaal after Fendrax's arrival, Lerma was walking towards the dwelling which he and Horven shared when a searing pain flared across his chest. He stumbled, gasping for breath, but managed to reach the doorway dragging in some air as the pain subsided a little. Opening the door, he entered and collapsed into a chair. His thoughts were confused and the pain, although lessened, was still there and he felt very weak. It was then that he remembered his silent plea when Halika and Mareen were slowly fading in the grip of the terrible illness. How, in that desperate moment he had pledged his own life in exchange for theirs. He recalled his relief at the miraculous arrival of a cure that somehow, rightly or wrongly, he felt was a direct result of his plea; and he remembered his and Horven's joy at the rapid recovery of their spawnlings as they regained their strength. In the intervening days he had forgotten that pledge, but deep in is mind he felt sure that a bargain had been struck.

Lerma took in a deep breath and tried to gather his thoughts.

<Varnahrin, are you there?>

<Always, Lerma.>

<I am right, aren't I? About the bargain I made?>

<Yes. Your life for theirs. The Balance is All, Lerma. The hour of your passing is approaching, your heart is weak. Lerma, while you did not suffer the blight in the same way as others, internally it has had a profound effect.>

<Then why was a bargain made? If I was going to die anyway why would the Intelligence care about the three of us?>

<Lerma, you ascribe Graaven emotions to a power that is neither good nor evil, cruel nor kind. Your plea was heard and judged worthy, as the Balance in all things must be maintained. Your life was shortened just a little so that theirs could be restored. Mareen and Halika have a role to play in the future of the Graaven people. You and the person that you have come to be, have played your part well.>

<Varnahrin I am afraid. I don't want to die alone.>

<You are not alone, my dear son; I am with you and Horven is on her way even now. I will guide you across. All will be well.>

Lerma felt the pain increase but then a strange lethargy came over him even as he heard the door open and with a cry of 'Lerma!' Horven came to his side. He felt her arms around him and his head cushioned against Horven's shoulder.

'Lerma! This is wrong, I thought we had many sem'chaal to look forward to together.'

'It is my time, Horven. Better here than on a battlefield, which I thought would be my fate. How much better to pass in your arms. Do not let Halika and Mareen forget me.>

'You fool, Lerma,' Horven's voice sobbed with emotion. 'I will tell them every day. Your strength, your kindness.' Horven could not continue.

'I am content, Horven,' Lerma's voice was the merest whisper. 'You and they are everything to me, Horven I…'

Lerma's voice grew silent and his breathing stilled. Horven, who had stood on countless battlefields surrounded by the dead and dying and thought herself inured to loss, was bereft. She had lost Mareen but the coming of Lerma and then their two spawnlings had filled a void she thought could never be filled; and now that terrible pain was back.

Lerma stood behind the weeping body of Horven. He placed a hand on her shoulder in comfort, but could make no contact with her and instead tried to send a mental message. Beside him stood a tall figure that seemed vaguely female but could not be discerned, so bright was the light that came from it.

<She cannot hear you or feel you Lerma, but she can sense your presence. Come now, it is time to move on.>

<Am I dead then?>

<Dead, Lerma? If you were dead, how could you be speaking to me? The form you see in Horven's arms was the shell that enabled you to exist in this place. It has served its purpose and for now you are free.>

<For now?>

<Yes child. For now. Who knows, you may return here some day in a different form but for now let us say you are on a holiday. Besides there are some you once knew who are awaiting you, one in particular you held in your heart.>

He felt great joy infuse him and the form that was Lerma fell away until he too was infused with light.

<That is so much better!> Varnahrin laughed and it was as if the sun, rising into a new and bright dawn, had been transformed into music.

<Come now, follow me.>

The spirit of Lerma merged with the light that was Varnahrin and disappeared. An echo of laughter faded into nothing.

The voice of Varnahrin spoke into Horven's mind.

<Come, child. Lerma has passed on in gladness free from all pain and suffering. Even as he is now, he will not forget you and his love for you, Halika and Mareen will endure. Though you may not touch it or hear it, it will be there in your heart, you have but to reach out to it.>

'But Varnahrin,' Horven sobbed aloud. 'I have been so busy, I should have seen this, I should have spent more time, perhaps we could have prevented this.'

<Horven, do not distress yourself with 'could have' and 'should have'. Lerma knew his time had come and he was content. He did not pass alone; you were with him and he has crossed over, laughing. Cherished as he is, what you hold in your arms is but the body. Lerma has no more use for it.>

Horven took a deep breath, she knew the words of Varnahrin were true and they helped her through the first shock of Lerma's passing. She struggled with how she would tell Halika and Mareen, but taking a deep breath she placed her forehead against Lerma's for the last time.

<We will never forget you, my dearest one. May you find joy in the Lands Beyond. Forgive us if we grieve for a time over your passing.>

Standing quietly, she left in search of their spawnlings and steeled herself for the news she must impart to them both.

ooooOoooo

Grakh, Pershivon and Drenyk, aided by the seemingly tireless Hrv, used the gateways established by the Graavens to not only transport doses of the cure but also to establish new sites for the propagation of the seeds that the Hrv had brought with them, and to set up new facilities to produce and stockpile the cure. Its effects were no less remarkable when taken by Benshin, Xotic and Ma'Vessick sufferers and there appeared to be no visible side effects.

Not everyone could be cured; some were simply too far gone or had other conditions that adversely affected their recovery, but the vast majority were saved until it seemed that the period of the sickness was some nightmare from the past.

One morning, several Graaven dak'chaal after the Hrv's unanticipated arrival, Horven met with them to discuss their return to their own lands. The seasons had turned and the time of Carminac Gar – the Season of Abundance – had begun.

She stood quietly as the four Hrv entered the Council Chamber, six other Graaven councillors behind her following her lead. When the Hrv were before her, Horven and the councillors bowed low to them as one, Horven speaking to them and indicating that she did so on behalf of all present.

'When first you came to us you said you had come in need, not out of friendship. It took courage for you to enter our lands and your journey to us was a long and dangerous one. We here can never express in words to you our gratitude for what you have done for our people. I know I do not speak for the Graaven alone. Whether you desire friendship or not, you have ours and that of all the peoples you have saved from a terrible death. Our pledge to you is as we have agreed. The lands of the Hrv are sacrosanct to us. If you have need, call upon us and we will aid you as we may.'

Now it was the Hrv who bowed low.

'You have honoured our bargain,' said Sarrt. 'Nothing more was required of you.'

'But,' said Zekkr, 'in journeying here and staying these many days with you, we also have acquired knowledge and understanding of your people that was unknown to us.'

Nedr nodded. 'Our knowledge was based on the history of our Race and our treatment at the hands of those of ancient times. Wrongly, we did not think that your people would be any different and we also did not know that some of our own had caused pain and suffering to you and others. For this we are ashamed.'

'If the hand of friendship is raised toward us,' said Trrz, 'we willingly accept it and hope that a new dawn of cooperation may begin. The journey back to our people is long, but we know there will be much gladness when we return.'

'As to that,' said Horven. 'The least we can do is to ensure that your return journey is incomparably faster than your one here. If you are willing, we will travel by ImXin and you will be the first Hrv to fly.'

In response to this, each Hrv made the clicking sound that Horven now knew was their equivalent of laughter.

'Have I said something funny?' Horven was curious as to the Hrv response.

'Horven Var, it has been a long time, but each of us has flown before now. As hatchlings, we emerge with wings, but as we grow to maturity these shrivel and drop off. I speak for all when I say we would be delighted to travel with you and we thank you.'

The Graavens exchanged looks of surprise.

'Truly there is much still to learn of our Races. I look forward to hearing more about your people. Then come friends, we will make our way to the ship that will carry you home and if you are willing, we will greet those of your kind and reiterate to them our gratitude. Let us hope, as you have said, that a new and beneficial relationship between us will begin.'

'Let it be so, Horven Var,' said Trrz.

Without further ado Horven and the six councillors led the Hrv to where the ImXin lay awaiting their departure. It had already been decided that as Pershivon and Drenyk had taken a leading role in the circulation of the cure to all parts of Tarvuli and worked closely with the Hrv, they would escort the Hrv home and speak on behalf the Graaven and all their allies.

So, with the giving of parting gifts and cries of farewell, the ImXin lifted from the ground, much to the excitement of the Hrv aboard the craft, and set off for their lands.

ooooOoooo

Grossa stood looking at the lands of Percassia in the light of a new dawn. They lay just upon the other side of the bridge that spanned a great ravine, stretching as far as the eye could see in both directions, which formed a natural border between the lands of Crosh and Percassia.

Fifty sem'chaal had passed, as the Graaven reckoned years. Fifty years during which his people had united all of Crosh under his leadership. By a process of diplomacy, bribery and open warfare, all the tribes had submitted to Grossa and his people. Some begrudgingly, some through brute force and some willingly. All had prospered.

The Graaven had adopted the gods of the Hagalan peoples, more for expediency than any real desire to follow a belief in divine beings of whom they had never heard prior to their arrival, and who meant nothing to them as a people. However, it served to give them a common interest with those that they would seek to embrace in the new order, and dispelled some of the fear and mistrust among the Hagalan that the alien aspect of the Graaven instilled.

Their Kamehan friends had proven to be staunch allies and, like the Graaven people, they too had grown in numbers and wealth since the days of their first alliance. Now Grossa stood poised to cross the bridge that lay before him, the first step in a continuing program of conquest and assimilation.

Despite Graaven and Hagalan attempts at diplomacy the Percassians had thrown all overtures of friendship back in their faces.

Now Grossa stood silently, eight thousand Graaven and three thousand Hagalan warriors in ranks behind him awaiting his orders to advance. Where diplomacy had failed, force of arms would now determine fate. Foolishly, the Percassians had neglected to destroy the bridge, arrogantly believing that their greater numbers would successfully repulse any attempt by their enemies to cross into their territory.

Grossa shook his head impatiently; it need not have come to this. Borka stepped up alongside him awaiting orders and he turned towards her as she spoke.

'It would appear that the reputation of the range and effectiveness of our bows has failed to make an impression on these people.' She pointed to the thousands of soldiers gathered on the far side, banners and flags of many colours bearing the geometric designs that denoted the various clans of Percassia waving in the wind. They milled restlessly but made no move to cross the bridge and commence hostilities. 'If nothing else, our arrival has united them all in opposing us.'

Grossa grunted. 'Yes. Defeat them here today and we defeat them all in one blow. We take prisoners today Borka, as many as possible and particularly the clan leaders.'

Borka nodded. 'As you command, Grossa. Shall we get started?'

He turned away and once again focused his eyes on the masses that stood an easy bow shot away. He uttered just one word.

'Begin.'

Borka strode off towards a group of Graaven and Hagalan warriors that stood nearby. She looked at each individual intently before speaking.

'You have your orders. You know what to do. Are there any last questions?'

No response was received.

'Very well. Join your units and may Bekkor watch over you.' As one, the many turned and moved away with purpose.

Borka's gaze shifted to the Graaven signallers who stood quietly by the massive drums that, along with Hagalan horns, would relay commands to the allied forces.

Drawing a deep breath, she gave the first order.

'Sagit advance ten paces and commence attack.'

In response to a patterned series of drum beats and the call of horns, four thousand Graaven sagit advanced the required distance. Each carried forty shafts tipped with heads easily capable of piercing chain mail, even though few of the enemy appeared to have little more than hardened leather helms and breastplates, if anything at all.

Four thousand bows raised as one and on command, four thousand shafts were released towards the enemy in a rush of sound that could be heard even above the wind that blew across their front. Four thousand more followed just moments later, followed by yet another volley, so that the sky above them seemed to darken momentarily as they followed their trajectory.

The screams of the wounded reached Borka's ears as the devastating impact smashed through the Percassian forces arrayed in easy range of the Graaven war bows. It was simple carnage. Thousands lay dead and dying in a matter of moments and still the waves of shafts smashed into their diminishing ranks.

In response to a further series of drum and horn calls, columns of Graaven and Hagalan hoplex crossed the bridge armed with long spears and rectangular shields woven from the tough reeds that grew in the swamplands of Crosh, as the rain of arrows continued to fly above them. Their passage across was unopposed.

By mid-morning, the Percassians had been defeated, their forces decimated and their will to oppose, destroyed. Hundreds had been captured and thousands more had died trying to escape the horror of the battlefield, impeding each other in their terror and falling victim to the arrows of the sagit who had now crossed the bridge and fanned out in a mopping-up exercise that was as clinical as it was relentless.

Most of the leaders of the seven clans of Percassia had been captured, the bulk of their generals killed. Honour-bound they had chosen not to flee and so had perished. In one stroke, the combined Graaven and Hagalan forces had overthrown the enemy and while isolated resistance might still be encountered, the province was theirs.

Grossa sat outside of the great leather tent that formed the command post in the centre of the allied camp. Kneeling before him on the grass, their heads bowed in defeat, were all that was left of the clan leaders. Grossa shook his head in frustration; this had all been so unnecessary. If they had but swallowed their pride… his thoughts gave voice to his words.

'This carnage is on your heads; it could have been avoided and we could have united in friendship and trade, if you had only swallowed your pride for the greater good.'

One Percassian lifted his head, a sneer crossing his face.

'We will never surrender to such as you, do to us what you will. I spit on you. For as long as there is breath in my body, I will oppose you!'

Grossa threw back his head and laughed, a sound which made all those on their knees shudder.

'Borka, have this fool thrown into the crevasse, he can count his breaths on the way down.'

Struggling uselessly, the speaker was dragged bodily away, his piercing scream as he was thrown down penetrating the ears of the clan leaders.

'Does anyone one else wish to join him?'

Grossa waited for a response and let the moments go by, as the silent consternation of the prisoners grew with each breath they drew.

'You think my people and I are aliens bereft of feeling, savages even. Yet the lands of Crosh are united with us. We live in peace, we prosper. You have defied us and paid the price. I tell you now that the lands of Percassia will join us. No retribution will be suffered by your people unless they continue to foolishly oppose us. As with Crosh, all will prosper, willingly or otherwise. You can choose life for yourselves and your people with the hope of future peace and prosperity, or you can choose death. What say you?'

ooooOooooo

The evening was drawing on apace and the three moons hung overhead. The wind had finally died to nothing and the air was pleasantly warm. Grossa and Borka stood together looking out over the bridge they had taken.

'So, they chose peace,' said Borka. 'The fate of their comrade may have been a salutary lesson.'

'They do not trust us, Borka. Yet. But we will make good our words and they will unite under us in time. A few more salutary lessons may yet be required.'

Borka nodded. Behind her, thousands of camp fires twinkled in the darkness and the smell of meals being prepared combined with the subdued sound of conversations and laughter.

'And what then, Grossa?'

'Then? Beyond these lands Borka, lie others. In time they too will unite under Graaven rule. Our people will grow, as will our armies. Some will resist, but nothing will prevent us. All will prosper in time to come; I have seen a vision of it, Borka. We have taken the first steps toward a Graaven Empire.'

ooooOooooo

Pershiva al Dur stood at the foot of the Pohlan Kar's bed and watched him with mixed feelings. A thousand sem'chaal ago, long before there was an empire, the band of Graavens who emerged out of the east had been led by Grossa. It was his vision and single-

190

minded focus that had forged its beginnings: befriending some and conquering other peoples, he continuously expanded Graaven influence. Those leaders that came after, both male and female, had followed in his footsteps capitalising on the physical size and strength of their people and their great talent for war, counterbalanced by their equal ability to forge lasting peace with those they conquered. Strangely, Graaven society itself had become atrophied over time, becoming steadily more rigid and stratified. Now, clans were differentiated by skin markings, thus consigning many with talent to roles of servile inconsequence.

In life, Dur ab Shemma had bordered on the tyrannical even by Graaven standards. He had driven all with a relentless arrogance and belief in his own power. His own spawnlings had not been spared from his exacting standards and were meted out punishments where, in his view, they had not applied themselves. All were wary when coming into his presence. But, as Pershiva reflected, he had consolidated the Empire as no ruler had done before him. Although tyrannical, he was neither overly cruel nor sadistic. True, those who disappointed him seldom lived long after their failure, but in the main their executions were not made into a public spectacle, and were quick.

Both Menkh and Pershiva had a healthy respect for him and were able to see past his faults to his achievements. However, it was also clear that there were those among the prominent Graaven clans in the Court that surrounded him, while living in fear of his wrath, nevertheless secretly plotted his downfall.

That he had been poisoned even unto death was an established fact that Menkh and she had discovered long ago. Despite this knowledge, the Pohlan Kar had refused to even remotely entertain the possibility that any Graaven would have the temerity to think of plotting against him. His own arrogant certainties left him deaf and blind and Menkh and Pershiva's secret entreaties to those few whom they thought might listen, were discounted. The political manoeuvrings of Peremon, Fazor and Hema, the heads of three powerful clans, had been such that they had been unable to counter them.

Even now Pershiva was unsure how they had achieved their ends. Dur ab Shemma's decline had been so gradual, one could only surmise a lengthy and drawn-out illness. Pershiva and Menkh knew better, though it was the 'how' that they could not ascertain. Food and drink these three clan heads had always shared, so if poison it was, and it had to be, they themselves were immune to it or had dosed themselves with an antidote.

Sycophants and lickspittles to his face, their sole aim was to establish their own dominance. They perceived Pershiva to be weak and ineffectual, a belief that was actively encouraged by Pershiva herself, a calculated plan to give them a false sense of security in their plotting.

Now having successfully arraigned Menkh for a charge of treason against the Empire following his brilliant attack and peace settlement with the Percassian rebels and the Pohlan Kar's debilitating illness which left him virtually incapacitated, Menkh was even now returning to the capital under guard. Dur ab Shemma had neither the will nor the strength left to oppose them. Their aim was clear: to remove Menkh as the next in line for the throne and set up Pershiva as their puppet.

Menkh and Pershiva's plans were well thought out. Pershiva recalled their last cautious meeting before Menkh had left for Percassia.

ooooOoooo

'You are sure this is the only way, Menkh?'

Menkh nodded. He and Pershiva sat in one of the palace gardens far from prying eyes, the sounds of a fountain covering their whispered voices.

'We will defeat these Percassian rebels though it will not be easy, they have fled into the wilds of Gromdesh with the last remnants of their people. It is my intention to conclude a peace deal with them.'

'Peace!' said Pershiva in amazement. 'Menkh you cannot be serious; our Sire will never allow it.'

'Never is a long time, Pershiva. I will argue the logic of it to him. Gromdesh would provide the perfect buffer between the Empire and the Steppes of Portis. It is sparsely populated, just a few Terrax farmers. Our enemy may be the last of the Percassian rebels but they are wily fighters and well organised. So, if I can conclude a peaceful settlement, it will be enough I think to draw our conspirators out. Their opportunity to move against me in condemnation.'

'But Father would never countenance such a move.'

'No, he would not. But I think that this will be a spur for them to bring their plans forward. My belief is that the Pohlan Kar will be neutralised.'

'Then we must warn him!' Pershiva was growing increasingly agitated and fearful that this could all go terribly wrong.

Menkh took hold of Pershiva's hands. 'Sister, have we not tried to warn our Sire on multiple occasions? He has dismissed our concerns every time. He cannot conceive of even the remotest possibility that any Graaven would have the courage to move against him.'

Pershiva nodded. 'They are clever, these three. They have ingratiated themselves so that they appear to have become indispensable.'

'Yes,' Menkh agreed. 'You must keep up your act. They perceive you to be weak and indecisive, so you will be their perfect puppet in my place.'

Pershiva's countenance became grim. 'Oh yes. They think they know me well.'

'Good. During our absence you must make sure that your personal guard is totally loyal to you. Be wary of spies; our conspirators will, without doubt, have informers even among the Baran Mec.'

'Do not worry on that score, brother. I have known some of them since I was a spawnling. Their loyalty is unquestioned and they bear no regard for our conspirators.'

Menkh stood still, holding Pershiva's hands in his own. 'Then there is nothing left to say, but much left yet to do.'

Touching foreheads with Pershiva in the Graaven way of affection, Menkh turned and walked purposefully back to the palace. At dawn he would march off with his Impisch to war.

Taking a deep breath, Pershiva followed the disappearing form of Menkh along a pathway which wound its way past groves of ferns and artfully planted beds of flowering plants. Silently, three Baran Mec emerged from places of concealment and bowed low to her.

'We watched carefully Supremacy. No one came anywhere near where you and the Pohlan Harac sat.'

'Thank you Tremm. You also Jessic and Paltor. Watch your backs over the coming meh'chaal, we must all be prepared.'

The three Baran Mec bowed once more and falling into step, followed Pershiva back into the palace. Her confident steps and posture subtly altered as she entered the palace itself, shoulders somewhat bowed, steps rather hesitant, her head turning left and right as if fearful of seeing or meeting someone.

Tremm smiled to himself. Pershiva was a consummate actress, though where the talent came from, he had no clue, it was certainly not from her Sire. Things were definitely going to get interesting as she had told them, but whatever resulted he, Jessic and Paltor were determined that no harm would come to their charge; they would kill and die for her without a second thought.

CHAPTER FOURTEEN

Menkh and Crixac journeyed back along the Threadway to Tarvuli faster than thought. Both he and Crixac could not dismiss the deeply unsettling feeling that the Enemy pursued them. It was like trying to flee a nightmare with some horror just one handbreadth away from catching you in its deadly embrace.

Rarely had Menkh experienced terror, but while the passage of time back to Tarvuli was brief it nevertheless felt as if time itself had slowed, invested with a creeping sense of paralysis underscored by the all too real fear that they would simply arrive back too late to be of any assistance in the battle to come. While they had no clear indication of the Enemy's intentions, both Menkh and Crixac were convinced that their feelings and those they had discussed with the adepts at the Balancepoint concerning the Enemy, were completely accurate.

At the same time that Menkh and Crixac hastened back to Tarvuli, so too did Tishan. Like Menkh, she was filled with an overwhelming sense of foreboding and the belief that there was only one course of action their foe would now take, its sole purpose the eradication of their world and the enslavement of

Varnahrin. Should this be achieved… Tishan's mind shuddered away from what might then follow.

Both Menkh and Tishan materialised out of the Threadway at almost the same moment, appearing on the other side of the shield that Varnahrin had shaped from a pillar of energy that arose from the Complex far beneath them, bolstered by the beacons on the three moons.

Varnahrin's voice entered their minds like the peal of horns before battle.

<It comes! It comes! Prepare!>

Passing inside the protective rim of the shield, Menkh and Tishan floated in space high above their world slowly orbiting far below them, their Adept forms shrouded in a glow of white and red light. Alongside them, a vast luminescence of light and energy hung suspended, which now drew into itself, coalescing into a form that appeared vaguely Graaven but was neither male nor female.

<Varnahrin?> said Menkh.

<Who else, Menkh ab Dur. The time of trial is upon us!>

In the instant of time that Menkh perceived the presence of Varnahrin, the Enemy smashed into the shield with cataclysmic force. A blinding coruscation of light bore witness to its terrible impact and the golden shield buckled. The power generators on the three moons were driven in that moment to critical levels of stress and the failsafe mechanisms built into their construction began a shutdown process. The pulsing lines of energy that joined the central core began to flicker as their power faded. Without their concentration of supplementary power, it was clear that the shield would not withstand a further impact of such force.

The Enemy, a formless mass of inky blackness, screamed in outrage, seething with uncontained rage and spite. Its blackness expanded, increasing to a size that could swallow not only Tarvuli but all the worlds that formed its planetary system.

A roar equal to the sound of a tidal wave, thundered in Menkh's and Tishan's minds as the Enemy again threw itself against the barrier. This time the shield shattered, the great pillar of energy emanating from the Complex instantly evaporating.

The voice of Varnahrin called out. <Now is the time. Focus your wills and join with mine!>

Within the Complex far below, the machinery powering the core deactivated instantly in response to the shutting down of its outlying generators, thus dampening the energies that had been so violently broken. Now the final defence of Ta'Morin itself increased its intensity; above the heads of the Graaven in Ta'Morin, the faint blue haze that they were used to seeing high over the city, hardened into a deep blue lattice work of interlocking geometric shapes. Beyond these could be seen in the sky far above a hovering pinpoint of intense white light....

Long had Varnahrin prepared for this day; the combined will of all those living was yet another source of energy that could be drawn upon in the struggle.

Varnahrin now exerted control and, as one, all the peoples and sentient creatures of Tarvuli looked upwards and focused on that point of light. Held in a kind of stasis, the Xotic, Benshin and Ma'Vessick along with the peoples of the yet undiscovered lands that surrounded them, stood silently, their gaze turned upwards as Varnahrin drew on their minds and their very life essence to aid the battle being played out far above them. Prides of Gonverdeem lifted their muzzles and gazed intently into the sky. Within Ta'Morin, Fendrax, who had regained her full strength, let out a mighty roar, both a cry of defiance and a challenge to the thing that threatened all life. Far away the Hrv also stood motionless and they too leaned their mind-strength into the battle.

Exposed directly at last to the power of the Enemy, a feeling of terrible and gloating exultation crashed into their joint minds.

<Now you are mine! All that you are will be as nothing, and I will consume you and you will enter a living nightmare as all you know comes crashing down around you!>

As these words of hatred and malice echoed in their minds, the visible force of energy that was Varnahrin intensified and began to expand. Menkh and Tishan stood behind a golden wall of light crafted by the Spirit of Ta'Morin. The power of the Enemy was beyond comprehension, it was a manifestation of evil so intense that despair threatened to overwhelm their senses. Menkh gripped his staff, which now blazed with an intense light, and more than ever before he felt his will mesh with that of Crixac in an unspoken accord of resistance. Tishan focused her mind and using the Rod of Klemish, calmed her fears and let the titanic fury of the Enemy slide over her.

Even with the combined will of all life on Tarvuli and the forces of Menkh and Tishan, they struggled to contain the Enemy, let alone counterstrike. At that precise moment Varnahrin began to sing. Eerie and discordant at first, the voice sounded utterly alien and without recognisable meaning, yet it was filled with an inescapable sense of wonder, spanning a range of notes so low that the very space around them seemed to vibrate, then so high that any mortal ears would have shattered. To Tishan's mind it was as if the very stars of the heavens had taken voice. Up and down the scale it went and whatever its meaning, it had a profound effect on the Enemy so that, despite its efforts, it seemed to shrink in size.

But then the Enemy responded pushing back with redoubled force, so that the power of the voice diminished and despair and defeat arose once more in their minds. Against the renewed assault, the music emanating from Varnahrin changed once more and it sprang anew with light and hope and unalloyed joy. A school of Gathanax suddenly appeared out of the ether, followed by another and another and yet another. Their complex harmonies joined with the voice of Varnahrin.

<We are here Mother. We have heard your call!>

They sang as one.

Screams of rage formed a counterpoint to the joy of the song which was anathema to the Enemy. Now, faster and faster the blackness of the Enemy condensed, swiftly shrinking despite all its powers of resistance; yet its fury and malevolence remained undiminished and as before Apocris fought back with mind-numbing power.

ooooOooooo

At first, Menath couldn't describe the feeling. It was like rising up from a warm and luxurious bath, or perhaps emerging from a deep and dreamless sleep into soft light. Yet, it was both of these feelings and more besides and underscoring all of that there was sadness and something else…. she thought more about it as her senses restored themselves. Yes, the feeling was tinged with melancholy and loss, but what that loss was she could not yet determine and now, with clarity of thought returning, she became aware of something else. Turning her thoughts outwards, she assessed the external events that increasingly impinged on her mind. She felt power flowing through her, energies that were not created *of* her, but rather *through* her as a conduit of that power, another will that focused on something else.

Menath made a further discovery: it was not one will but two working in such close accord and harmony as to be almost inseparable from each other. Behind this, she sensed something else, an emotion she had not experienced for a very long time: love. A love born out of a mutual need and grown into a profound respect and friendship that transcended into something greater still. Two beings unified, yet with all their attention currently concentrated on something else. For a time, Menath puzzled over this; it seemed that she too was a part of this fierce attention. A part of it and yet somehow separate from it. How was this possible?

Her senses continued their inexorable journey towards complete restoration. She remembered a room and she remembered holding a rod of crystal. The feeling of sadness and melancholy grew and then she remembered. Her consciousness had flowed into the crystal and she had become one with it. A feeling of peace and contentment had flowed over her and who she was; what she had been had become supplanted by something else – what she had now become. A union with another intelligence, unfathomable, all-consuming. As Menath considered this in light of her returned capacity to review events, she also realised that there was a complete sense of rightness about this. Far from feeling threatened or frightened, she had surrendered willingly to it and that surrender felt like walking into the embrace of a beloved parent, like stepping into light and warmth from the darkness and finding total contentment.

Until this moment.

What had changed?

What had caused this reemergence?

With her restored ability to range outside of herself, Menath now followed the energies being directed through her and away from the focus of the two minds she had encountered. Her consciousness danced along the lines of that power, a focused beam of light of enormous strength now directed towards something else entirely. Abruptly she halted at the very ends of that energy, for here she encountered something else that made her recoil in revulsion. It was a vast and sentient intelligence, implacable, loathsome and ultimately corrupt. A cloud of evil created from the horror of a million, million tortured and devoured souls. It had only one purpose founded on the absolute certainty of its own pre-eminence, its own need, its own hunger. That purpose was the complete destruction of Balance, the overthrow of light and reason, of love and compassion. A new reality where chaos would be supreme and where this being could give its ravenous hunger full reign.

She turned her mind away from the terrible reality of this evil and looked back along the thread of energy that pulsed towards it. In that moment all her memory returned to her. She saw the crystal staff that pulsed with indefinable power and realised that it was herself. She looked beyond the staff and saw a humanoid figure, familiar to her eyes from a time long ago and yet different in ways that she had not the time to consider at this moment. She looked beyond that figure and drew a mental breath. Here was another sentient being bathed in light like a veritable sun. In every way imaginable, it was the opposite of the corrupt presence that sat behind her. Stern and all powerful as it was, it was imbued with a compassion that would have filled the cosmos, a love for all life that instilled in Menath a feeling of profound and pure joy. Yet there was something else. Will. A single-minded and implacable purpose, the equal of the corrupt power it strove against. A will that would make any sacrifice to maintain Balance, not with evil intent or selfish greed but a preparedness to preserve and protect.

As Menath became more aware of her surroundings she realised that this titanic struggle was occurring in space. A living planet turned slowly far below, and three moons could be seen orbiting that world. From the planet's surface, threads of energy flowed into the golden light supplementing its power, but this energy came at a cost. It was drawn from the life-force of the sentient beings that occupied this world, indeed the very life energy of the planet itself. In that moment memory stirred and Menath recalled the name of that world as realisation flooded back. Tarvuli!

With recognition of the name, memories of her siblings Kortsan and Tambel returned with painful clarity. Their arrogance, their surety that they were right and that all others were wrong. Their success in fleeing the Balancepoint and establishing a new world using the power of a stolen crystal. Their triumph and ultimate failure and subsequent descent into despair.

Yes, it all came back to her now. How she had welcomed her transformation and absorption into the crystal as a means of escaping her guilt. The strange matter she had discovered by accident so long ago on a world that had no record of existence, undiscovered and overlooked – till she had stumbled across or been drawn to it – even though it lay not far from the Balancepoint. Where, as an Adept of the Red, her sworn duty was to preserve the Balance itself.

She had taken samples of this new crystalline matter, its constituent properties so different from that which were found anywhere else in reality. Fascinated, she had experimented endlessly with it and its ability to hide itself. Ultimately it had provided the means to achieve her siblings' plans and, she was certain, had even guided them to Tarvuli.

Menath ceased her introspection. While it had taken but moments in time, the battle yet raged around her in the silence of space. Like the crystal that she had bonded with, her presence went unnoticed. Now, she became aware of other things. A shield of energies was rapidly reaching a point of collapse. That shield was the same one she and her siblings had created to hide the world of Tarvuli, cunningly refashioned into a powerful defence field. More disturbingly, she knew that despite their striving against the evil power that sought to gain dominance, those that opposed it would not win. The shield would fail and at that point all hope would fail also. Unless.

In an instant of time, Menath's consciousness flowed back into the crystalline staff. As great as the energy was that the two beings manifested, it was nothing compared to what she herself could conjure if she wrested control of it away from them.

Her thoughts flew to the being of golden light.

<You cannot triumph here. This creature is too powerful even for you.>

Varnahrin recoiled in complete surprise. Not something which had ever happened before.

<Who or what are you? Be quick, even this small distraction weakens my power.>

<I am Menath. I am also the crystal staff your friends are wielding with great effect. However, they cannot last, they will tire and when that happens their focus will diminish, along with the energy they use to hold the enemy off.>

If Varnahrin was further surprised by this revelation, no sign of it manifested to Menath.

<What do you propose?>

<I will resume power and directly attack this thing. As it was for you, so will it be a complete surprise to the Enemy. It will recoil and, in that moment, you must split open the fabric of space and push it into the Place Between.>

Varnahrin's voice was coldly matter of fact, despite the battle that raged around them.

<You know I cannot. To attempt to do so will invoke the fifth immutable law. There is no power here that can achieve this thing.>

<Just as you were oblivious to me, Varnahrin, so are you also oblivious to that which sits within your grasp. The Rod of Klemish is of the same material as that which I now am. The properties of this crystal are not affected by any of the immutable laws of this Universe, they vibrate to a different harmonic. With all your combined wills channelled through the Rod, and with my aid, you can achieve this. It is the only way if you wish to restore Balance.>

<You expect me to trust you, Menath? The Adepts still refer to you and your siblings as the apostates. You abandoned the preservation of Balance for your own ends.>

<Only partially true. Will you debate this with me now, when all around is on the verge of collapse?>

<I do not. Now I see a pattern that was hidden from me before. The Intelligence works behind this. Very well Menath, proceed, we will do our part.>

<Think of this as atonement for myself and my siblings and remember me more kindly in time to come. In our arrogance and pride, my brothers and I thought we had achieved our ultimate goal; I see now that we were delusional and all that we did was governed by the Intelligence, ultimately to preserve Balance.>

<The Balance is All,> Varnahrin replied. <You have my blessing. Go now Menath and may the Intelligence guide you.>

ooooOoooo

Tishan gripped the Rod of Klemish in her right hand; she had been uncertain of her role in the battle, but now she knew. With resignation, she accepted her fate, realising that the trial she had endured to activate the shield with Menkh had been but a prelude to what she must do now. She was filled with both a profound sense of rightness and also of sadness, but she was Graaven and a warrior. As Guardian of the City, she would gladly give her life to save others. Mentally taking a deep breath, she prepared to throw herself into the heart of the blackness and distract the enemy using the power of the Rod and so allow Varnahrin to triumph.

As fast as Tishan moved it was not fast enough to prevent what happened next. In that moment of decision as Tishan leapt forth, the staff in Menkh's hand dissolved. In its place a huge humanoid figure took shape, its facial features undoubtedly female and mirroring those of the two statues that guarded the Causeway Bridge in Ta'Morin. In that instant of recognition both Menkh and Crixac jumped to the same conclusion

<Menath!>

Tishan felt herself dragged back, pushed to one side.

<This is my task, Tishan Dar. My moment of redemption. You have other tasks. I wish you joy of them!>

The figure of Menath shot like a flaming comet into the heart of the Enemy. In a split second, there was an incandescent bloom of light accompanied by a scream of rage and pain that echoed across the Cosmos, silencing even the song of the Gathanax. Just as swiftly, the light extinguished. Menath had disappeared, absorbed into the heart of the Enemy which still floated in space but diminishing rapidly. In the place of furious rage and unending assault on the senses came utter silence. It was akin to being battered in a violent storm when suddenly in the midst of the fury the eye of the storm passes overhead and all becomes still.

But something more had changed. Deep within the heart of the Enemy's darkness, lights flared like gigantic forks of lightning. Once again, a titanic scream of rage echoed in their minds as the Enemy fought back. Menkh and Tishan saw in horror that despite Menath's assault, the form of the enemy began again to grow, even while its power appeared to be lessening. Hope in the minds of the defenders dwindled once more.

ooooOooooo

Deep within the Balancepoint, in a room that was not a room but rather a construct to limit any feelings of disorientation, several Adepts sat in conclave around a circular table. The table and chairs appeared to be made of rose-coloured stone, yet none of the Adepts could have said precisely what the material was. Like the room they sat in, the items of furnishing were also a construct to provide some familiar reference point. In any event, where they were exactly and what they sat upon, was not the focus of their meeting; rather they concentrated on the several spheres which floated above the table. Around the central larger sphere rotated three others, smaller in size. If it were possible for an outside observer to have entered this space they would have been struck by the spheres' remarkable resemblance to a planet and its moons and as they drew closer, they would have noted with fascination that it was indeed a planet in perfect miniature, its violet atmosphere and land masses clearly discernible.

Morgath, Plakar, Frzath, Denith and T'klath focused their thoughts not so much on the world of Tarvuli, which indeed this was, but rather on the cloud of inky blackness which sat menacingly above that world, held seemingly at bay by a shield of golden light. Energies of great power were being unleashed from the darkness, colliding with the field of light only to be deflected back in coruscating beams of dissipating energy. Each Adept felt rather than heard the crackle of power and explosive percussion of sound.

<We must lend aid to our friends; they fight bravely but I fear their shield is weakening,> T'klath's thoughts expressed their shared misgivings.

<The course of action we take in this matter is dangerous; we are tasked with defence of the Balancepoint, what then if we fail?> said Morgath.

Frzath looked at each in turn. <If the darkness triumphs, then we are all lost. We will activate the failsafe. Should we be eliminated, the Balancepoint will self-destruct in the moment the last of us dies. We can do no more than this.>

The Adepts nodded in agreement.

<Then we are all agreed, we will meld. My dear friends let us hope that our intervention will tip the balance in favour of those who fight for the light. Balance is all,> said T'klath.

Their combined thoughts echoed in response.

From the table's surface rose up an intricate tracery of crystalline filaments encasing each Adept and growing ever upwards from their bodies, the tracery finally enveloping the spheres that slowly rotated above their seated forms.

Within the cocoon of filaments, the consciousness of each Adept flowed through the weblike structure, coalescing into one united and disembodied power that pulsated with red, blue and white strands of force. The whole then began to throb with power, flowing on through the construct until the entirety of the floating orb was surrounded with energy. The light condensed, becoming ever brighter, ever sharper, until it was unleashed in a blinding flash against the darkness.

ooooOoooo

Within Menkh's mind, Crixac occupied a world within a world. As a symbiote, Crixac was nurtured by the spirit of Menkh and in turn empowered his host with healing energy and knowledge. The union of Menkh and Crixac, originating out of mutual need as Menath had perceived, had grown into something profound. A bonding that was beyond even Crixac's considerable power to fully explain. But there was another side to the power of a symbiote, and one which Crixac had briefly alluded to when he first made contact with Menkh. Rooted in ancient times, the first symbiotes had invaded their hosts, forcibly controlling their minds and bodies, feeding on their energy before madness and death had consumed their unwilling prey. If the invasive symbiote failed to find an alternative host in time, then it too suffered the same fate as its quarry.

Such a meaningless and savage existence had been replaced over time. Crixac's symbiote forebears had learned how to nurture their hosts. Benign and enduring unions of mutual benefit were ultimately achieved, and the savage earlier times relegated to history. However, buried deep, a spore of that former power remained.

Through Menkh's eyes and perceptions, Crixac observed the Enemy, drawing his own conclusions as to what the next course of action must be. Menath still battled on, evidenced by the flaring lights manifest within the body of the Enemy. Clearly however she could not win – not alone, without aid.

Slowly, imperceptibly, Crixac withdrew his tendrils of power from Menkh's body until all but one remained. He took a mental breath and reflected on the years of his existence and the delight and comfort he had felt in his final union with Menkh.

<You will always be my friend Menkh. I wish you everlasting joy.> Crixac's voice whispered in Menkh's mind.

<Crixac! What are you saying?>

Out of Menkh's body, an intense ball of blue energy leapt across space and, as Menath had before, disappeared into the Enemy. This time however, there was no connecting thread left joined to Menkh.

All too late, Menkh's voice called out in despair:

<Crixac! No!>

Within the darkness of the Enemy the blue energy that was Crixac pulsed into incandescence as it merged with the power of Menath.

<Suspend me in a tree will you, you piece of shit!> Crixac screamed.

Somewhere, the voice of Menath laughed aloud and joined with Crixac, so that their efforts redoubled. At the same time, out of nowhere a beam of pure energy swirling with a pattern of red, blue and white light, smote the darkness that was Apocris, piercing deep into its shadow.

In the Balancepoint, the Adepts slipped into unconsciousness, drained of all energy as T'klath pulled on the last reserves of their combined power.

The Enemy screamed out in agony.

<Now Tishan!> The voice of Varnahrin thundered in her mind.

<Now is your task at hand! Employ the Rod and cast the Enemy out!>

Without thought Tishan raised the Rod of Klemish and, concentrating all her mind, pointed it towards the vicinity of the Enemy. Something outside of herself seemed to supplement her will and to open up the very fabric of space, a rent no bigger than the length of the Rod itself.

Despite its diminutive size, the rent exerted an irresistible and terrible force, dragging everything inexorably towards it.

Reeling from the abrupt sacrifice of Crixac and the dissolution of the staff, Menkh now drew back his focus to observe something becoming gradually clearer on the other side of the rent. Could he see a vast shape moving there?

Still screaming in fury, the Enemy was sucked into the rent, faster and faster, like water disappearing down a drain. Despite its vastness and its great effort to resist the pull, it met with an overwhelming force and was inexorably drawn into the tear, stretched and pulled through the fissure in space and time. Deep within its blackness, white and blue energies still flared, battling and confusing it, so that it could not focus its will on extricating itself from the rift that continued to slowly widen.

Menkh now saw Tishan reeling from countershock. Bereft of Crixac and without his staff, he had no focal point on which to exert his will; instead, he entered Tishan's mind and channelled his strength to her. Thus revived and re-energised, Tishan refocused the Rod, and, with one last despairing scream of pain, the Enemy's form disappeared through the rent.

The force emanating from the tear was beyond measure. Suddenly Varnahrin's voice echoed in their minds.

<We must close the rent! If we do not, everything in this reality will be drawn into it!>

Menkh and Tishan were horrified at Varnahrin's words: their failure to close the rift would result in the total annihilation of everything. While the Enemy may have been defeated, Balance itself would cease to exist. In that moment, Menkh and Tishan felt another power enter the fray. The voice of T'klath sounded in their minds.

<Menkh, we must aid Tishan in closing the rift; if not, as Varnahrin has said, all will be destroyed.>

Menkh redirected his will towards Tishan, and now Varnahrin also lent power to the Rod, but despite the immensity of their combined will the tear grew still larger.

As their united strength fought to seal the ever-widening rent, a different voice spoke into Tishan's mind. Despite the battle that continued around her unabated, she felt herself detach from her surroundings. The voice was crystalline, dispassionate and aloof from all that was occurring.

<Listen to me Tishan Dar, you know what has to be done. Only by your passing through the rift with me can we repair the hole in space and time. If not, we will not succeed, despite combined wills, and all you have fought for and suffered will be in vain.

<Who are you? How do I know I can trust what you say?>

There was desperation in Tishan's thoughts. Fatigue and despair assailed her mind.

<I am that which you hold in your hands. Let us go before it is too late. Only we can achieve this thing. The Balance is All.>

It was these last four words that truly spoke to Tishan. She steeled herself for what she must do. Deep down, she had known it from the start; her situation was uncannily like one of the tests she had undergone in Ta'Morin when she and Menkh were activating the shield generators. Perhaps that was a preparation for this very moment. Drawing on her years of military training and discipline, she pushed aside all thought of self, of Menkh and of their spawnlings. She was the Guardian of the City, her life was required to save it and if that was required, so be it.

Still with a lingering doubt, she tightened her grip on the Rod. With a surge of effort, she threw Menkh's consciousness away from her and before even Varnahrin could react, sped like a comet through the rift and into the space beyond.

Menkh's despairing voice screamed into her mind, <Tishan!>

In a blink of time, both Tishan and the Rod of Klemish expanded to a colossal size and they passed through the rent into the nothingness beyond. The Rod seemed to dissolve and become one with the very substance of her hands and she felt a coldness seep into her body as the rift thundered shut behind them.

Despite the vacuum she was in, Tishan heard a sound like an immense boulder sealing the mouth of a great cavern. Briefly, she felt a terrible and overwhelming pressure, then all life fled from her body.

The countershock of force as the rift closed, smote Menkh and flung him like spindrift on the sea. Abruptly his passage was halted and he was held in a warm embrace of golden light. Menkh called out in despair. He had suffered many losses in his life, but he was unprepared for the passing first of Crixac and then of Tishan. At worst, he believed he would die but that she would live on after him. Grief and pain struck his mind until Varnahrin enfolded him into a deep slumber, and carried him back to Ta'Morin where the long process of healing could begin. It was with a profound shock of realisation that Varnahrin too was moved in an unfathomable way by Tishan's sacrifice. Varnahrin was changing in unexpected ways.

CHAPTER FIFTEEN

Far below, across the lands on the world of Tarvuli, those who had lent their life force to the battle collapsed to the ground, physically and mentally drained. As many sank into unconsciousness, some never to revive such had been the drain on their life essence, yet was Tarvuli tinged with euphoria, a lightening of spirit and sense of unfathomable joy. This was perhaps supplemented by the close proximity of the many Gathanax whose song had resumed and continued unabated overhead. But there was more to it than this. A sense that a great calamity had been averted, an implacable enemy defeated whose final overthrow they had all contributed to in a way they could only guess at, but which still brought with it a belief in victory accomplished.

Menkh sat in silence, communication of any kind beyond him since Tishan's closing of the rift. Even Varnahrin was silent, although they were all refreshed and bathed in the song that the Gathanax wove around them. Then, one by one, each school shot away, their song tinged with an echo of farewell as they disappeared in the merest blink of an eye to continue their endless journey and their eternal song of joy and hope.

Even as the last school disappeared, Varnahrin's form was sur-rounded by a nimbus of white light, brighter than the sun. In the minds of all, whether they still stood in joy, or slept deeply in ex-haustion, a voice spoke, its tone deeply soothing, quietly triumphant and ultimately reassuring.

<Balance is restored, equilibrium is achieved.>

From nowhere as if in echo, a myriad voices responded.

<The Balance is All.>

Menkh woke slowly from a dreamless slumber to the harsh re-ality of the loss of Crixac and Tishan. Even the staff that had been passed to him was gone. In all his life, Menkh had never felt so bereft and the sense of grief and loss threatened to overwhelm him.

<Menkh, I am so sorry. But you must know that the willing sacrifices of Crixac and Tishan, as well as that of Menath, were critical to our success in defeating the Enemy. You and Tishan achieved what was believed impossible. Equilibrium has been re-stored. Tishan's sacrifice and her use of the Rod of Klemish was a master stroke; even I could not have predicted that to seal the fis-sure was the correct course of action. There is much to ponder here. A form of sentient matter, hidden even from me. Who would have thought it possible?> Varnahrin's voice was quietly consol-ing.

Despite Varnahrin's words, Menkh's mind was still reeling in the aftermath of all that had happened.

<They were both more than my friends, Varnahrin. I feel as if a part of my soul has been ripped away. There is no chance that they may have survived?>

<I wish that I could reassure you Menkh, but there is none whatsoever. Truly, nothing can survive on the other side of that rent in space. In achieving success, we broke one of the immutable laws. I think we can all see why such a law exists. We breached the buffer which separates one reality from another, one universe

from another. Even I cannot bear to think of what may have oc-curred had we not sealed the gap that had been created. You must take time for yourself, to recover. Tishan and Crixac gave them-selves for you, for all of us, so that we could live without fear. We have a debt to ensure that their sacrifice is not forgotten. Though in your grief you may not feel it now, truly a time of healing and renewal has begun. It is not often that one can claim to have saved the Universe!>

Menkh closed his eyes, the pain of loss still too raw for him to acknowledge Varnahrin's words, even while he knew them to be true.

When Menkh opened his eyes moments later, having felt no discernible movement or disorientation, he found himself within the Complex standing in the rooms he and Tishan habitually used when they were in Ta'Morin.

The voice of Varnahrin ebbed away and Menkh was left alone to mourn.

ooooOoooo

Several meh'chaal passed and Menkh battled with his grief. Slowly the pain lessened with time and yet Menkh could not believe in his heart that both Tishan and Crixac were gone. Despite the euphoria of their triumph, the loss of Crixac left an emptiness inside him that refused to heal.

In order to turn his mind to other things Menkh had been learning all that had happened on Tarvuli during their absence and he spent as much time as possible with Drenyk and Pershivon, who were also bereft after the passing of Tishan. He was proud of their efforts in assisting the Hrv with the delivery of the cure to their friends and allies, and he became aware that since travelling to the land of the Hrv a keen desire to explore further had been ignited in both of them.

Menkh grieved too over the loss of life due to the contagion, but recognised how much worse things may have been without the Hrv. He saw also that as Varnahrin had drawn on the energy and life force of all living things in the great battle, there had been a strange lethargy that seemed to permeate everyone as balance was slowly restored and vitality regained.

The funeral for Tishan Dar took every last drop of his self-control to get through. Visitors from all over Tarvuli made the journey to attend, including Trrz and Nedr representing the Hrv. In the great crystal pyramid that Varnahrin had created and where the faces of fallen Graaven cycled endlessly, Tishan's visage could now be seen, though Menkh could not summon the courage to look at it. Near him, Horven wept unashamedly and she was not the only Graaven to so do. Those still living who had survived the flight from Tarmech, the Graaven capital, honoured Tishan's courage and fortitude and mourned the passing of the years.

Menkh stood alone long after the others had departed to the funerary feast. He could not stomach the thought of food. He sent his thoughts out to Tishan.

<I would have gone in your place, my dearest one. I lost Pershiva and now I have lost you and I must journey on alone into the bitter years ahead.>

Try as he might he could not shake off the malaise that gripped him. Sadness for Tishan and Crixac and even the loss of his staff compounded the effect; after trying hard to distract himself by involvement with the Council, he found he lacked the energy for the work that was required to restore what had been lost.

Several dak'chaal after the funeral and after some precious time alone with his spawnlings, sharing their grief and recalling happier moments, Menkh was sitting near the Ta'Morin gateway when he felt a familiar presence loom over him.

The great head of Fendrax, now completely returned to her former strength, bent near his own and snuffled him gently.

'You and I have indulged ourselves in grief for too long, Menkh ab Dur. I am going hunting and you are coming with me. We both need a change of scenery.'

Menkh looked up. His first instinct was to refuse but he was exhausted by grief, and tired of feeling sorry for himself. Fendrax was right. Somehow he must lift himself up and move on. How much better than on the back of a Gonverdeem.

'So, can you carry me in your weakened state?' Menkh's attempt at humour was feeble but it was a start.

'Luckily you are not as fat as Horven Var, so I should manage well enough. Come, let us go.'

'What now? I have made no preparations.'

'What need you of preparation Adept of the Red? No excuses. We hunt. Now.'

Menkh climbed to his feet. He noted with interest that for the first time since the battle, he was filled with anticipation for what was to come.

'Come then my friend. Let us hunt.'

Eschewing the gateway Fendrax leapt straight up the pathway and together she and Menkh exited Ta'Morin, passing like smoke on the breeze.

For many weeks they traversed the lands, visiting the Xotic and Benshin and even passing through the gateway to the lands across the Great Water. It was in every way a time of healing and renewal for both Menkh and Fendrax.

During this time, a compulsion began to grow in Menkh's mind. Somewhat amorphous, at first he felt it as a vague longing to be somewhere else. Over several days, the tenuous feelings became sharper, more focused, and took on form and shape. In his mind, a picture of a planet grew. A star system far from Tarvuli but whose location became fixed in Menkh's thoughts. As yet, he could not name the system nor the particular planet that increasingly filled his waking thoughts, but the urge to journey there became overwhelming. A compulsion he could not ignore, yet felt constrained to keep to himself. He could sense no evil intent in this need, rather that the journey itself was the only way to rid himself of it.

Finally divulging to Fendrax his need to return and the strange longing he felt, they journeyed back to Ta'Morin.

It was a happy return.

Menkh was greeted by Horven Var and his two spawnlings, now grown to full adulthood, all of whom were relieved to see him recovered from his pain and grief. Fendrax snuffled Horven's face as Drenyk and Pershivon, Mareen and Halika came running up.

'So Horven Var,' Fendrax said. 'You are now so fat even I could hardly bear your weight.'

Horven nodded. 'Yes, now that you are old and feeble, I can clearly see the effort would be beyond you.'

Fendrax emitted a coughing grunt that was the Gonverdeem equivalent of laughter. 'It is always good to see you Horven Var, and your offspring.'

'Now is the time for parting. I will return to my pride-lands; Menkh ab Dur and I have been away from our loved ones too long, but he and I will meet again in time to come.'

Fendrax snuffled Menkh's face in farewell and turned her attention once again to Horven who stood alongside him.

'I will miss you Horven Var and I grieve for you at the passing of Lerma. We have all lost those we hold dear in our hearts; there is always a price to pay though it tears our soul apart.'

Horven stepped forward and reached up to caress Fendrax's mane.

'I too grieve for your loss, my dearest friend. Do not be away too long.'

Fendrax leaned in close and sniffed at Horven. 'Watch over those two cubs of yours. I look forward to seeing them again soon.'

Without another word Fendrax turned and within moments disappeared from their view.

'I still don't know how she does that!' said Menkh.

'I think she enjoys it, it's part of her mystery.'

'You are doing well as Head of the Council, Horven Var, who would have believed our journey would bring us here?'

Horven smiled at Menkh. 'Who indeed?'

'I will leave you to your duties. Send for me if you need to, although I feel the pull to travel.'

'Travel? You have only just returned to us,' said Drenyk, his sentiment echoed by Pershivon.

'I know. I'm sorry, I cannot explain it, but I will walk to the Complex and think on it for a time.'

'We will come with you. Pershivon and I have something to tell you, so now is a good opportunity.'

Menkh looked at them enquiringly.

'Let us go together then. You have me intrigued.'

Horven waved them farewell, saying, 'I will leave you to your musings. Anyway, I have a Council meeting to attend. Shall we meet for dinner?

'An excellent suggestion, Councillor Var. We will see you later.'

Menkh, Drenyk and Pershivon made their way over several bridges, accompanied by the sound of water rushing below them. They passed between the twin statues of Menath, where Menkh paused awhile musing on the battle and Menath's role in it. Finally crossing over the causeway bridge, bathed in the mist from the maelstrom of merging waters below, the three made their way to the rooms Menkh occupied within the Complex.

Once comfortably seated, Drenyk and Pershivon spoke of their desire to take the ImXin and explore the lands far to the North, lands unknown to any that now lived. Menkh nodded and smiled at their enthusiasm as they sought his blessing.

'Go, my children. You have my blessing, but on one condition which I hope you will indulge me.'

'Of course Father,' Pershivon replied.

You must take a tetran escort with you. It would allay any concerns I have as you enter unknown lands.'

'Horven Var has already set the same caveat,' said Drenyk.

'We hope you don't mind Father, but we have already sought Council approval for this expedition. Receiving your blessing, however, is important to us.'

Again, Menkh nodded and smiled.

'You are both grown and in charge of your own destinies. I wish you well in your endeavours and look forward to hearing of your adventures in time to come. So; tell me of your plans and your hopes for your expedition.'

The rest of the evening passed in deep conversation about the forthcoming trip and Menkh was pleasantly surprised at the level of planning and organisation that had been done.

Several dak'chaal later and following Fendrax's departure, Menkh too stood in farewell as the ImXin rose silently into the air with Drenyk at the controls. He and Pershivon waved as the craft sped off.

Horven looked at Menkh.

'Part of me wants to travel with them.'

'Me also Horven Var, but this is their time. How fortunate we are that all this is possible.'

Horven nodded. 'I feel the need for a beaker of clshmik. Will you join me?'

Menkh smiled. 'I believe I will.'

ooooOooooo

Some days later, after overcoming the effects of a sizable hangover, Menkh stood on a balcony high in the Complex and looked out over the city. Without informing anyone of his intentions, and for reasons that he could not explain even to himself (though doubtless Varnahrin already knew), Menkh's thoughts crystallised. Focussing his will he ascended the Threadway and disappeared.

It seemed to him an age had passed since he had first experienced the wonder of travelling along the lines of energy. While his ability to travel could have had him at his intended destination in moments, his chosen speed allowed him to linger over sights which still left him in awe. Observing as majestic planets, great multicoloured clouds of gas and debris where emerging new planets that might one day develop life, and other celestial bodies flew past him, he felt totally renewed. It was a balm to his soul and a new and sharper awareness of the Cosmos took shape in his mind.

At ease, he reached his destination: a planetary system remote from Tarvuli consisting of several worlds, two of which were home to flourishing civilisations, yet it was another world he knew to be the true focus of his compulsion.

As he drew closer, he saw that its lands were fertile and verdant yet seemingly uninhabited by intelligent life. Smaller than Tarvuli, from far above he observed its many different features. Unlike the violet-coloured atmosphere of Tarvuli, this world's atmosphere was a vivid blue. Great mountain ranges dominated its surface, abundant streams of water flowed in mighty rivers and plunged in great waterfalls to form lakes or to flow into vast oceans teeming with aquatic life. Forests of towering trees shrouded huge areas of land.

As he descended through its atmosphere, he spied ancient ruins; great pyramids of stone poked above a dense jungle canopy in many places, their sides choked with vines and other plants. Everywhere, vividly coloured birds filled the air and all kinds of animal life thrived in what was clearly a rich and fertile land. Strangely to his mind, given the environment of the planet, of living people there were none, despite evidence that some race of beings had once populated this place.

He passed over a clearing which seemed to beckon to him and so he gravitated to earth and stood upon the ground. A field of strange blue flowers grew everywhere, their long stems covered in sharp thorns which formed a contrast to the delicate beauty of the blooms which reached up towards the warm light of a single sun, giving off a heady perfume that wafted through the air from tubular petals. Red, multi-winged insects darted in and out of the flowers, their wings making a buzzing sound clearly audible in that open space.

At first Menkh could discern no reason as to why the jungle did not encroach on the place where he stood. Several paces away in all directions save one, a dense jungle of trees and vines grew and it was only after he moved forward that he realised that the ground he stood on was not earth at all, but stone. Further investigation showed that only a thin layer of soil covered great flagstones which had apparently prevented the jungle from covering the area, other than for these flowers which obviously thrived in this artificial environment.

Immediately ahead of him lay an opening in the trees. He guessed the same flagstones which paved the area on which he stood, were also the cause of the gap. Although he had been drawn to this place from above, it was impossible to tell if the opening led anywhere, as the density of the trees blocked out most of the light and hid any potential pathway from view.

Stepping forward he waded through the blue flowers, avoiding as far as possible trampling their stems and warding off the insects that rose in protest at his disturbance. Reaching the edge of the clearing where he now could clearly discern the beginning of a pathway, he peered into the gloom of the forest. His Adept's eyes adjusted to the scarcity of ambient light and piercing the shadows he saw that it led onwards. Here, the flagstones were covered by a detritus of fallen branches, leaves and other matter, but Menkh could sense no danger, only a feeling of great age. Where the surface of the flagstones was visible, he could make out vague geometric shapes and patterns along with traces of colour, faded yellows and purples, the last vestiges of what must once have been a brightly coloured and highly decorated pathway.

He walked on. Under the forest canopy, only faint light penetrated. There was little noise of any kind save for the occasional call of a bird that could be heard but not seen and tree limbs moving above his head to a wind that made no impression at ground level. While time was very difficult to measure in this dark place, Menkh felt he had been walking for some time when he came to an abrupt stop. The perceptions of a bonded Adept were not those of any ordinary being and he sensed danger close by. He had no sooner halted than he heard a low-pitched popping sound. It was loud enough to indicate that whatever was making it was large and the effect of the sound was one of complete menace.

Drawing upon his will, a blue protective aura then surrounded Menkh and he vainly wished he still had his staff, or had Crixac to speak to in that dark and eerie place. No sooner had he shielded himself than a huge shape dropped down from an overhanging branch, effectively blocking his passage forward.

Other than four greenly glowing points, which were most likely its eyes, the rest of its body could not clearly be seen as it blended into the gloom. That it was a predator of some kind Menkh felt certain, but without waiting for the expected attack he lifted both hands and, concentrating his mind, sent a stinging bolt of force at the creature. In the light of the energy before the bolt struck, he could clearly see a long and sinuous body covered in scaly skin from which protruded barb-like projections. Two large forearms culminated in sharp talons and above all, was a skull like head, its four glowing eyes set above a maw full of many large and serrated teeth.

As the bolt struck the creature it howled in shock and pain. Having experienced nothing like it, and judging in its primitive mind that here was a creature it wanted nothing to do with, the beast leapt up with sinuous grace and disappeared back into the gloom of the canopy above. Menkh peered for a few moments into the trees but, even with his enhanced vision, could not see or hear anything of the erstwhile predator.

Maintaining his protective aura, he continued his journey along the pathway. No further incidents occurred other than a gradually increasing sense of isolation and a feeling that he was hopelessly lost. Still, he continued on, until all sense of time deserted him. Abruptly the path came to an end. Here great tree trunks blocked his forward passage and dense undergrowth of some spiky plants reached up head-high, obviously adapted to growth in the deep gloom and filling any possible openings between them.

Menkh stopped a few paces from the barrier in some confusion, however it was not soon enough as the ground under his feet suddenly fell away and he slid down unceremoniously on a slippery carpet of leaf matter before sprawling on his face some distance from where he initially fell. Rolling onto his back Menkh gave in to embarrassed laughter even though the was completely alone. His thoughts considered what Tishan might have said at his predicament, no doubt supplemented by Crixac's pointed observations about lack of due care and attention. His laughter was a sound unheard in that place for untold years, hardly carrying at all in that deserted place.

Climbing to his feet, reflecting that his dignity would have been in tatters had there been anyone present to witness his accident, he now saw that he stood upon a stairway, so covered by plant matter that it was undetectable even to his eyes, which led steadily downwards. There was something else there too, poking out from the leaf litter. At first, he thought they were merely sticks among the debris, however, it was the discovery of a skull alongside them that set him back, and he peered closely at it.

Large and elongated in shape, it had wide holes where its nose might have sat, much bigger than that of a Graaven, and sizeable teeth which projected from a strong jawline. Fragments of material could also be seen, although now mostly rotted away in the time the body had lain there. Menkh pondered how the body had come to be here and what errand the creature had been sent upon. Perhaps they had been dragged here by some beast, for many of the bones were scattered around in the leaf litter.

Picking up a serviceable branch that lay on the ground close by, Menkh used it to carefully probe the drifts of dead leaves, but finding nothing else of interest, he pondered the answers to a puzzle he knew would never be forthcoming. Cautiously, he continued to make his way downwards, entering a tunnel whose features he could barely make out in the gloom, occasionally slipping on rotting vegetation which gradually lessened as he descended. His eyes adjusted to a darkness even deeper than the murk of the pathway above and he eventually reached level ground where he halted for a moment. Against his skin he felt the slightest sensation of moving air and he again stepped out. In his right hand he still held the branch, it gave him a surprising degree of comfort in place of his lost staff, even resembling it in size and shape.

The air movement increased and he saw, far ahead, a tiny pinprick of light that at first, he dismissed as an optical illusion. Instinctively however, he increased his pace and the light grew greater with each step. The walls of the tunnel he was progressing through became clearly discernible. High above his head he saw they were made of individual blocks of a stone-like material that fitted seamlessly together. The walls on either side and the floor beneath his feet, were covered in the same geometric designs and symbols he had glimpsed earlier, but whether there purely as decoration or full of meaning lost in the echoes of time, he could only guess.

Finally, he emerged from the confines of the tunnel into a large, open circular space filled with light. Whether it was the act of stepping into warmth and light or some other quality of the space he now entered, his spirits lifted and he felt refreshed and re-energised.

Around the circumference of that space, six tall pillars of crystal refracted the light in a myriad of colours which in turn reflected off the clear waters of a tiny stream which bubbled from the ground and flowed along a crafted stone trough and on into a large pool.

Verdant sedges and other grasses grew around it and an overflow of water kept the ground moist. Small froglike creatures of a startling green colour, darted in and out of the plants, their calls a whirring sound that added to, rather than diminishing, the serenity of that magical place.

Menkh closed his eyes and took a deep breath. Upon opening them he spied a stone bench covered in something like moss; he sat down upon it in quiet reflection. He had not felt such peace for what seemed a lifetime. As he looked around, soaking in the beauty of his surroundings, he wondered what had drawn him here; he now saw that a plain stone cup, unnoticed before, stood upon a small pedestal next to the pool of water, within easy reach of where he sat.

It was a natural reaction to pick it up, rinse it in the clear water, fill it, and take a deep draught. It was like no water he had ever tasted. Sweet and refreshing, yet there was something else which lingered on the palate. Replacing the cup and still seated on the bench his gaze turned once again to his surroundings.

Something had changed. Before, when he had observed the crystal pillars their faceted surface had refracted the light. Now he could see that deep within five of the pillars, shapes moved and shifted. Rather than refracting light, they seemed instead to absorb and magnify it. Menkh felt no alarm or sense of danger, and simply watched in growing fascination as the swirling shapes inside the pillars gradually condensed. Abruptly they coalesced into humanoid figures and emerged from the pillars into the light. Again, Menkh felt no alarm at this strange occurrence; in some deep corner of his mind he knew he'd expected something like this would happen.

The figures were unlike any people he had seen before; their facial features seem to shift and change, making it difficult to tell what they looked like. They were clad in translucent, garments which flowed with a motion akin to the waters of the little stream, effectively obscuring their bodies from any closer inspection.

Several voices spoke in harmony within his mind, their sound was musical and not vastly different in tonality to the froglike creatures which lived in that place.

<Greetings to you, Menkh ab Dur. It is an age since anyone was drawn to this place.>

Menkh shook his head in wonder.

<How is it that you know my name?>

<We knew who you were the moment you emerged from the entranceway. You cannot be host to our kind without your mind and spirit becoming accessible to us.>

<You mean that you are symbiotes? Is this the birthplace of Crixac?>

<We see that your bond was very deep. We grieve with you in his loss. But you have heard the call and come to receive his gift to you.>

<Gift? I am sorry, I don't understand. I miss his presence every day but I have no knowledge of any gift.>

Laughter echoed in his mind.

<The compulsion that drew you here is part of it. Within you Crixac left a tiny fragment of himself, a seed if you will. But that seed cannot be activated without journeying here. It cannot form within you without your willing acceptance.>

Menkh spoke aloud with joy. 'You mean that Crixac will return?!'

<Yes and no. If you allow Crixac's gift to energise then it will have all of his memories and experiences. In effect it will be a clone of Crixac, though it will call itself by another name. You formed your bond in a time of mutual need when solemn promises were exchanged. Crixac could not leave you bereft. Now, that which may emerge also has need of you, if you will allow it. Together, as you once did with Crixac, you will grow strong.>

Menkh's thoughts sobered. He thought of the alternatives and that he could deny the 'gift' that had been left him. But how could he do that?

Even if the reality of the situation was ultimately one that he could not live with, he could always seek out an alternative host for the replacement. Crixac had done this in the extremity of the situation at the time and in the knowledge that Menkh could not, would not refuse.

Menkh came to a decision.

<I will not refuse this gift of Crixac's. Tell me what I must do.>

<Stand, Menkh ab Dur. Next to the pool of water there is a plinth. Step up on to it and open your mind fully to us. You will feel a sense of euphoria for a brief moment followed by a feeling of dizziness which will quickly pass. You will feel as if you are in a waking dream. When you emerge from that state and fully regain your senses, our physical presence will be gone from here. Fare you well Menkh ab Dur, we will not meet again.>

<Wait, please wait! Will you not tell me something about yourselves? What this place is and how you came to be here?>

The voices spoke among themselves for a moment in a language that even Menkh with his abilities could not fathom. Then a single voice responded.

<When the great transformation came upon our people, six of us fled in fear to this place which was sacred to us. We did not then understand the transformation. In desperation we believed the waters that flow here might save us from a terrible end and we felt a powerful compulsion to travel here. We had seen what happened to others of our race who fell ill and what happened when their physical bodies died. Only five of us made it. Pokara Ne Takasha, the chief of our band and who held the greatest power, fell in terrible agony. In the final extremity he resisted the change and so died.

At the last, reaching here in our final extremity, we drank of the waters and as the transformation came upon us our new forms were drawn into the pillars you see. They nourish and sustain us, as we nourish and sustain this place that we call Harama Te Polia, the Place of Renewal. One day a new people will arise from here and they will seek us out. We have knowledge and wisdom to share and await that day with longing.>

<So, it was you who drew me here?>

<In the moments before Crixac sacrificed himself his thoughts reached us. We knew that you would make your way to us. As you carry the seed of Crixac, the compulsion to come here is indefinable yet irresistible.>

Menkh nodded in response, a thousand further questions burned in his mind.

<Our time with you is brief, Menkh ab Dur. If you are determined to accept Crixac's gift the time is now.>

<Then I thank you my friends and I wish that your waiting will soon be over.>

<Now that you have restored Balance, Menkh ab Dur, we feel the time approaches. It is we who thank you. The Balance is All.>

Standing quietly and leaning the branch he had found against the bench, Menkh made his way to the plinth which projected a little above the ground. In the middle of the plinth, a circle of multi coloured stones with a flat top protruded and it seemed natural to stand upon it. Composing his thoughts and clearing his mind, he closed his eyes and waited, somewhat nervously it had to be said, in anticipation of what was to come.

Around him the light from the pillars increased tenfold so that even with his eyes closed he could yet see the brightness that surrounded him. He felt bathed and drenched in light. A tingling sensation suddenly manifested from his feet to the top of his head and suffused him with a feeling of joy; he felt as if he floated in a vast ocean of warm water that drew him into a dream where he was released from all cares. His thoughts passed away into nothingness.

Slowly his consciousness returned, his thinking a little confused. Somewhat dizzy, he sat once more on the bench beside the pool of water. Remembering the branch that lay propped against it, he now reached out and took hold of it once again and, despite his recent experience and nervous anticipation, his eyes were drawn to it.

<Strange,> he thought. <Now I look at it closely in this clean light it looks like no tree branch I have ever seen.>

He turned in response to a sound he thought came from behind, yet there was nothing to see. The pillars once again refracted the light, they had ceased to swirl with internal colour and no shapes turned within them. There was no evidence to suggest that they were anything other than columns of stone. No other sound could be heard but the song of the green frogs which still reverberated around him, and the clearing in which he sat was empty of any other life. His brow crinkled in thought and turning back he continued his inspection of the branch he had picked up, his thoughts still somewhat hazy.

Moments later his mind snapped out of introspective observation in response to a whispered sound that came from within, not without. Closing his eyes Menkh formed words in his mind.

<*Crixac?* Is that you?>

The sibilant whisper grew in volume and slowly a clear voice spoke.

<Greetings, Menkh ab Dur and thank you for the gift of life. I am Crixon. He that went before, knowing he would not return, left a spore from which I have grown. His memories are mine but I am not truly him.>

Menkh paused in profound consideration of Crixon's words. The newly awoken presence of Crixon brought him great comfort in that the memories of Crixac would be preserved but therein lay the kernel of a possible dilemma. It was not Crixac and the bond that had grown between them would have to be forged anew. If he did not reject Crixon.

<Yes. I understand your thoughts, Menkh ab Dur. Of course, you are right, I am not Crixac though he is my progenitor. You are free to reject me, but as with Crixac before, I would only ask that you allow time for me to find a new host. Having only just come into consciousness, the thought of my rapid demise is not one that I care to think about.>

<I understand. Let us make a pact then, Crixon. We will allow some time to acclimatise to each other and if, after that time has passed, I cannot accept your presence then we shall find a willing host. I would not suffer the spawn of Crixac, my friend, to perish,> said Menkh.

<Thank you Menkh. That is very fair. I too need some time to fully assimilate all of Crixac's memories stretching back as they do over millennia. My thoughts were somewhat scrambled after you activated me. I am not sure though if that is the right term.

<The word 'birth' hardly seems appropriate,> said Menkh.

Crixon laughed quietly.

<It is of no consequence, Menkh. Your willingness to undergo the rite has brought me into existence. I see that Crixac correctly predicted your reaction.>

<Yes. Even now your presence feels so much like Crixac's that it brings me great comfort.>

<I too share your sentiments. We will have much time to adjust to these new yet familiar feelings.>

Menkh felt overcome with emotion and sat once again on the stone bench. His mind was in a turmoil of thoughts that seemed to swirl around without focus. Pushing them to one side in an attempt to settle his mind, he engaged once more with the branch, holding it in both hands and gazing at it. Crixon, adjusting to his new awakening, also turned his attention to the object that drew Menkh's curiosity.

<I see your thoughts about this tree branch; you are puzzled over it. Have you reached any conclusions?>

<No Crixon. No conclusions as such. You can sense for yourself that it doesn't feel like wood. It is cool to the touch yet it is neither stone nor crystal, as was our previous staff. It has whorls and knobby protrusions akin to wood and the apex of it ends in these twig-like strands. It seems to have no weight at all and the texture of the surface feels more like bone.>

<Yes, I see what you mean. Also, it lacks a definitive colour, it seems more to absorb light. It is a most curious object. Might it have been part of some device or fashioned out of this material by unknown hands perhaps?>

<Hmm. Curious indeed. It lay near the body of one who did not reach this grove so I am of the view that he may very well have carried it, in which case if I am right, it would have some specific purpose, I think. Maybe religious, or something else. Shall we focus our wills upon it and see what other qualities it may have?>

<A good thought, but we will need to take it slowly. This is all very new to me and if we invest too much power or go too quickly it may have undesirable results.>

<Like blowing apart in our hands?> Menkh chuckled aloud. <Yes, you are quite right. Come then; a trickle of energy and let us see how it reacts.>

Focussing his will and aided by Crixon, Menkh channelled a small amount of power into the staff. Acutely aware that this may cause it to react violently, he did it with infinite slowness, until after some moments he paused.

<Do you sense anything?>

<Nothing at all> said Crixon. <It seems to have completely absorbed that energy without any unwelcome reaction. Shall we try a larger flow?>

In accord, Menkh increased the power without any untoward reaction from the staff other than a faint vibration.

<Whatever this material is and wherever it has come from, it is quite remarkable. Its reaction, or should I say lack of reaction, is completely different from the staff that Crixac passed on to me.>

<Yes. We should try to ascertain what it is. It must be from something on this planet. Perhaps if we scan from above, we might locate its source.>

Unconsciously nodding his head in agreement, Menkh left the clearing and the glowing rock formations circling it. While only a brief time had passed, he was rapidly acclimatising to the presence of Crixon; it was a remarkably satisfying feeling.

Their journey back to the first clearing seemed to take much less time and on reaching the area where he had originally descended, levitated upwards. They had not risen far above the canopy and into the light when Menkh and Crixon felt a strong pull being exerted by the staff, as both of them now thought of it.

Letting it dictate their movements they travelled rapidly away passing at great speed over the forest which stretched beneath them, as far as the eye could see. After some time, ruins appeared below them which were much more extensive in both size and scope than those Menkh had discerned earlier. Given the scale of what must have once been a huge city, the jungle here had failed to cover it completely. Great pyramid buildings of alien aspect reared upwards from the ground, which was paved in multi-coloured stone. Some of the buildings had partially fallen in, but many bore only the slightest damage when seen from above.

Finally, in the very centre of a great plaza, a tree of gargantuan size lifted bleached white limbs to the sky and soared above its surroundings.

Menkh set down and walked towards it.

CHAPTER SIXTEEN

s the rift closed behind her, Tishan was surrounded by an intense light. Before her eyes the shadowed menace that was Apocris was torn into shreds before dissipating into nothingness, its passing accompanied by a wail of terror and hatred that descended into total silence. For a few lingering moments, a flickering pool of blue energy merged with a similar pool of white light until that too drifted away like smoke in the wind, but unlike the shadow, their passing was tinged with a sense of triumph.

In the short time that Tishan observed this she was overcome by a terrible pressure that assaulted her senses and probed into her mind. Like the Enemy, she was now subject to irresistible forces, which threatened to tear her apart. She thought she could hear something, but the unrelenting pressure in her head prevented her from focussing, and then suddenly as if it had been but an imagined pain, the pressure vanished. Now, impenetrable darkness surrounded her and she felt as if she moved at tremendous speed. Merging with the sensation of movement, came an extreme coldness that pierced to the very core of her being. Even in the midst of these tumultuous events, a part of her mind aligned the feeling of cold with something like the passage through a gateway, yet the sensation of raw iciness and its duration seemed to stretch onward without let. Overcome at last by the chill and disorienting emptiness, she fell into darkness; her last coherent thought that death had finally claimed her.

Yet she was not dead.

As if emerging from the darkest depths of the ocean, her senses returned gradually to her and with consciousness, she found herself sitting in a garden whose beauty revived her in a way that nothing else could. A small waterfall fell with a tinkling sound splashed lightly into a pool surrounded by ferns and flowering plants that gave off a heady and delightful scent. Several trees gently waved long sinuous branches in a fitful breeze, providing a welcome shade from the warm sunlight.

She sat upon a comfortable chair at a small metal table, while around her brightly coloured small birds provided a melodious accompaniment to the sound of the waterfall. So peaceful was this place that it seemed an age had passed before Tishan began to wonder where she was and whether in fact she had travelled to the afterlife. Then she dismissed her thoughts, as any propensity to worry was impossible in this quiet place. She closed her eyes and took a deep breath of the pure air, feeling new energy flow into her.

'Yes, it is a truly wonderful place, Tishan Dar.'

The voice, which she recognised, caused her to open her eyes. Sitting opposite her on a chair she was sure had not been there a moment ago reposed the form of Thatras – albeit a much smaller version than she remembered.

'Thatras? Is that really you?'

'I see you still have the habit of stating the obvious,' Thatras observed drily, followed by the small trill of laughter that Tishan remembered.

'It is very good to see you, my dear child. I must say well done indeed, for without your considerable efforts and the sacrifice of Menath and Crixac, the shadow could never have been defeated.'

Tishan knew she should be feeling a range of emotions but the tranquillity of her surroundings allowed for no negative sentiment or even surprise, merely an acceptance of what had gone before. There was, however, a small sense of satisfaction in the accomplishment of her task.

'So, what happens now?' asked Tishan. 'I don't really understand where I am or what is to become of me. Strangely none of these considerations gives me any disquiet. I feel a kind of detached curiosity.'

'Yes. Well that really is in the nature of where we are, or you might say where we aren't, which is probably closer to the mark.'

Tishan's brow crinkled and she smiled.

'As ever, you speak in riddles Thatras.'

'I am sorry my dear. It is a very annoying Acclydian habit, I realise. This place, like the Hall of Gateways, is merely a construct to give you a frame of reference that you can understand. In part it is drawn from your memories, which is why you may feel some degree of familiarity with it. You see, your presence here poses rather a conundrum. In breaching the fabric of space and entering the nothingness that separates one universe from another, which of course you had to do in the circumstances, you broke one of the immutable laws; in doing so, your fate should have mirrored that of the Enemy. The fact is, in addition to being a bonded Adept something else completely unpredictable happened to you, and so the rules as we know them apply rather less in your situation.'

'Unpredictable? In what sense?'

'Unpredictable in that at the moment you entered the rift, the Rod of Klemish somehow transformed itself and melded with your physical body. Despite the terrible pressure that was being exerted upon you in that place you proved totally resistant to it.'

'So, I should have died but didn't?'

'That's what I just said dear. Do try and keep up.'

'Well, if I am not dead, am I actually alive?'

'Very good Tishan Dar, there you have it. You aren't actually dead, but nor are you actually alive. This is compounded by the fact that nothing can stay in the place beyond the rift and nor can you stay in this place. So, it is somewhat of an understatement to say that steps need to be taken in terms of what to do with you. As your transformation is unprecedented and has revealed a presence in this Universe previously completely undetected (which I can tell you borders on the impossible), I have been sent here to help you, to answer any questions you might have and in general provide you with a familiar and hopefully not unwelcome face.'

'I am very happy to see you Thatras and your presence here does help. Still, can't you just return me to my previous reality?'

'Well, no. That is part of the problem. You see, where you come from you are in fact dead. You could not return in your previous form even as a bonded Adept; that's another of the immutable laws. So, if you are to be sent back, it must be in a different form entirely, which strangely, nor do I believe coincidentally, your recent physical change may actually assist with. Of course, the mere fact of your insertion back into reality may itself disrupt the Balance. All in all, it is a very delicate matter.'

'Yes, I can see that. You mention a different form? Can you be more precise?'

'That is going to depend on a number of factors.'

'Such as?'

'Well, your willingness to do this, for a start. You can be coerced of course, but that is a totally undesirable outcome and may ultimately lead to a number of very serious consequences. Then again there is a time factor. You cannot re-enter your reality at the same moment as you left it for reasons that would take a lifetime to explain to you. So, your insertion must occur at a time and place that will cause the least disruption possible.'

'Somewhere in the distant future?' asked Tishan.

'No Tishan Dar. The future is yet to be written. No, your insertion must be in the distant past.'

Tishan's brow wrinkled in thought. 'But I thought that travel in time was another immutable law?'

'Indeed it is child. However, the Intelligence can manipulate it – and has done so before on extremely rare occasions and then only when the risk of imbalance was predictably low.'

Tishan shook her head. 'I cannot even begin to grasp the complexity of what you are saying. Let us take it that I fully accept what you are telling me. If I am inserted back into reality, what happens to me as I am now: my thoughts, memories, experiences? Will the essence of who I am be lost?'

'I will not mislead you, Tishan. You will experience profound changes, but the core essence of who you are remains. It is these things that will help shape and determine what you will become.'

Tishan struggled to rationalise what she was being told and closed her eyes in an effort to control her emotions.

Thatras's voice changed in timbre, and now resonated with warmth and compassion.

'The Intelligence will not abandon you, Tishan Dar. That which is being offered to you is unique. The only alternative is death. The fact that there is an option before you is not only in recognition of all that you have done, but also because there is something else beyond my powers of comprehension that the Intelligence foresees. I am empowered to tell you that there will come a future time when you will be reunited with all you hold dear. That which you will become will endure throughout the ages, untroubled by grief or regret. A new path will be set for you. All that you have achieved as Tishan Dar will not be lost. Your passing will be mourned by your people, but your name will never be forgotten.'

Tishan's eyes stayed closed and silent tears rolled down her cheeks. Thatras did not speak any further, but allowed her the time to reconcile her thoughts with the enormity of the decision before her.

'I had thought myself dead. As a Graaven warrior you come to expect death in battle. When I took the action I did, I knew it was the right thing to do, really the only thing to do; I was reconciled to it and buried any regrets deep inside. Here, now, I do not wish to die.'

Tishan took a mental deep breath. 'I will trust in the Intelligence and in the great Balance. I will take on a new form, whatever it may be, and I will follow the path laid down for me in the hope that one day in time to come, I will be reunited with my true self in whatever way.'

Tishan opened her eyes to find that Thatras now stood before her and was bowing deeply to her.

'Tishan Dar, there are no words in any language spoken or thought that could convey to you my profound respect and gratitude. I have lived for millennia and I will tell you now that my existence has been blessed by meeting you. This Universe is a better place for having you in it, in whatever aspect. You will not be disappointed in the form that will be chosen for you. May the Intelligence watch over you for ever. The Balance is All.'

Before Tishan's eyes that which was Thatras melted away and the construct that had held her, vanished. A warmth spread through her body and her perception of that which surrounded her began to change; her consciousness expanded even as the memories of what she had been diminished, fading to the background and no longer holding the importance they once did. She felt her body altering, her arms and legs transforming into multiple

branches while the opaque whiteness of her Adept form intensified and became luminescent.

Finally cocooned in an aura of intense light that surrounded
her like the shell of an egg, Tishan felt herself catapulted outward
into space. Myriad stars flickered past her in a blur until she saw in
her mind's eye a planet approaching at tremendous speed that she
knew was to be her new home.

ooooOoooo

They were a primitive people, few in number and on the edge of
extinction. Hunter-gatherers, for whom most of their lives was a
constant battle against the elements and the unknown perils of
wild beasts and malevolent spirits that ruled their world.

Several family groups were gathered around small fires to eat
the bare amount of food they had been able to scavenge that day.
Their communication was limited: verbal gestures, facial expressions and some distinct sounds were sufficient for their purpose,
but they were intelligent and quick to learn and might, in time,
grow and develop into much more but only if they could somehow
survive. Deep inside their bodies, dormant and unknown to them,
they carried the seed of something else, a mutation which might
come into being, given the right circumstances. Only time would
tell.

As one, they looked upward in sudden fear. The darkness of
the sky was illuminated like the brilliance of stars, lit up in an alien
glow of intense white light. A sound like the roaring of the sea in
a storm reached their ears, followed by a shaking of the earth beneath their feet that left them calling out in fear. Finally, a pulse of
light so bright that it dazzled their eyes, flared briefly and then, in
a matter of moments died away to nothing and all became still
again.

The tribe exchange frightened looks. Females gathered up their
infants, others grabbed weapons. A large male and female, the

dominant pair, looked at the other members of the group. Nodding their heads in accord and gesturing to indicate that the group should stay, the pair set off to investigate. Wary of the creatures that prowled the night, they passed silently, barely disturbing the ground they traversed. Occasionally they stopped in perfect stillness to sniff the air, their sensitive nostrils alert to the scent of predators.

Finally, they came to an area of flat land covered in a tall grass which gave off a susurrating sound in the slight breeze. Ahead of them, a strange white glow could be discerned. Reaching an incline they cautiously scaled it, then dropped flat to furtively peer over the top. What they saw left them in amazement and wonder. There before them emerging from the ground, growing and spreading like a tree of huge proportions they saw a luminescent multi-limbed structure reaching up towards the sky. To the creatures watching in intense amazement, it was godlike and beautiful. It gave off a palpable aura of power, neither threatening nor frightening, which called to them. In unspoken accord they stood and walked towards it until they stood beneath its spreading limbs. It then spoke to them within their minds and in so doing, wrought profound changes. Unbidden, all the others of the tribe had followed and they too stood in the radiance of the Presence and bathed in its light.

Millennia passed.

The people of the tribe had flourished and grown. In communion with the deity they worshipped, they had developed knowledge and skills over the ages. Their cities spread across the world, their culture at one with their planet, and they basked in the benevolent radiance of the Presence. They mined precious ores and materials to beautify their buildings and laid offerings of precious goods beneath the spreading branches of the Great Tree. With the invention of new technologies, their kind spread to other worlds and made contact with other Races; the people exulted.

One day, a group of miners uncovered a hidden stream of milk-white fluid that gave off an irresistible smell of earth and richness. The liquid so resembled the luminosity of the Presence that they thought of it as a gift and drank of it. They carried some in flasks and gave it to others of their kind, not suspecting it carried a pathogen that would have far reaching consequences, a trigger to the dormant mutation that lay in each of them. Those who had partaken of the milky fluid fell into a terrible fever that ravaged their bodies and wrought a terrible transformation. As their bodies died, so new creatures were formed. Intelligent and parasitic, these new symbiotes could not live without a host and in desperation they invaded the bodies of others, enslaving them until in madness the host died, often along with their parasitic invader. Thus the cycle repeated itself, spreading beyond the confines of their planet. The contagion took a terrible toll on the people until, on their home world, they ceased to exist.

Slowly the surviving symbiotes learned to harness their power until finally a balance was achieved and their malignancy passed. They mourned those who had died so terribly, their guilt changing them in thought and manner. But their numbers too had diminished and those that were left journeyed out across the universe with their hosts, anxious to make amends for what they had done.

Their once great cities fell into ruin as the centuries passed by. Now, that which the People had worshipped as the Presence, was alone. No one visited the world that had once hosted their civilisation, fear of the parasitic contagion being documented and firmly rooted in the minds of those who might once have travelled there.

But the Presence endured in hope and waited for that which had been promised.

CHAPTER SEVENTEEN

As Menkh and Crixon floated above the gigantic tree the pull from the staff abruptly ceased and a feeling of warmth spread through it, seemingly in reaction to the towering structure below.

Descending rapidly to the ground Menkh stood and looked up in awe. The tree – if such it was – stirred strangely profound feelings inside him. He couldn't tell if it was a naturally occurring growth or something more sinister like the Tree of Tangoreth. Up close however, it now appeared that its life force was diminished; perhaps it was dying, as it lacked the vibrancy he had expected to find, given the staff's reaction.

<It feels nothing like the Tree of Tangoreth, Menkh. I cannot feel any sense of evil but this is very similar in some ways to that place where Crixac was imprisoned. It may resemble a tree, but it is not. It looks dead and yet I can feel a thread of energy flowing out of it, and something else, something I cannot quite grasp.>

Crixon paused in thought.

< It seems clear that our original branch came from this thing, but seeing there is no debris of any kind on the ground at its base, I wonder how the branch came to be where you found it?>

<Perhaps we shall never know, though my suspicion is fixed that it was held by the sixth member of the group who died trying to reach their sacred place. I really do think that it is less a branch and more a staff, which is a wonder all by itself. Crixon, I feel a powerful urge to place a hand on this thing, it is as if it calls to me in some way. Can you sense any danger in doing so?>

<No. I sense the same feeling. There is almost a feeling of longing, of suppressed emotion, though how that can be I cannot begin to comprehend.>

<Well then. Let us do it, it seems somehow right.>

Menkh walked forward until he stood under its mighty branches. Not without some trepidation and still clutching the staff in one hand, he placed the other on the smooth surface of the trunk. Immediately he felt a shift in reality and his head spun. Suddenly all around, a clamour of voices could be heard. Turning, he saw that the plaza was no longer empty. Many stalls selling produce of all kinds were scattered about and tall people with silvery skin and clad in brightly coloured garments of shimmering material, bartered for goods. Their faces were long, with angular eyes set above a prominent nose and protuberant lips. Without exception, some part of their garb sported multi-coloured feathers. Whether as a part of long cloaks or tall headdresses of fantastical design, they varied in complexity. Some people were almost completely covered by feathers and Menkh wondered if this was a sign of wealth or perhaps social status.

The aspect was one of energy and vitality, but insubstantial, and Menkh realised that they were watching an image of something that had long passed into history. Suddenly a sound like trumpets rent the air. All talk stopped and the people stood quietly. At first obscured by the vast trunk of the tree, a group of six individuals now appeared. They were uniformly covered by exquisite cloaks of red, blue and yellow feathers. Ornate headdresses fashioned from the skulls of some large birdlike creature covered their heads.

The long-fingered hands of all but the one who walked in their centre clutched objects which gave off a bell-like sound when they were lightly struck. Menkh's eyes were rivetted on the figure in the centre. Much taller than all the others, he or she bore the staff Menkh now held in his hands, or one very much like it. As they passed, the people in the market raised their hands in the air and bowed, but other than the bell like tones that rang out in the air, the people made no sound at all.

<Priests of some kind, do we think?> queried Menkh.

<Or perhaps the rulers of this city – or even both. The memories of Crixac contain no clue at all as to the existence of these people. I can provide no explanation, Menkh.>

They had no further moment to ponder this because the scene disappeared. The air shimmered and resolved. The picture now was grim. Dozens of bodies lay upon the ground, twisted grotesquely and bearing terrible lesions on their skin. The six priest-like figures they had observed earlier, moved past them, their distress obvious, the tall figure who led them clutching the staff, tottered drunkenly, clearly in a much worse state than were the others. Bereft of feathers and head dress, its silver skin was also covered in the black growths. It was impossible to tell if it was male or female, or if it had any sex at all. Reaching an abandoned gold-coloured object that, albeit smaller in size, resembled an ImXin such as the Graavens themselves had discovered in Ta'Morin, it fell upon it in exhaustion, followed by the rest of the group. Within moments, the golden object rose into the air carrying the six and sped away from the plaza bearing its forlorn passengers. Menkh had a good idea where they were headed.

<I begin to understand what we are seeing, Crixon. We wondered about the origins of the staff and here we are being shown.>

<Yes, to a degree, but it raises more questions than answers. Who are these people? Was this terrible affliction a natural contagion or one which they themselves manufactured? Are these

beings my distant ancestors and if so, as would seem highly likely, why can I find no clue in Crixac's memories?>

<There are some things we may never know for certain, Crixon, but in any event our suffering friends have left the plaza so I'm not sure if we will see....>

Menkh did not complete his thoughts as the scene shimmered once again, bringing with it a feeling of disorientation not unlike standing upon the Eye of Malavak. Now though, even as the tree stood motionless alongside them, they peered into the clearing where the pathway led to the standing stones. It took some time to realise it was the same place they had been, as the jungle was well clear of the area. Where Menkh had traversed in the darkness of a veritable tunnel covered over by encroaching trees, here they could clearly see a wide paved area open to the light. A broad pathway of many coloured stones led to the grotto via a covered walkway and ramp. In every respect the place where the stones stood was unchanged and the waters of the small stream flowed placidly into the pool.

No sooner had they observed these things than the figures they had so recently seen in the city staggered into view. Falling heavily, the tall figure dropped the staff on the ramp and crawled desperately on hands and knees in a vain effort to reach the dell before finally collapsing motionless. The five others, now also in final extremity, made it into the dell. Frantically they filled the stone cup and each drank of the water before dropping to the ground. Their bodies seemed to dissolve into nothingness, but at the same time there arose from each body a blue haze of light, fine as smoke. These plumes paused momentarily, then abruptly sped away, each entering one of the standing stones that circled the dell. As they did so the stones glowed faintly. Then all was quiet.

Both Menkh and Crixon were too amazed to form a coherent thought until at last Menkh spoke aloud.

<I think we have seen the origin of your species, Crixon.>

<There is no question of it, Menkh. Crixac has no memory or knowledge of these happenings. As to the origins of these people, this remains shrouded in mystery. It does explain how the staff came to be there. That the staff is a branch of our tree-friend is inescapable, but what its significance is I cannot say.>

Menkh nodded in agreement, his mind racing. Once again, the lifelike image flowed before their eyes until they stood in the ruined plaza, which was once again bereft of all life.

<Obviously there were reasons for coming here other than awakening you, Crixon. I feel the hand of the Intelligence at work once again. Discovery of the staff was no accident or coincidence though it has lain undisturbed for untold sem'chaal.>

<I agree. Many things lie unexplained. I wonder if there are other trees like our friend here, and other locations like the one we were drawn to when we arrived.>

<We can spare some time to do a sweep over the surface before we depart,> said Menkh. <Perhaps in some future time we may return and explore further but for now it would seem we have achieved our purpose.>

<You will take the staff?> Crixon queried.

<If the tree permits.>

Unselfconsciously, Menkh lay his left hand upon it and spoke:

<I believe the staff is a gift but I do not wish to depart without some sign of your blessing. I am no thief.>

In response, Menkh felt a tiny yet powerful thread of energy flow along his arm and into his body. With it came an inexplicable feeling of euphoria. He felt his consciousness shift as if he stood somewhere else, and could sense another presence that stood with him. Without conscious volition he transformed, setting aside his Adept form and assuming his Graaven body. Then before his unbelieving gaze Tishan Dar coalesced before him and looked deep into his eyes.

Menkh was utterly incapable of rational speech or thought. Tears flowed down his face mirrored by those of Tishan Dar and with one accord they stepped into each other's arms and simply held each to the other in an embrace that neither wished to end.

Eventually Menkh choked out some words, whispering into Tishan's ears, 'How is this possible? Is it a dream? My dearest one, how can it be you?'

'That is a story very long in the telling. I thought that this moment would never come. But I had faith in the Intelligence and I am reunited with you once more.'

Menkh stepped back a little from Tishan, his face suffused with joy. 'Then you may return with me? We can be together?'

Tishan smiled, though there was a hint of sadness in that look and Menkh felt his happiness diminish; there was something else to be told.

'Yes. I can be with you and we can leave together.' Menkh was about to speak but Tishan placed a finger on his lips.

'I can be with you Menkh but only in the form of the staff you carry. I cannot stand alongside you as Tishan Dar, as I once did. I am not sure that you would want that.'

'Not sure? Tishan Dar. I would have you at my side in any form. Our reunion is a miracle. You can read my mind so you must know the joy I feel that you are alive.'

Tishan smiled at him, her face reflecting his complete happiness.

'As we stand here together, we are both slightly phased out of reality, so we can meet and talk like this, but when we step back into phase I will be present as the staff. You will know this, but your communication with me will be limited. It will be like it was when you had Crixac's staff and little did you know then that the spirit of Menath was contained inside it.'

Menkh nodded his head.

'I understand, Tishan. The knowledge that you are nearby will ever be a comfort to me. It is a day of wonders indeed. To have you back in my life when I thought you dead and then to have Crixon….' Menkh could not form his words coherently.

'Yes. I detected his presence. I am so pleased. But Menkh, Crixon will have no knowledge of me. As we entered this other reality his presence remained outside of it. You will have to explain this to him.'

Menkh renewed his embrace. 'That will be an interesting discussion. But he can read my thoughts anyway so he will know the circumstances.'

Tishan pressed her forehead against Menkh's and they clung together in an enduring embrace, oblivious of the time, but savouring their contact and the wonder of their reunion.

At last they drew apart.

'I look forward to the time we spend together, there is so much to discuss. So much I want to tell you,' said Menkh.

'Then it is truly time to depart. I will not be sorry to leave this place at last, though part of me will forever remain here.'

'Then we shall go. For once I will get to surprise Varnahrin!'

'A moment to look forward to indeed, my Heart.'

With those words Menkh's surroundings flickered, his Adept form reasserted itself and he came back into reality.

<Well, if that wasn't an unqualified blessing, I am a parasite!>

Crixon's words echoed in Menkh's mind. It was so like a wry observation Crixac would have made, that Menkh laughed out loud. His words were apt even though he had no idea of what had passed between Menkh and Tishan. The potency of the staff in his hands, which had been welcome before, now increased tenfold. Whatever the future held, he would not be alone to face it and he felt reenergised and renewed in the most profound way

<Well my friend, you are a most welcome parasite! Come let us leave this place. I feel the need to return and visit the Balance

Point and see how our friends there are faring, I have yet to thank them for their involvement in the battle with the Enemy. As we travel, I have some news to give you. You should prepare yourself for a surprise. This day is one that I will never forget!>

ooooOooooo

Crixon listened amazed as Menkh recounted the events that had occurred. Even knowing what Menkh now told him, he was then completely unable to communicate with Tishan despite his efforts at probing the staff. Without the knowledge that Menkh had provided and his access to Menkh's thoughts, he would have doubted the occurrence at all. On reflection, the inability to sense any presence other than the physical reality of the staff itself, precisely mirrored Menath's presence in Crixac's staff until the moment she had revealed herself. It appeared the material their new staff was made from differed from the other's crystalline substance, yet neither Menkh or Crixon knew how that difference might manifest in time to come.

There was much to ponder, and knowledge of the two staffs merely led to a whole new series of questions, not least of which were the circumstances –thousands of years in the making – that had led to the awakening of Crixon as well as the reunion of Menkh and Tishan, albeit in a strange new form. The circumstances behind this were such that the mind shied away from them.

Their journey to the Balance Point had been deliberately slower than it might have been, to allow them the opportunity to talk. Merely channelling their will toward their destination took them unfailingly in the right direction, no matter where it was located in space.

At length they approached a star system where a huge gas giant and several moons orbited a distant sun. After the defeat of the Enemy, the Adepts had relocated the Balance Point, choosing one of its several moons as their new home. As Menkh and Crixon descended, they were able to see that the selected moon boasted an atmosphere where ice-covered mountains reared up above a vast ocean of water.

In the moments before they arrived Crixon spoke into Menkh's mind:

<For reasons that are unclear to me at this time friend Menkh, I believe you should say nothing about the presence of Tishan within the staff we carry. In fact, I am suspicious that if nothing is said then the presence of the staff will be overlooked unless attention is drawn to it. There is something about its construct that seems to deflect any notice being paid to it. I think there is a purpose behind that and so I would suggest, that at least for now, we keep it to ourselves. If you agree?>

<You have arrived at your conclusion quicker than I, but I share your thoughts, Crixon. Agreed. We shall say nothing for now and will see if it is as you surmise.>

There was no further time to talk on these matters or even to evaluate their location in terms of the presence of life in the waters below, before they stood once more upon the Eye of Malavak inside the Balance Point itself.

Standing alone and waiting for them was T'klath who greeted Menkh warmly.

'Welcome Menkh ab Dur, welcome indeed. The importance of your victory over the Enemy cannot be put into words, but all of us here rejoice.'

'It was not my victory alone, T'klath. Varnahrin drew on every vestige of power possible and even then, along with the self-sacrifice of Crixac and Tishan, it was your intervention here that gave us the final triumph.'

T'klath nodded and switched to mind-speech to better express his feeling.

<You have our deepest condolences, Menkh. The loss of Tishan and Crixac must have been overwhelming for you. But. Do I detect another presence here with us?>

<Indeed. Before giving up his own life, Crixac left a seed of himself as a gift. T'klath meet Crixon, who has awakened in place of Crixac.>

T'klath bowed his head.

<Greetings Crixon. A gift indeed. We know little enough of your kind, but the ability to do as Crixac has done is a wonder of itself.>

<Thank you T'klath. I am not Crixac though I have his memories. I am no less grateful to Menkh for his acceptance of the gift that enabled me to emerge. Even the short time we have had together since then has been a revelation.>

<Then I wish you both joy of it. Your return here has been timely. Frzath, Denith and Morgath are all still in stasis. The energy draw that was required drained them of almost all their vitality. They will recover, but it will take time. So, in the meanwhile we can turn to discussing your role going forward, Menkh.>

<My role?>

<Yes. As a bonded Adept you will have much to do in assisting Equilibrium. There has been significant disruption due to enemies meddling with the Threadway. Much will eventually regain Balance as it was intended, but some direct aid will be required in other places.>

<I had realised that there would be tasks to be done once we had gained the victory, but I am only one; how much can I alone achieve?>

T'klath smiled.

<But you are far from alone, Menkh. It is true you are a bonded Adept with powers far exceeding other Adepts such as myself who are bound to the Balance Point, but even though it has been a

revelation for you, you have only scratched the surface of what the Balance Point actually is.>

<How so?>

<Look around us Menkh. How many doorways do you see?>

<I know from having been here that there are hundreds of them, T'klath.>

T'klath nodded his head.

<Yes Menkh. Every one of those doors connects with a myriad of Balance Points, each of which has Adepts whose tasks mirror those of us here, that is, to watch and subtly manipulate where we can, to maintain Balance. Only a bonded Adept such as yourself can directly intervene, as you have been doing.>

<You mean there are thousands of Balance Points? I thought they were few in number, at least that is what I came to believe.>

<There is only one Balance Point, Menkh. These doorways are merely an extension of it. The Balance Point coexists with the Threadway to which it is inextricably linked. Go through any of these doors and you will stand upon the Eye of Malavak as you do now, though the Adepts you meet will have beings occupying them totally unlike us, but all united in purpose. We travel through the doorways from time to time and we will also get visitors here, some unexpectedly.>

Menkh closed his eyes. He thought he was used to dealing with baffling concepts and he had experienced so much of late that he believed he was beyond surprise, but once again he found that he was profoundly wrong.

<Did you know any of this, Crixon?>

<I will tap into Crixac's memories and see what he knew.>

<Of course, my apologies Crixon. I am thinking that you have instantaneous knowledge of all Crixac's experiences. We will have time to explore this further.>

T'klath spoke again in a conciliatory tone.

<I am sorry Menkh. I realise that this is a totally new disclosure, but given all the events that have led us to this point, perhaps you can forgive us for telling you only what you needed to know in order to complete the task before you.>

<Then what of bonded Adepts? How many of us are there?>

<Certainly, there will be more now. In light of all that has happened it is clear that many more will be required. But you need not concern yourself. The fact is, we will be here to aid and to guide you when needed. For the time being though, and until the others here are fully restored, you should return to Tarvuli. Rest, recuperate. When you are needed, we will call on you. Any questions you may have we will answer and you can journey for yourself through some of the doorways if you wish.>

The idea of a return home was a welcome one and it would certainly give him a period to strengthen his bond with Crixon and check that all was well on Tarvuli.

T'klath could see that his suggestions had met with Menkh's approval.

<Go, my friend. Take some time for yourself. I can promise that you will be busy in time to come. Farewell Crixon, I look forward to our future collaboration.>

Without further words Menkh focused on the Threadway and departed for home.

CHAPTER EIGHTEEN

Menkh's return to Tarvuli was in every way different from his departure. He returned reinvigorated and in a state of profound happiness which was noted and remarked upon by everyone who knew him.

Both Crixon and Menkh had noted T'klath's complete failure to refer to the staff, even though all the Adepts knew of the circumstances around the old one. It was now very clear that there was a mysterious power at work within the staff that turned the mind and attention of others away from itself.

Even the meeting with Varnahrin upon their return led to mutual amusement that they did not share with any other. Menkh had thought that perhaps the newly acquired presence of Crixon may be a surprise but even before he spoke Varnahrin's voice entered his mind.

<Nonsense Menkh. I am never surprised.> The voice paused momentarily. <Let us say that I have been surprised once and that, very recently. Greetings Crixon, your existence fills me with joy knowing that Crixac lives on in you. Despite Menkh's understandable caution, your presence will be a comfort knowing what has been endured.>

<I thank you, Spirit of Ta'Morin. That which was Crixac is preserved in me it is true. Having achieved the impossible we know now that there is still much left to do.>

<Yes, but you have time to celebrate. Menkh remains a bonded Adept of the Red. Equilibrium is restored but there are many who will need assistance. As Agents of Balance this is your primary task.>

Menkh nodded his head in agreement.

<Then how long do we have?> he asked.

<Let us say that when the Season of Hordeth Gar approaches and winter grips the land, you must journey to the Balancepoint. T'klath will direct you from there in your first task.>

<And what of Tarvuli?>

<You will always be free to return for a time. But you must be aware that in the years to come all that you know will change and those whom you have known will be no more.>

<That is true, and it is a knowing that has been in my mind for a long time,> said Menkh. <But their descendants and our descendants will live on and we will cherish and protect them. Crixac and I long discussed this between ourselves.>

<Then there is no more to be said. You have time to rest and reflect and to prepare for your departure, knowing that you will return. However, Menkh ab Dur, I detect a very annoying sense of amusement between yourself and Crixon over something but I cannot uncover what it is. That in itself leaves me wondering. Care to enlighten me?>

<Not at all, completely trivial, Varnahrin. Just a feeling of joy at being back.>

<I see.> There was a long pause before Varnahrin spoke again. <It would seem that the presence of Crixon has had a profound effect on you, Menkh ab Dur and not all for the good. I will leave you for now. Enjoy your stay.>

Menkh felt Varnahrin's presence leave. If it was possible for a non-physical entity to exit in a huff, he would have said that was exactly what had happened.

Menkh laughed aloud and Crixon joined him in his amusement.

<Do you think we should tell Varnahrin?> Crixon asked.

<Definitely. Let's say, in a hundred sem'chaal or so. I'd like to build up the element of surprise. I think I'm owed that much for a few surprises of Varnahrin's in the past.>

<Yes. Well, it would seem that not only can our staff divert attention from itself from a being as all-knowing and powerful as Varnahrin, but even your thoughts regarding the existence of Tishan or indeed any thought connected with it at all, seem also to be shielded.>

<Yes. It remains a mystery. We will see what the years ahead reveal to us. Now, let us go and say hello to our friends. Your presence will be a welcome surprise to them, if not to Varnahrin.>

ooooOooo

Over several meh'chaal, Menkh and Crixon travelled extensively throughout the lands visiting friends and providing comfort to those still grieving the loss of loved ones. In all, it could be fairly said that a feeling of happiness and satisfaction in the aftermath of victory remained dominant. While some grieved in their hearts for those lost to sickness or the great battle, it was not the grief of despair; the sadness of loss was offset by the promise of renewal and hope.

During this time, Menkh and Tishan took the opportunity to meet frequently and tell each other of all that had passed during their time of separation, and also to speak of the future. Their meetings occurred mostly at the end of the day, when Menkh chose to regularly retire early and, as they occurred in that curious place outside of reality, which was one of the powers that could be exerted by the staff, the time spent together, however long it seemed to them, was virtually no time at all once they phased back.

Tishan's consciousness and her memories and experiences as a being before her melding with the Rod of Klemish, was subsumed when her form once more merged with the staff. It was a mysterious dual existence which over time she grew used to and became comfortable with. Menkh also slowly grew accustomed to the situation, but it never diminished his wonder at the circumstances that had led to their being reunited. Another aspect of their meetings was that Crixon was never aware that they were taking place. Whether this was a power vested in the staff, to exclude others, or part of the alternative reality that they occurred in, was a mystery. Menkh found their privacy, even from Crixon, pleasing. It was time reserved wholly for himself and Tishan where they could open their minds to each other in a way that would not otherwise have been possible.

The seasons turned in happiness until finally, there came the day of departure.

In the great square of Ta'Morin where stood the crystalline memorial which Varnahrin had raised in memory of those Graaven who had fallen, the people gathered to say farewell to Menkh. Among the crowd were Benshin, Xotic and Ma'Vessick peoples; with even several Hrv in their midst. Their development of the cure for the terrible disease had transformed the earlier suspicion of them among the people into one of enduring trust and friendship.

Horven Var had tears in her eyes as she shyly embraced Menkh, who she still thought of as the Zaltec. Behind her, Halika and Mareen stood quietly, holding hands.

'You will return to us. You will not forget us?'

'Horven Var, who could ever forget you, my dear friend. You will ever be in my heart. Of course I will return, and we will drink clshmik together and look back on old times.'

Horven nodded and smiled through her tears. 'Then I am content. It is strange, I feel as if Tishan were very close to us. I know she has passed, but it is the strongest sensation.'

Menkh looked into Horven's eyes. 'I agree with you. I feel her presence very strongly.'

Horven's brow crinkled at Menkh's words and she briefly wondered if there was a hidden message within them which she couldn't quite grasp, but then she shook her head.

'You take good care of yourself. I will be very angry if you get hurt without me to protect you.'

'I will take that as an order, Horven Var,' said Menkh. 'And you look after yourself also.'

'I have these two to watch over me,' said Horven, indicating Halika and Mareen and reaching behind her for their hands. The two walked forward and took hold of Horven's hands, looking up and smiling at Menkh.

'Will you journey far?' Mareen asked.

'Never so far as to forget you and Halika, or Ta'Morin,' he answered.

From the crowd of well-wishers, Draachnull and Tlkcha came forward. To Menkh's eyes Draachnull was looking old and he still carried the slight limp from the leg he had broken when Menkh first encountered him.

'Safe travels to you both. You journey far beyond the lands of the Benshin but our thoughts will go with you always,' said Draachnull.

'May the Sky Father watch over you,' added Tlkcha.

'Thank you, my friends; the Graaven people are blessed by your friendship,' said Menkh.

'No less than are we, Menkh ab Dur. It has been a long journey since first we met,' said Draachnull.

Menkh nodded and smiled in response.

Then the huge form of Fendrax padded forward and loomed over him. Her mighty head lowered and she snuffled Menkh's face. Despite their long friendship, it was still daunting to stand still while that mouthful of razor-sharp teeth drew close. Impulsively, Menkh reached up and ran his hands through Fendrax's translucent coat.

Fendrax's voice rumbled:

'I am glad I do not have to carry you on your journey, you too have grown fat. Bad enough I have to carry that one,' Fendrax rolled her eyes indicating Horven standing to one side.

'I am sure you will manage, my friend,' said Menkh removing his hands.

'Time for you to go, I hate long goodbyes and if Horven sheds any more tears she will melt away. I look forward to your return. We will hunt together.'

Menkh smiled, 'That is something I will look forward to.'

Finally, Drenyk and Pershivon stepped forward. Menkh and Tishan's spawnlings had grown straight and tall and unlike Graavens from the former Empire who generally avoided physical contact, the three stood in a close embrace.

'Listen to Horven, follow her advice and fare well wherever you wander till I return,' said Menkh quietly.

'Our journey north has whetted our appetites to travel yet further. Drenyk and I fly the ImXin to the lands of the Hrv. We have trade goods and it seems the Hrv have developed a taste for clshmik, so we return Tlkcha first to Xotic lands before continuing our journey.'

'Then take care. You are both becoming quite the adventurers! Look after each other.'

After a few more brief moments touching foreheads they all stepped back.

'Farewell my friends. Look to a celebration when I return,' said Menkh.

Taking a firm grasp of his staff and his thoughts of the form so dear to him that lay within it, he focused on the Threadway which then coalesced, drawing him away from Ta'Morin and the world of Tarvuli.

<All will be well on Tarvuli, have no fear. Frzath and the others have all recovered and they are expecting you.>

The voice of Varnahrin echoed in their minds in parting, as they set forth for the Balancepoint.

<The Intelligence guide you, Menkh and Crixon. The Balance is All.>

To all those who stood witness it seemed as if Menkh simply vanished from sight.

They stood in quiet reflection for several moments before slowly dispersing.

There was much to do, a bright future of promise beckoned.

EPILOGUE

Draachnull laboured up the stony path that led to the outcrop he often favoured when he wished to watch Avlar rise, heralding the new day. What was once an easy journey now took a considerably greater time and Draachnull felt the weight of his many years. He was, he reflected, the oldest living Benshin Elder and if nothing else, his many aches and pains were evidence of his age. Still, his progress was determined, as he had felt a strange compulsion to make the journey to the rocky perch high above the forests that his people called home.

As he reached the summit and gratefully lowered himself with care onto the ground, he felt an uncomfortable fluttering within his chest, as if a small bird was trapped inside him, trying to get free; he found that breathing was difficult. After some moments the strange feeling subsided and as his breathing became easier, he looked out with deep satisfaction over the panorama of forest and meandering rivers that lay beneath him.

Not altogether unexpectedly he felt another presence join him on his perch and he nodded his head in acknowledgment.

'I thought perhaps you might come,' he said.

<You are as perceptive as ever despite your great age,> the voice of Varnahrin spoke in his mind, edged with dry humour.

Draachnull chuckled aloud. 'I must seem like a veritable new-born to you, Varnahrin. What is age to an immortal?'

<Immortal? Even I have a finite period in this dimension, Draachnull of the Benshin. But yes, as you say, your age is but a whisper in the wind in this life. However, the fact is that you are considerably older than the years you have spent on this world.>

Draachnull nodded. 'You perhaps speak of other lives and other places, but I have no recollection of them, just the here and now and the beauty of these lands.'

<That is as it should be,> said Varnahrin.

After a period of time spent in what felt to be companionable silence, Varnahrin spoke again.

<You recall the last time you were here and what occurred?> It was a statement, not a question.

'I can never forget such a momentous occurrence. In fact, it has increasingly been in my mind in recent days.'

<There is a level of consciousness that you could not access when last you travelled. The gates that barred that path lie open to you now.>

Draachnull turned his eyes towards the first glow of Avlar lifting above the horizon and he was overcome by the beauty of that moment.

'You speak of death I think,' he said quietly. In his voice, there was a hint of sadness and trepidation.

Draachnull felt a comforting warmth envelope him; it was like being held in an embrace. The words of Varnahrin spoke quietly into his mind.

<What is death Draachnull of the Benshin, but a form of re-birth. A return to that which you truly are.>

'It was in my mind that I would not return from this place. It comforts me that you are here with me. It is good to be in the presence of a friend, even one as unfathomable as yourself, Varnahrin.'

Varnahrin laughed and the sound in his mind was so full of joy
that Draachnull joined in the laughter.

<What is life without surprises and a little mystery, Draachnull?>

Draachnull nodded. 'What must I do? I haven't died before.'

<Never was such a simple statement so full of errors. But you
will know that very soon. So, breathe out and as you breathe out
stretch out your hand and we will lift you up.>

'We?' asked Draachnull.

<It's a mystery,> Varnahrin replied.

Draachnull looked out one last time at the glory of Avlar as it
rose over the forest and rivers he loved and, nodding to himself,
took a deep breath and blew it out attempting to stand at the same
time. For the briefest moment the fluttering in his chest pained
him but in a single heartbeat all discomfort left him and he stood
with joy, pulled up by the presence alongside him. He felt his hand
gripped tightly but when he looked at himself, he saw that his form
was insubstantial, a ghost of himself; looking up he perceived a tall
figure clothed in light who stood with him and held him close.

'Varnahrin?'

Tall like a Graaven, its shape was vaguely humanoid in form.
Its features, which shifted as the light which made it changed and
swirled, were neither male nor female. Draachnull felt not the
slightest fear, he knew that he was held in love like a mother with
her child.

'Well, this is a surprise,' he said.

The swirling features resolved into a face that smiled broadly.

<Told you so. Come. Now we travel.>

Had any living eyes been able to see it, the pulsating streams of
light that comprised the forms of Draachnull and Varnahrin, shot

upwards into the heavens and a peal of laughter, joyous and uncontained, echoed for a moment in the wind that blew over the
rocky ledge and then was heard no more.

The lifeless body of Draachnull slumped forward on the ledge,
while far out on the horizon the glory of Avlar lifted fully into the
sky, heralding another morning and a new day of promise on the
world of Tarvuli.

Acknowledgements

A s ever, no book simply appears without help and support.

To my wife Marilyn and my children for their encouragement I love you guys!

To Nina Smith for her wonderful map of Tarvuli, my Editor Jo Smith for her fantastic assistance and input and last but by no means least my publisher Leschenault Press and Ian Hooper, without whose involvement this story would not have been written.

About the author

Robert C Littlewood was born in London in 1957, emigrating with his parents and sister – all now deceased – to Australia in 1964.

Prior to completing a Bachelor of Education at Murdoch University in 1992, he undertook many different jobs. After attaining his degree, he worked as a state schoolteacher for a number of years before leaving teaching to take up other interests, including semi-professional work as an opera singer.

Robert is married with three grown children and resides in Bunbury in the south-west of Western Australia.